MURDER IN THE GROTTO

Also by Amy Myers

The British Stately Home mysteries

MURDER AT TANTON TOWERS *

The Nell Drury series

DANCING WITH DEATH *
DEATH AT THE WYCHBOURNE FOLLIES *
DEATH AND THE SINGING BIRDS *

The Car Detective series

CLASSIC IN THE BARN *
CLASSIC CALLS THE SHOTS *
CLASSIC IN THE CLOUDS *
CLASSIC MISTAKE *
CLASSIC IN THE PITS *
CLASSIC CASHES IN *
CLASSIC IN THE DOCK*
CLASSIC AT BAY *

Marsh and Daughter mysteries

THE WICKENHAM MURDERS
MURDER IN FRIDAY STREET
MURDER IN HELL'S CORNER
MURDER AND THE GOLDEN GOBLET
MURDER IN THE MIST
MURDER TAKES THE STAGE
MURDER ON THE OLD ROAD
MURDER IN ABBOT'S FOLLY
THE MAID OF KENT MURDERS

The Tom Wasp Victorian mysteries

TOM WASP AND THE MURDERED STUNNER
TOM WASP AND THE NEWGATE KNOCKER
TOM WASP AND THE SEVEN DEADLY SINS

** available from Severn House*

MURDER IN THE GROTTO

Amy Myers

First world edition published in Great Britain and the USA in 2025
by Severn House, an imprint of Canongate Books Ltd,
14 High Street, Edinburgh EH1 1TE.

Paperback edition first published in Great Britain and the USA in 2025
by Severn House, an imprint of Canongate Books Ltd.

severnhouse.com

Cover and jacket design by Piers Tilbury

British Library Cataloguing-in-Publication Data
A CIP catalogue record for this title is available from the British Library.

ISBN-13: 978-1-4483-0999-3 (cased)
ISBN-13: 978-1-4483-1813-1 (paper)
ISBN-13: 978-1-4483-1000-5 (e-book)

All Severn House titles are printed on acid-free paper.

Typeset by Palimpsest Book Production Ltd.,
Falkirk, Stirlingshire, Scotland.
Printed and bound in Great Britain by
CPI Group (UK) Ltd, Croydon CR0 4YY

The manufacturer's authorised representative in the EU for product safety is
Authorised Rep Compliance Ltd, 71 Lower Baggot Street, Dublin D02 P593
Ireland (arccompliance.com)

Praise for Amy Myers

"Fans of classic British cozies will enjoy"
Booklist on *Murder at Tanton Towers*

"An enjoyable read with a bit of history, a touch of romance, and a tight circle of suspects"
Kirkus Reviews on *Murder at Tanton Towers*

"Gently paced and enjoyable . . . a promising start to a new series"
Mystery People on *Murder at Tanton Towers*

"Satisfying . . . Vividly portrayed characters and engaging plot twists"
Booklist on *Death and the Singing Birds*

"Believable characters"
Kirkus Reviews on *Death and the Singing Birds*

"Buoyantly amusing . . . fans will be pleased"
Publishers Weekly on *Death at the Wychbourne Follies*

"Myers has discovered a no-fail recipe for suspense as she dishes up another delectable cuisine-centric caper"
Booklist on *Death at the Wychbourne Follies*

About the author

Amy Myers has written a wide range of novels, from crime to historical sagas to contemporary romance. She is also well known for her mystery short stories that have been published in *Ellery Queen Mystery Magazine* and many anthologies.

Her traditional and cozy mystery series include the Jack Colby, car detective mysteries, co-written with her husband, American-born car buff James Myers; the Auguste Didier series; the Tom Wasp, Victorian chimney sweep novels; the Marsh and Daughter mysteries; the Nell Drury mysteries; and the new British Stately Home mysteries.

amymyers.net

Acknowledgements

No man is an island, as John Donne pointed out, and no book is a book without the input of many talented people. For *Murder in the Grotto* I am so very grateful to Rachel Slatter, editorial director at my publisher, Severn House, to Piers Tilbury, head of its design department, and to my agent, Sara Keane of Keane Kataria Literary Agency, for all their thoughtful expertise. I'm very grateful too for the staunch support of Sally French, Martin French, Gaye Banyard, Annette Tomarken and Edward Tomarken. Professor Tomarken's splendid books on Dr Samuel Johnson made me realize that in his journeys to his much-loved Kent Dr Johnson might have dropped in to see the newly built Tanton Towers had his death in 1784 not intervened. Although he plays no part in this novel, his portrait in the Great Hall allows his benign eye to witness what happens when the Towers' usually peaceful life is hit by murder in its gardens. I am also grateful to the late Stephen Finnis for his expert input on the ghostly career of Sir Reginald Farran Pryde of the Royal West Kent Regiment. Reading fiction suspends disbelief to good effect, and my thanks to all the above for giving *Murder in the Grotto* the opportunity to do so.

ONE

A celebration?

Cara had been mystified about why Max and Alison had invited her over to the Tanton Towers family wing this evening. That wasn't unusual, but she knew Max's eccentric Aunt Izzy would be present and – fond as she was of the Dowager Lady Lendale, or Lady Izzy as Cara had been commanded to address her – Max and Alison had hinted there was something special about this visit. She'd decided it was probably just family business that would have little or nothing affecting her own realm, which was running the Happy Huffkin Café in the Towers' gardens. On the other hand, it had sounded exciting – and a celebration at Tanton Towers counted as exactly that, Cara thought, as Lady Izzy revealed the reason for her visit.

The stately Tanton Towers, owned by Max Farran Pryde with his wife Alison, was something special in itself. With its crazy architecture starring turrets, gables and towers, and its general non-conformist approach, it sat benevolently perched on the hill above the River Syn in Kent, overlooking the small village of Tanton nestling beneath. But what was this celebration? And where did she, Cara Shelley, fit into this?

Lady Izzy chuckled. Sitting there in her bright purple tunic over equally bright red trousers, she was a mesmerizing figure. 'Such fun, Cara dear,' she said. 'Did you know I'm honorary president of the Tanton Ghost and Phantom Society? And did you know that the society has just pinned down its twentieth ghost?' She giggled. 'I don't mean literally pinned down. After all, it was in a bedroom, and who would want to be in bed with a ghost?'

Cara laughed. 'Especially if it snores.' She had known Lady Izzy for some years now. It had been she who had recommended her plans for the Happy Huffkin to Max and Alison, and so begun the most exciting venture of her life.

'Dear Berowne would defend you against any manifestation anywhere,' Lady Izzy assured her. 'I expect you know him, of course, and as chair of the society he'll be in touch with you very soon.'

The name clicked. Cara remembered meeting Berowne Dyer once or twice. He lived nearby with his wife Rachel at Ellum Place on the outskirts of the Tanton estate. He seemed pleasant enough, maybe in his mid-forties and a natural leader – which must be a gift in his working life, probably with some financial outfit.

Ghosts though. This was a step into new territory, although as she lived in the village she had heard about this society. There were even rumours of ghosts at Tanton Towers, but she had never taken them seriously – and never seen them either, save for the weird shiver now and then. She'd occasionally wondered on spooky nights whether her own fifteenth-century cottage harboured any, lurking ready to leap out on her. Don't be so daft, she always told herself.

'Berowne will want to discuss the menu with you,' Lady Izzy chattered on. 'It will be such fun. And in the evening, of course, because of the ghost hunt after the feast—'

'*Hunt?*' Max broke in, aghast. 'But where, Izzy? I thought this was an evening dinner for the society committee in the Italian garden if it's fine weather and, if it isn't, then in the folly. Is that acceptable to you, Cara? You'll take care of the catering?'

She certainly would. No grumbles about that from her. Far from it. She loved running the Happy Huffkin Café in the old folly in the grounds. She had been here for four years now. That meant every day she could climb the hill up through the woodland from her cottage in the village and share in Tanton Towers' peaceful happiness – well, she amended, it was *almost* always happy. Even when it wasn't, the Towers was majestic enough to rise above any clouds that threatened it.

The Towers was open to the public on Wednesdays to Sundays, courtesy of Max and Alison. Max, a former professor of medieval history, was a direct descendant of the eccentric Sir Jeffry Farran, who in the eighteenth century had built his dream house here. Dream house for him, anyway. The staff must have had different views on that, Cara thought. They had to struggle with the twisting passages that led nowhere or in a circle, the spiral staircases and the mysterious doors that didn't seem to open into rooms. Lengthy corridors ran through the Towers' majestic building, but would suddenly turn unexpected corners, as did the servants' wing that abutted the main building, together with the family wing and orangery.

The Happy Huffkin had never had an evening commission before, but why not? She could cope. It was Friday the ninth of June today, which was ages before the proposed Tuesday the twentieth. This was June after all, and the weather would be fine. Cara performed a mental song and dance. This was a new adventure. Perhaps one of the ghosts would turn up as a guest.

'Of course it's acceptable. I can't cater for the ghosts though,' she replied brightly, her mind already racing with visions of ghostly waiters running up and down the twisting stairs of the folly if it rained.

'I'll pay extra for each paranormal guest who appears, Cara dear,' her ladyship anxiously assured her.

Alison quickly intervened to Cara's relief. 'You'll be relieved to hear that the archives don't reveal any hauntings in the Italian garden or in the folly, Izzy. Those hideous ghouls and gargoyles were designed to frighten them off,' she assured her, straight-faced.

'Of course,' Lady Izzy said happily, 'I'd prefer to hold the dinner in the grotto.'

'The *grotto*?' It was Alison's turn to flounder, and Cara could see that Max had his 'I'll take a speedy step or two back' look about him.

'The grotto?' he echoed valiantly. 'I'm not sure that's practical, Izzy.' Cara knew from his tone of voice that there would be no chance at all of that happening.

And no wonder. The grotto, Cara knew, was perhaps the most eccentric of Sir Jeffry's eccentricities, when he had indulged himself not only with designing the Towers in 1784 but the gardens and ancillary buildings including the folly. He had added a final flourish just to show what he was capable of: the grotto. Not just any old semi-underground grotto for Sir Jeffry. This one was larger than most and much of it now ran underground. In the last year another small cave had been unearthed (literally). Once a narrow stream had run through the middle of the grotto, but had now been diverted from its appearance in a gruesome but imposing lion's head fountain at its entrance, and now ran underground. The grotto still had its defences against invaders though, as statues and carvings of Greek gods and heroes still glared down at all those who braved an entry into their territory.

Their territory was indeed spectacular, as from beginning to end its walls and rounded roof were covered with oyster shells. Sir Jeffry had made the most of Tanton's proximity to the kingdom of Kent's abundance of seafood on its eastern front, something of which Jane Austen was fond, according to Alison Farran Pryde. Looking at the oyster shells now, Cara inevitably wondered whether the great novelist had lunched on any of those facing her in the grotto. With her brother living in Kent not far away, it was quite possible.

Even if Jane had munched her way through a few of them, there was no way the grotto would provide a welcoming venue for the superb dinner that the Happy Huffkin would serve. Cara would back Max up to the hilt on that. The Italian garden was much more suitable, and anyway the grotto was only fifty yards or so away from it. The path from it led straight to the Italian garden.

Lady Izzy beamed. 'I do so agree, dear Max,' she said brightly. 'It's no use your trying to talk me out of dining in the Italian garden. I am quite set on it.'

Relief all round, to Cara's amusement. She was never sure how much Lady Izzy was deliberately putting on her old woman act or whether it was indeed unconscious.

'After all,' Lady Izzy continued, 'this will be a celebration not only of the achievements of the last ten years under Berowne's leadership, but for the life of his predecessor, my husband's nephew Thomas Chalcott.' She turned to Cara again. 'My dear, you would not have known Tom. He died after a ghost hunt in the grotto ten years ago. A heart attack apparently. Tom led the society for ten years and had just handed over the reins to Berowne. He felt that there might have been something amiss in the society and it needed a new guiding hand. Darling Tom. Such a splendid man. I always hoped he'd marry. Tom would have been thirty-seven then. He paid such enjoyable visits to us, no matter where my husband was posted. My husband would have loved . . .'

Thankfully Alison cut in, as Max was looking flummoxed. 'It was very sad, Izzy, and we were very fond of Tom. Cara, you never knew Tom of course. He died not in the grotto itself but on his way home. Max and I weren't living at the Towers then, but we heard about his death with great sadness.'

'Of course, of course.' Lady Izzy looked disconcerted. 'No ghosts were involved with that. But,' she added wistfully, 'it would be very nice to have the feast in the grotto. I feel sure that Tom will be with us. There have, so I'm told, been unexplained presences there.'

Back to square one. This could run and run, Cara thought, much amused. Max would have to deal with this. She had strong suspicions that Lady Izzy was deliberately winding Max up.

'I'll have a word with the grounds manager, Len Redman,' Max said firmly. 'I'm sure he'll insist on the Italian garden.'

Lady Izzy sighed. 'Very well, but of course the *hunt* will be taking place in the grotto. And I understand they'll all be sleeping overnight there.'

'*What?*' Max roared.

Time for Max to put his foot down, surely. It was staggering news and Cara waited on tenterhooks, trying to hold back a giggle. She could see from Alison's face that this was new to her. Cara had even more doubts about 'the hunt'. She wouldn't be directly involved with it, but from what she'd heard of ghost hunts, there would be a lot of equipment coming and going and a lot of waiting around, even without the added complication of bedding down for the night. Anyway, what ghosts were thought to be in the grotto? She'd never heard of any ghost sightings, although she could see that it might be a suitable place for them to gather – if there were any hanging around.

However, regardless of the ghost position, Cara reminded herself, this was going to be a fun event. No doubt about that. The Italian garden would be a splendid venue to dine in, especially as it had a large arbour which could shield guests and tables from the worst of the rain if there was an unexpected shower, and it had a generally good atmosphere. Like the grotto, it had many gods and goddesses, true to the orthodox Renaissance approach. The eighteenth-century Sir Jeffry didn't do orthodox, however. At the main entrance to the Italian garden, instead of conforming to the usual glares and flexing of muscles of classical sculptures, two huge statues of Romulus and Remus greeted the visitor, grinning their heads off in welcome.

'We'll begin the ghost hunt after our celebration dinner,' Lady Izzy chattered on, then giggled. 'I shouldn't call it a hunt really. Dear Berowne prefers to think of it as a tour to feel those presences. I don't know exactly whose they are, but I expect dear Tom's will be one of them. They will be visiting us from the other world, if only in some cases to point the finger at the injustice of their premature passing.'

Max's turn to sigh. 'If you're thinking our Horace will be there, Izzy, forget him. He only haunts the woods and the Towers when he feels like it.'

'Perhaps he'll pop over and have a look at us all,' Cara said solemnly. The prospect of the ghost hunt was taking on a lighter touch. Horace was the reprobate crazy twin brother of Sir Thomas Farran who had inherited the Towers from his father Sir Jeffry, and was reputed to haunt it. Horace was given to prancing around in the nude, whether he was inside the Towers or cavorting naked down to the village. It had taken the addition of Pryde to the family name some considerable time later to restore due prestige to the Towers.

'Horace may not know his way to the grotto,' Lady Izzy said anxiously.

'Maybe he'll need someone to look after him. I'll have a word with Len Redman,' Max muttered.

'Perhaps not while we're eating,' she said more cheerfully. 'Berowne could ask Horace to wait until after we've finished.'

'This Berowne Dyer, Izzy,' Max said. 'I know him, of course, but not well enough to know why he came to be running a ghost society, apart from taking it over from Tom.'

Lady Izzy looked surprised. 'The prestige, Max dear. The society is very highly thought of because of its careful approach to the supernatural world. Not everyone believes ghosts exist, you see, and so they have to be very careful and have lots of evidence before they declare something is a ghost. That means the society's leader plays an important role. Besides,' she added, 'everyone loves Berowne.'

Everyone loves him? That's off-putting for a start, Cara thought, as she hurried back to her Happy Huffkin Café across the lawns. What was so special about this guy Berowne that made him so lovable? She was getting curious about him. He hadn't seemed particularly special on the few occasions she'd seen him around. At least, she comforted herself, thanks to today's meeting, she had some idea of what this celebration feast would be about and her role in it. She would leave the ghosts for Berowne to organize. She'd have to talk to Len about the feast, however, because there would undoubtedly be complications about the proposed celebration supper: how to serve; where exactly to serve; access for the necessary vans, and so on. She got on well with Len and he was sensible enough to quash any nonsensical plans. Looking after the grotto was part of his job, but guests sleeping there plus a dinner party in the Italian garden might be a step too far. As for the food, that had to be organized pronto, but Cara was well aware that having such a party might cause friction with the Towers' new events manager, so she needed Len's co-operation.

She would do her best to ensure it was a splendid occasion, she told herself, as she gave her customary wave of thanks to the Towers as she dashed past the servants' wing jutting out from the main building. It was already seven o'clock, way past the time that normally she would have left the Happy Huffkin for the day.

She was entering her fifth year of running the café, and the Towers was the best of all possible places to run it, quirks included. The folly alone confirmed that, with its gargoyles and ghouls greeting her as she reached it. The front of the tall red-brick building was plastered with them, and on the other sides two or three more sternly studied the landscape for potential enemies on the higher level. There were even one or two peering out from the tumbledown mock temple columns on the stone terrace surrounding the folly, from which one could admire the views.

There was plenty to admire inside too. The kitchen was modernized, of course, but the carvings on the panelling upstairs were pure eighteenth century. The Farran coat of arms predominated. Sir Jeffry had left his mark everywhere, and the panelling displayed carvings of the pious Edward the Confessor, the crusader Richard I, and various other monarchs, all looking approvingly upwards at the heraldic shield.

With luck, her faithful and dependable assistant Sammy would still be around, and she could put him in the picture, Cara thought thankfully. She was well used now not only to rising to the occasion, but leaping there whenever she could. Virginia Harding, a distant cousin of Sammy's, organized daytime events held at the Happy Huffkin, usually bringing her own team of cooks and waiters and with Cara superintending. Nearly all of Virginia's team lived in the village, at the edge of which was Cara's home, Knights Cottage. Small, but easily large enough for her now that her daughter Kate had spread her wings and graduated from university. Kate's father had been absent from the day she was conceived – to Cara's relief. Some mistakes in life can be overlooked and, after struggling for some years, she was now as happy at Tanton as it was possible to be. Every day was a celebration – well, almost every day.

Ah, good, there was Sammy standing at the folly door, no doubt eager to get home. He looked as grumpy as usual, but that was a mask and she had learned to live with it. He must still be in his forties, not that much older than she was, but his detached outlook on life and tanned wrinkled face made him seem ageless.

'Big celebration coming up,' she called up to him as she reached the steps.

No reply, but she hadn't expected one.

'A party on Tuesday the twentieth, in the evening.' Too late she realized that not only were Tuesdays usually Sammy's day off, but he would be planning to spend it at his home from home, the bowls club. No wife for Sammy, not now anyway. She noted that he had his cap on, which was a subtle hint that he'd been here long enough today.

Still no greeting from him. Sammy was taciturn and abrupt at the best of times, but perhaps she had gone a step too far.

'I'll be calling Virginia,' she told him as she ran up the steps to the folly. 'Evening. Dinner for a dozen or so, either here or outside in the Italian garden.'

He spoke. 'Who?' he asked, with his usual economy of words.

She interpreted this to mean not Virginia but an enquiry after the customer. 'The Tanton Ghost and Phantom Society,' Cara replied.

A grunt. Was it one of approval or disapproval? The latter. 'Could mean trouble.'

She summoned up all the brightness she could on the spur of the moment. After all, Lady Izzy always had Sammy's seal of approval, luckily.

'Lady Lendale is honorary president of the society,' she explained. 'And she gets on well with the chair, Berowne Dyer. Have you ever run into him? He owns Ellum Place and is generally very popular, she says. Everybody likes him.'

That must have struck a chord, for silence fell. A meaningful one. 'Trouble,' Sammy eventually pronounced again.

Best to ignore that, she decided. 'The society seems to take itself very seriously,' she assured him. 'They're not just after fun and jokes. Their quest is to winkle out the truth about the stories they're told; it's not just giggles and gasps.'

Then something made her add, 'Ten years ago it came to the grotto and her nephew died of a heart attack. You weren't here then, were you?' The Happy Huffkin hadn't existed then, of course, but she knew Sammy had worked at the Towers before that.

But Sammy was Sammy. All he replied after a long pause was: 'Party. How many?'

'Italian garden?' Len Redman thought this over. 'Don't see why not,' he eventually pronounced.

That was a relief. At least they had the gardens' manager on their side. Talking to Len and his wife always gave her a different perspective from the Towers' indoor staff, or even from that of Max and Alison. Len was on the outside looking into life at the Towers, in much the same way as Cara was. He and Josie were in their late thirties, and lived on the estate, which meant it was far more comfortable chatting to them in their cottage rather than in Len's shed tucked away in the woodland behind the Italian garden and grotto. Josie was a gardener too, but not for the Towers, although Cara knew her almost as well as Len as she sometimes helped out on Victoria's team from the village. Josie's liveliness was well balanced with Len's more dour and suspicious approach to life, although he too was fond of a good laugh.

Len ran his own estate gardens team here, managing them with his popular young assistant Harry Bright, currently the 'gardener's boy' – as Len had been himself at Tanton before progressing up the ladder twelve years ago. Harry was working for a degree in landscape architecture and design, and affably did any job that came along. He didn't even object to being referred to as the 'gardener's boy', Cara noted, although that might have had something to do with the fact that he had a reputation for chasing the young female members of the Towers' staff.

So far so good. Cara mustered up her strength. Now for the tricky bit. 'As Max or Alison will have explained, it's for the Tanton Ghost and Phantom Society,' she said lightly. 'And they want to have dinner in the Italian garden, followed by a hunt in the grotto afterwards. I gather they plan to sleep there overnight.'

As she had expected, that did not go down well. Both Len and Josie looked distinctly unimpressed. 'So Mrs Alison told us,' Len said grimly.

'Why the grotto?' Josie said at last, glancing at her husband. 'I've never heard of any ghosts there.'

'Forget the ghosts,' Len said darkly. 'It's those ghost hunters cause the trouble. One of them's young Harry – he's joined them for fun, he says. Not much fun to my way of thinking. There'll be trouble, you mark my words. And no open candles. Don't want to see the arbour bursting into flames.'

Cara hastened to reassure him. 'Understood.' His usual sense of humour had certainly vanished.

'It's more than candles,' Len muttered. 'I don't want soup chucked over the begonias and messy food hurled around. Broken glasses and all that. Don't want the risk in the Italian garden or the grotto.'

'Darling,' Josie said firmly, 'I'll make sure I'm on Virginia's team and that everything's under control.'

'I don't think they'll be hurling things around,' Cara reassured him brightly. No laughs from him today. 'Unless there's a poltergeist around.'

'I'll go along and play being a bloody ghost myself.' Len glared at her. 'That'll scare them off.'

If he didn't thaw, Cara thought, it would be up to Alison to step in. She was the Towers' manager. Max would be the last port of call, chiefly because most of his time was spent either lecturing on history or at his favourite occupation of admiring his own gallery of the work of the sixteenth-century artist, Lavinia Fontana.

Cara tried again. 'Their chair will keep order. I expect you know him. It's Berowne Dyer of Ellum Place.'

'Yes, we do.' Josie took over again. No thaw yet from Len. 'We know everyone round here with a garden that needs work done on it,' she continued. 'Especially me. I'm a jobbing gardener, and I did a few jobs for Berowne and his wife Rachel.'

'I don't know him well, but I'm told everyone seems to like him,' Cara said, a trifle tentatively. There didn't seem to be much enthusiasm for him here. Perhaps she was wrong though, because thankfully Len seemed to be warming to the idea.

'Give me the date, time and numbers, and I'll get it all ready,' he said almost cheerfully. 'Bringing all their paraphernalia with them, are they? I'll organize the mattresses and their precious equipment in the grotto's side passages. Have to make sure they don't get damp. We don't want that equipment of theirs littering the rose-beds or falling into the water in the Italian garden.'

Paraphernalia? Cara had only the vaguest idea what this might involve. A camera, obviously. Their iPads, electro-recorders of some sort, probably. Would everyone have this equipment with them or only the leader? How did one catch a ghost on screen? With the help of the latest technology, presumably. Somehow the idea of a troupe of people marching into the grotto began to feel ominous. No, she was being stupid, she told herself. How could anything go wrong? The side passages on each side of the main path through the grotto would indeed make suitable individual rooms for the ghost hunters.

It was a pity, Cara thought, that the stream had now been diverted from the grotto's centre, but that would undoubtedly not have helped the smooth running of the ghost hunt. Would it be smooth? Each of those hunters would eagerly be awaiting signs of the ghosts of the past. Nothing could go wrong, even if the ghosts failed to oblige by turning up.

'I'm Berowne Dyer.'

Taken aback, Cara stared at him, belatedly recognizing this smiling man. Of course it was him. She hadn't recognized him out of context, but he had turned up unexpectedly at the Happy Huffkin door. She would have expected to be summoned to his presence rather than be sought out by the man himself, and yet there was nothing out of the ordinary about him. He looked – well, likeable. He was good-looking without pushing it, medium height, medium build and quite nice eyes. It was Sunday, an open day at the Towers, but not until two o'clock, so it was a good time for him to choose, even if she was setting up for the first flood of visitors and Sammy was busy in the kitchen. Though Virginia brought most of the food, the café also served specialities she or even Sammy provided. Sammy's favourite was his precious huffkins, said to be invented centuries ago by the Kentish cherry pickers. They were rather like scones, only more interesting in Cara's view, considering they provided a dent in the top for a quickly snatched fruit.

'Of course. You're chair of the Tanton Ghost and Phantom Society,' she greeted him.

He grinned. 'Rather a mouthful. But not all ghosts are phantoms and not all phantoms are ghosts. There's no universal agreement on that, but in Tanton feelings run so high that in a small village we have to cater for all beliefs. After all, suppose I'm a ghostly figure of your imagination. How do you know which I am?'

She laughed. 'You've proved your point.'

'Good, because I need your help.'

Whooh! What was all this? she wondered. 'About the menu or a ghost?' she enquired.

'For the current lie of the land. There have been several ghosts reported in Tanton Towers, but after our hunt in the grotto ten years ago, we haven't been back since.'

'So Lady Lendale told me,' Cara said. 'Her nephew was the organizer of the hunt and chair of the society. Correct?'

'Yes, Tom Chalcott,' he replied promptly. 'This celebration is a tribute to him. His death here ten years ago was a shock, a very sad one. So much so that it overshadowed the findings that we made. We know that the ghost of the great Horace still appears to haunt the grotto as well as the Towers itself. In the last year or two, as well as the occasional presence, we've also heard reports of the Laughing Lady.' He must have seen the blank look on her face because he laughed. 'Another ghost. Sometimes there's a cackle heard without the lady and sometimes the lady is grinning but in silence.'

That was one she hadn't heard of. 'I can't help you find her,' she joked. 'I'll be looking after the feast itself, not the grotto hunt. You need Len Redman for that. Or Harry, Len's garden assistant, who's a member of your society.'

'Ah, but he doesn't know much about the history of the Towers and its grounds. I want to know what other ghosts might be lurking there and the stories behind them. At present I only know bits and pieces. I need someone to give me a serious tour.'

Careful here, she warned herself. Likeable though he seemed, this was not her job, so why was he here?

'Then you need to talk to Alison Farran Pryde, the Towers' manager as well co-owner. You must have met her.'

'Yes, but I don't want an insider. I want someone who can see things objectively.'

A year or so ago, she thought uneasily, when tragedy had struck the Towers, someone else had said that to her. 'I'm not sure I can help,' she replied firmly.

'I'm sure you can.'

Phew. He was trying it on big time – and yet for some reason she felt that he meant it.

'I'm not a scammer,' he added.

For once she felt blind-sided and that was annoying. 'I'll clear it with Mr and Mrs Farran Pryde first.' She hesitated. 'But if I do it, I'd like to know more about the ghost hunters who are coming here. Including,' she added boldly, 'yourself. What interests you so much about ghosts that you devote your free time to them?' She was going to be working hard for this celebration evening, and there was no way she wanted to get embroiled in the field of the paranormal – or in village feuds and disagreements.

'I'm a writer,' he replied.

Nice one, she thought. That told her nothing. 'What sort of writer?'

'A ghost writer.'

Stonewalled. All she could do was laugh.

'You wanted to know about the other members of the society,' he continued. 'I'll tell you and you can ponder over them after I leave. Ready? You'll probably know many of them,' he continued when she nodded. 'For a start, there's my wife Rachel. Staunchly on my side at all times. We both work for her family property firm. Doesn't believe in ghosts but believes in my right to do so. Then there's Charlotte, married to Pete Brandon, landlord of the Farran Arms, so I'm sure you know her at least by sight. Stunning to look at, coming up for her fortieth, jealously guarded by Pete. Pete, too, you must know. Reasonably popular publican, but not a bundle of laughs.

'Then there's Luke Claxton,' he added. 'Divorced and thinks he's God's gift to women; he's a handyman and computer enthusiast who believes that technology is the one and only answer to our communicating with the spirit world. Hence, he is not one of my admirers since I do not. Young Harry Bright you already know about, and there is also his grandfather Oliver. Every society requires a grand old gentleman, and Oliver Bright is ours. He was once the leader, the organizer of every hunt over twenty years back, before retiring to be succeeded by Tom Chalcott. We do a maximum of ten years each as chair, but Oliver considers himself the *real* chair of the society and had his eye on succeeding me. Unfortunately for him, the society has made an exception and elected me for a second term.'

He was grinning so she had no idea how much – if anything – of the above was either correct or relevant. But so far the society certainly didn't sound as though it worked together harmoniously.

'Is that the lot?' she asked politely.

He clapped a hand ostentatiously to his brow. 'How could I forget? Of course there's one – no, I should say one and a half.'

'Nothing like intriguing the audience,' Cara observed.

He grinned. 'The one is young Jamie Dickens. No descendant of the writer, alas. Jamie represents Youth and the Future, which sweep all before him as he strives to show us the true path ahead with the help of the ancient spirit world. Today is nothing, the Past is the Guide because only the Future matters.'

'Sounds a handful,' Cara said drily. 'If he's your one, who's the half?'

'That's our latest recruit, dear Emily Hunt, whose love for the spirit world is severely rationed to the help it might provide in her pursuit of retaining Jamie's love.'

'Thank you,' she said gravely. 'And you? Who are you, as well as being the society chair, organizer and writer?'

'Me?' he said. 'I'm just Berowne.'

She wasn't having that. 'And your name? That seems special.'

'So Shakespeare thought, and my parents too. All the world's a stage, and they pushed me on to it, having bestowed me with my name as they'd been playing in *Love's Labour's Lost* the night I was conceived.'

'Are you – or have you been – an actor yourself?' she asked curiously.

'Never. The only time I tried, they booed me.' He laughed, and took his leave.

She watched him as he strolled away. What had she taken on? Not only had she the daily tasks to attend to, together with the planning and operation of an evening dinner party for umpteen people, but she had to fit in a tour – and a tour for which she would have to do some speedy research. What had made her agree to do that? Then she realized the reason. She too liked Berowne – or did she? She wasn't sure. He certainly had charm.

TWO

Virginia Harding had not spoken for some time. Not unusual, and Cara was obediently standing by until Virginia had delivered her verdict. At present she was busy assessing the Italian garden with a view to its potential or otherwise for her to provide next Tuesday's evening feast. June the twentieth was now only a week away, which suddenly didn't seem long for all the preparations to be made. True, there would only be twelve diners, but it presented a challenge given the unusual venue, not to mention the fact that the twelve included not only Max and Alison but Lady Izzy as well.

Cara waited on tenterhooks as Virginia strode around eyeing the narrow stream of water that so meekly flowed down its centre, keeping to its carefully controlled space. The arbour had already received its seal of tentative approval, so would the stream now prove a problem? Thankfully it seemed as though the verdict was favourable because Virginia finally gave a quick nod. Then she barked:

'What happens if it rains halfway through the meal?'

Cara could see her point. The arbour's 'roof' consisted only of a wooden framework for climbing greenery, roses and wisteria. Unfortunately, Virginia had an awkward habit of seizing on the flaws that Cara pushed under her mental carpet.

'We run for it,' Cara replied hopefully.

Virginia managed a grin. 'I'm not one for ghost hunts. And I'm not one for running.'

Her stocky build was a testament to the latter, but it was mid-June so it was a reasonable bet that no sudden showers would hit them in the middle of the proceedings. Even if they did, Cara knew full well that Virgina's team would deal with situation splendidly. Josie Redman had duly arranged to be on it, which was a bonus, and Len was on duty for the evening in the background. If there was an emergency, it would be a case of all hands pulling together.

'We'll have the field kitchen marquee on the lawn with the food warmers and trestle tables,' Virginia continued grimly, 'but that's not big enough for guests scurrying for shelter, and it's a long way to the Happy Huffkin in the rain.'

A slight exaggeration, Cara thought. The first floor of the Happy Huffkin would surely be the answer to this theoretical problem. Anyway, a rainy night was hard to imagine today. The Italian garden was looking at its June best with a sudden burst of sunshine; Cara was optimistic.

The arbour was ablaze with Madame Alfred Carrière scented roses climbing eagerly up and over it. Looking at it all, for some reason Cara's doubts faded. She had no idea who Madame Alfred Carrière was, but any gentlemen in her life must have been very happy. A pity that Sir Jeffry would not have been around to appreciate it when he built the Towers, but it would have received his blessing (even if he wouldn't have resisted popping a quirky surprise or two in with it).

'The menu then.' Virginia sat herself down on one of the arbour seats. 'Next Tuesday. What have you in mind? Four courses? Fish? Crab mousse? Fresh up from Winchelsea. Scallops? No, wrong season. Oysters same problem, though we can manage somehow. Stuffed avocados? Problem with that as they might quickly go brown. We'll cope somehow though. Chicken in tarragon crème sauce? Raspberries with raspberry compote? Cheesecake? Cheese? Vegetarian and vegan alternatives? I'll buzz off a menu for you later on today. I know you'll be hankering after all that fancy stuff they tell you about on the Towers tours now, but you can't beat good English cooking.'

Cara did indeed sometimes hanker after it, although this 'fancy stuff' was also English to the core. The new events manager was enthusiastically expanding the possibilities of the servants' wing by introducing the occasional live eighteenth-century cooking demonstration in the kitchens with its end products on show. Max had firmly put his foot down over selling them to the public, on the feeble grounds (feeble to Cara anyway) that the cost of registration and insurance would be too high and, as he saw it, Cara's café was the place for afternoon tea. The events manager, Cara knew, was not going to give up lightly, and had muttered to her that by this time next year there would not only be jumbals and the like available but – strictly privately to Cara – the Towers' formal dining room would be hosting eighteenth-century evening dinners, at a price! Alison had been reasonably interested in this, but Max had most definitely not.

Meanwhile Cara had satisfied her own curiosity and palate with her own version of Mrs E. Smith's *Compleat Housewife*'s lemon biskets, jumbals, and gingerbread (with coriander in it? – weird), which sometimes crept into the Happy Huffkin's kitchen too, though Sammy – so far – had not noticed their source.

'What about wine?' Virginia continued. 'Shall I supply it?'

'Max will be looking after that,' Cara said firmly. It hadn't yet been mentioned but she was sure of her ground here. No one other than Max would have a say in the matter. 'And,' she added, 'he'll deal with all the rest of the alcohol too.' That would also be ground jealously guarded by Max, especially as he and Alison would be present.

'It's all because of that crazy aunt of his, isn't it?' Virginia commented. 'I heard about that. It was some nephew of hers used to run this ghost society, wasn't it? The one that died up there somewhere after one of their meetings.'

Cara wasn't surprised that Virginia knew about that. A village has long memories and Virginia had been born in Tanton, whereas Cara had only come to the village fifteen or sixteen years ago. A mere newcomer! 'Have you ever been a member of it?' she asked.

Virginia snorted. 'No way. I know that Jamie Dickens is, he and his new girlfriend, Emily. Our Lucy won't like that. She was item number one with Jamie till a few weeks back, when he dropped her like a rotten plum.'

That wasn't good news, Cara thought. The Harding family was widespread in Tanton. Lucy Parkin, Virginia's lively young niece, was a big plus on the team. 'Will Lucy be on your team next Tuesday?' she asked cautiously, foreseeing trouble.

'You bet she will,' Virginia said grimly. 'She'd like any chance to kick Jamie where it hurts. *Or* that Emily.'

Great, Cara thought. She knew Lucy of old. She was a rock in times of trouble – unless her love life was under threat. 'Tell her there'll be no kicking next Tuesday,' she said firmly.

'I'll make sure of that,' Virginia assured her.

Over to her then. Of course there was always the chance of Lucy losing her cool on the spur of the moment, Cara realized, but some things in life one has to leave to chance. Talking of which . . .

'Do you know the society chair, Berowne Dyer?' she asked Virginia.

'I do. More's the pity.'

That shook her. 'What's the problem?' Cara asked. 'I thought he was popular.'

'Maybe, but ghosts of the past linger, don't they? They'll be there all right, even if you don't see them coming. It might be today's committee, but most of them were around then. The same faces, ten years older. That Berowne for one, and his wife, newlyweds they were then, and Oliver Bright, Harry's grandad , Pete and Charlotte, Luke Claxton – the whole gang will be there, no doubt of that.'

'That's usual in village clubs,' Cara said uneasily, doubts returning. 'People stay on. But there are those newcomers so the club's moving forward.'

'Moving back, more like,' Virginia muttered. 'Anyway, can't stay here all day. Work to do.' She grinned. 'Cheer up, Cara. There'll only be the odd ghost or two to reckon with. And they don't eat much.'

The problem with village life, Cara thought, as Virginia departed, was that its strength lay in its unity, and from what Virginia had implied it seemed likely that not everyone in Tanton village contributed to that. If so, the forthcoming banquet could well be a prime example. It might not be Madame Alfred Carrière roses all the way.

Cara looked at her watch. It was time to have that talk with Max and Alison to check that they were happy for her to chat away to Berowne Dyer about the Towers' history, on which she had never claimed to be an expert. Her own role was clear enough, but the idea of being drawn further into the ghost hunt, even in an advisory capacity, was not appealing.

Normally at five thirty, Max would still be lost to the world high up in the Towers, with his prized collection of Lavinia Fontana paintings, and Alison would be scurrying between the family wing and her duties in the public area of the Towers, getting ready for tomorrow's open day. Not today, however, as Cara had pleaded with them for their input in sorting out her question marks over this celebration. Virginia and the menu were no problem, but there were other questions to be asked, including her job for Lady Izzy.

'Why,' she asked, once established in the comfortable so-called Den in the family wing, where such semi-work problems were discussed, 'is Lady Izzy so very committed to this celebration supper? I know it's in honour of her nephew, but she seems so very set on how she honours him. Does she play an active role in the society? Does it fit in with her usual visits here?'

Max instantly looked perplexed. (His fallback position when difficulties presented themselves that did not affect La Galleria, home to his art collection.) 'I've no idea.'

Even Alison looked puzzled. 'I suppose she goes to the meetings, but I don't know whether she attends all their hunts. She told me that they have regular meetings where they discuss paranormal events and watch videos and so on, and every so often they get called out to investigate them, but this grotto hunt will be their first at the Towers since Tom's death, ten years ago. We took over the Towers the year after that.'

'To more or less have a rerun of the night he died still seems an odd way of celebrating Tom, though. And why just the grotto rather than the house too?' Cara countered. 'That really turns it into a replay of ten years ago. Aren't the Towers' ghosts worthy of a hunt?' Cara saw their expressions and added, 'I'm asking because Berowne Dyer seems to think I can tell him everything he needs to know about recent sightings of ghosts in the grotto underworld, which implies he hasn't much research material to go on. Is it OK with you if I flounder my way through it?'

'Only too happy. As far as I know,' Max replied blithely, 'in the Towers itself we only have good old Horace to brag about. There may have been one or two others in the past who have probably got too old to bother coming back to haunt us and died out.'

Cara laughed. '*Died* out? I thought that was how the ghosts were born, not lost.'

'Very funny,' Alison retorted. 'And you're wrong. They just get bored and give up if no one comes to see them or they're exorcized by the clergy. The village must be tired of old Horace's ghost. Everyone seems to know about him, because he prances all over the estate, as well as in the Towers itself, and pops down to the village on occasion too. There's Sir Reginald too, who narrowly missed being caught up in the Zulu War. He pops in occasionally.'

'Any in the grotto, apart from an occasional visit from Horace and the Laughing Lady that Berowne told me about?' Cara persisted.

'Ah yes,' Alison said. 'I've been making enquiries about that lady. She might be haunting the new cave we opened up there around the time you joined us, Cara. Sometimes her laughter is heard, but sometimes she's seen but not heard even though her mouth is moving. She probably lived at one time in one of the tumbledown cottages we had to demolish.'

'She sounds fun,' Cara said, 'so she doesn't seem to be bewailing her cottage too much. What did she have to laugh about if not that?'

'Rumour has it that she shot her husband in 1807,' Max said matter-of-factly. 'Don't let it give you any ideas, Alison. Izzy told us the society is keen to check her out.'

'I suspect,' Alison added, 'that Izzy will be right by your side while you're having your chat with Berowne in the grotto. Good luck to you if so. Love her though we do, she isn't the easiest of people to be shown round anywhere, and I'm sure that's what she has in mind.'

'Fine with me,' Cara replied. She could cope with that. 'But I still don't understand why the ghost hunt has to be held in the grotto, rather than just the celebration dinner.'

Alison sighed. 'Tell her, Max.'

Just as she had expected, there was more to this than just a celebration. Cara saw him hesitate, but eventually he said:

'My aunt might be confused from time to time, but not where the grotto is concerned. She has it fixed in her head that this nephew of hers, Tom Chalcott, saw something evil there ten years ago and that's why he had the heart attack on his way back home.'

This still didn't make sense. 'But that's a long time ago,' Cara pointed out. 'It's true she said something about Tom having thought there was something amiss in the society, but it can't have been serious as she hasn't followed it up since. Why didn't she, do you know?'

'Good question. Answer: she spent a lot of time abroad. Her husband was ambassador to half the world, and she didn't see much of Tom in those days. When Tom died, his parents were still very much alive. But by the time Izzy returned after the death of her husband, Tom's parents were no longer with us, so Izzy stepped into the breach.'

It still seemed curious to Cara. 'But why? Was there anything suspicious about his death?'

'Not that I know of, but it's Max's side of the family, not mine,' Alison replied. 'Izzy's never mentioned anything specific. Are you hoping he'll turn up as a ghost from the past?'

'Not while I'm there, thanks. Does Lady Izzy believe in ghosts?' Cara asked warily.

'No idea. But she does believe in Berowne.'

Believe in him? He certainly made his appearance as silently as any ghost. On Wednesday morning, Cara had no sooner unloaded the dishwasher in preparation for the day ahead than there he was. All five foot eight or so of him, sitting at an inside table twiddling his thumbs. Alison had rung earlier to say that Lady Izzy and Berowne would meet her here at ten o'clock. No sign of Lady Izzy yet, but then Berowne was rather early. Luckily, she was hardly rushed off her feet with the demands of the Happy Huffkin, and she was about to go over to join him when Sammy arrived.

'Good morning, Sammy,' Berowne greeted him as Sammy trudged past him on his way to the kitchen.

It was hardly surprising that they already knew each other, Cara thought. Tanton was a relatively small village, so this was just another case of older residents versus 'newcomers' like her. She remembered, however, what Sammy had said about the great Berowne. 'Trouble,' had been his comment, but whether he meant from Berowne himself or others wasn't clear. So far, Berowne seemed far from being a troublemaker, but she had no time to ponder on that as she had caught sight of Izzy, looking very determined as she marched towards them, clad today in tartan trousers and a bright pink tunic. It made Cara's own jeans and tee-shirt feel pitifully inadequate.

'Ahoy,' Lady Izzy shouted, waving her smart walking stick at them as Cara followed Berowne down the steps to join her. 'Ready for the grotto? If I'm going to make a speech at the dinner down there next Tuesday, I want to meet every stick, stone and Greek god.'

Berowne laughed. 'Zeus and his companions are in the grotto, but it's the Italian garden we're dining in,' he reminded her.

'Whatever.' Lady Izzy beamed. 'You're going to tell me all about the ghosts in this grotto, aren't you, Cara?'

'As best I can,' Cara said hastily. 'I'm not usually here in the evenings.'

'The very witching time of night,' Lady Izzy murmured. '"When shall we three meet again?" as Shakespeare's three witches enquired.'

'Answer: next Tuesday, at seven p.m.,' Berowne joked.

'Good, good, very good,' Lady Izzy said approvingly. 'Step forth, noble knight. Lead me to the land of ghosts.' She stopped short, surveying them severely. 'Before I go further, do you actually believe in ghosts, Berowne?'

'I've run the Tanton Ghost and Phantom Society for ten years, Lady Lendale,' he replied equably, 'and will be carrying the task forward.'

'You could be running it and still think that everyone but you is loopy,' Lady Izzy pointed out.

'I joined it,' he replied patiently, as they reached the entrance to the grotto from the lawn, 'but whether I believe in them is immaterial. The mere fact that they are believed to be part of the environment surrounding us is enough to render them part of the atmosphere. We enter a building, new or old, and sense atmosphere, sometimes barely discernible, but there's a presence there. Ghosts, phantoms, spirits: they all could be related to that.'

Did she agree? Cara wondered. It sounded almost too plausible. Still, her job – as she understood it – was keeping both Lady Izzy and Berowne au fait, as far as she could, with the recent activities of the ghosts of the Towers and the grotto. After all, this could be the first of many more evening celebrations for the Happy Huffkin Café.

Lady Izzy nodded enthusiastically. 'Good, good, onward then. Or rather downward into the grotto. I've got my speech to prepare.' She swept on, marching towards the slope leading down to the grotto. 'And of course, dear Tom died in here,' she added. 'That's why I'm sure he must haunt it.'

'He didn't die here, Lady Lendale,' Berowne pointed out. 'Sadly he collapsed near the car park after the ghost hunt was over.'

'Did he?' Lady Izzy stopped her progress forward and looked vacant for a moment. 'Well, that's close enough. Perhaps something frightened him here in the grotto. He did have a weak heart.'

Berowne looked concerned. 'It's ten years ago now, but I don't recall anything happening here that could have led to it. We left the grotto about midnight, except for Tom who must have followed on later. We all had to work the next day, so none of us felt like sleeping here all night, unlike this time when we'll be coming prepared.'

'Why did you choose to come here that night?' Cara asked curiously, wondering whether Lady Izzy was putting on a show of confusion, or if it was genuine.

'Yes, do tell us,' Lady Izzy said, taking her place on a bench provided by the entrance to the underground area of the grotto.

This small garden was a pleasant place, Cara thought, with the stream running from the Italian garden snaking its way along here between two great statues of Zeus and Hera, the god and his goddess wife in the Greek heavens. Not that there was anything heavenly about the shenanigans they and the rest of the Olympians used to indulge in, but in this form and with waving palms and ferns around them, they looked innocent enough. This was the point where the stream entered a stone fountain, presided over by a grim lion, and then disappeared.

'It was Tom's idea, if I remember correctly,' Berowne replied. 'He was the chair when the decision was made a week or two earlier, although I'd inherited the honour by the time of the hunt. I assume he chose the grotto because of the family connection with the Towers, plus I think there'd been one or two reports of manifestations. Even so, I've no idea why the hunt was just in the grotto and not the Towers itself. It didn't lead to any tangible result, but then,' he added with a straight face, 'ghosts aren't tangible.'

Cara laughed. 'It could be because the Towers seemed rather short of ghosts,' she suggested. 'Perhaps the society already knew about good old Horace and his naughty tricks of skimming through the Towers and then rushing off in the nude to the village. I don't know whether he bothers to run through the grotto as well. The other famous ghost haunting the Towers is Sir Reginald, who is still convinced that his wife was unfaithful to him.'

'Did you find out any more about this Laughing Lady?' he asked. 'What's her favourite area to haunt?'

'Yes, she probably lived in one of the cottages that were demolished a year or two ago. That's roughly when the ghost apparently began to appear in the grotto, because it was given an extension that runs right underneath where their old homes were,' Cara explained. 'So that would be the best area for you to concentrate on. And,' she ended triumphantly, 'the pièce de résistance could be that she laughs because she's just shot her husband.'

'Charming. Does the lady have a real name, or is she just a laugh?' he enquired.

'Other than the Laughing Lady? Apparently not. Just a giggler.'

Lady Izzy was growing impatient. 'She's nothing to do with Tom. What ghosts did he hope to see here?' she asked brightly.

Warning signal, which worried Cara. Lady Izzy was clearly set on discovering more about Tom's death, but it was far from clear what she was hoping would happen at the ghost hunt on Tuesday – or worse, at the dinner itself. Nor to what lengths she would go to achieve her aim.

Berowne wasn't fazed. 'I don't know, I'm afraid. Let me fill you in on the background of that night. The society records only mention Horace. As Cara said, the Laughing Lady appears to be much more recent. In Tom's time, there are reports only of presences and odd occurrences. Nothing attributed to a specific ghost. That's why I'm interested in the historical background. Tom had served ten years when I took over, and before him Oliver Bright, Harry's grandfather, had been chair. No more manifestations in the grotto seem to have occurred apart from this recent Lady.

Tom had to give up the leadership because he couldn't spare the time anymore. We had a meal that evening at the Farran Arms before coming to the grotto, organized by the landlord Pete and his wife Charlotte, both society members. Two others were here too when Tom died. Oliver was present as well.'

'Harry Bright works for Len Redman on the estate now,' Cara explained to Lady Izzy.

'He's a society member too,' Berowne said, 'although he'd have been a child when Tom died. The other society member who was there then and is still a member is Luke Claxton, village handyman and technology wizard. We'll have a little business on Tuesday to sort out before the meeting takes place, though that should be straightforward enough. It includes my plans for opening hunts up to non-members if they pay a fee, which I'm determined to implement even though it's not proving popular with all the members.'

Lady Izzy beamed. 'How splendid. What a good evening we're going to have. Such fun. Shall we descend to the grotto now, to tread in dear Tom's footsteps?' She rose to her feet and made for the slope that led down into the depths of the grotto.

Even though Cara had come down here on many occasions, it always seemed to her that the atmosphere changed from the picturesque quaintness above to what at first seemed to be an underground party for Olympian ghosts. Berowne had switched the lighting on, and Cara was struck anew by the impressive sight of the grotto. The oyster-shell-covered walls were dramatic, impressive and beautiful, but there was something cold and forbidding about them. She told herself this was sheer nonsense, and yet she was very glad that she wouldn't be sleeping down here on Tuesday night.

'What a fun place for all the ghosts to live,' Lady Izzy enthused. 'Perhaps dear Tom might have thought that all those statues of gods and goddesses were going to turn into ghosts? If so, he could be with them now.' She paused. 'Of course, one of them is Hades, god of the dead and the Underworld,' she added. 'That wouldn't have been very joyous.' Another pause. 'Where will you all be sleeping on the night of the celebration?'

'Ah,' Berowne said. 'Watch this, Lady Lendale.' He headed straight for what seemed part of the shell-covered wall behind a statue of a merry-looking plump gentleman. A moment later and part of the wall revealed itself to be a door, which he promptly flung open.

Cara remembered her astonishment when she had first set eyes on the statues. The frolicking gods and goddesses drew the eye away from what lay behind them, as the doorways were disguised by the shells making an apparently continuous wall.

'There are nine side passages,' he explained to Lady Izzy, 'and each of the gods has his or her own quarters hidden here, with their statues guarding its entrance. This is Aphrodite's boudoir,' he announced, pushing open a door a little way along for them to enter.

The weirdest boudoir she'd ever seen, Cara thought, as she helped Lady Izzy over the stony floor into this brick and stone dwelling for the gods. The events manager at the Towers had done his best to cheer up the walls with framed pictures of the sexy goddess, and one or two miniature Cupids pointing arrows at the visitors, but it was hard to imagine how it had looked to serious ghost hunters ten years earlier, and even less what it was going to be like for those sleeping in here next week.

'I asked Max once why Sir Jeffry went to such lengths to conceal them,' Cara said. 'He'd no idea.'

'Sex parties?' Lady Izzy suggested brightly. 'Tea parties?'

'Uncomfortable for either,' Cara pointed out.

'Let me point out my proposed quarters,' Berowne said, leading them to the far end of the pathway. He indicated a passageway a little longer than the others, which branched off and led deeper into the hillside. 'They're along there, at the end of this path,' he continued, 'some way from the main passage. That's because the path was only added in the last year or two, so Tom wouldn't have had this luxury. If I remember rightly, Tom sat in Dionysus, that's the one we've just passed at the entrance. That was the hunt's control centre, with the rest of his team and their equipment spread out in the other side passages.'

'Did anything happen in there to frighten Tom enough to fatally affect what might have been an already weakened heart?' Cara asked. 'Despite no ghosts being seen that night, something else might have happened. Even Scrooge had a real Ghost of Christmas Past to watch.'

'If something had happened, my Tom wouldn't have left without calling the others back to share the experience with him,' Lady Izzy said firmly. 'That's why I wanted to see this place and find out what happened here that night. Are you sure there's nothing in the records, Berowne dear?'

Cara had a foreboding that her doubts about the evening could be fully justified. This was clearly no idle wish on Lady Izzy's part to find out more about her nephew's last hours and the possible reason for his heart attack. It was a mission, but what sort of mission? Hats off to Berowne anyway. He was keeping his cool.

'No ghosts recorded, Lady Lendale,' he replied. 'Despite the tragedy of Tom's death, the secretary wrote up the findings and I've read them. There was very little activity recorded. There was a presence recorded from Apollo. His quarters, that is,' he added hastily. 'And ironically – as Hades is the god of the Underworld – that too had a presence, an evil one, whereas Apollo's was benign.'

'What was recorded on Tom's fancy equipment?' Lady Izzy asked. 'Did he take it all away with him?'

'As far I recall, we took most of our equipment back with us. Tom was going to return the next morning to bring the rest. I don't know what happened to that, and I didn't enquire about it because we were too upset by his death.'

'Suspicious,' crowed her ladyship. 'It's been destroyed. There must have been something. And what since then?' she demanded. 'Tom's ghost, or at least his presence, must have been around this place for years.'

Lady Izzy was going into overdrive, Cara thought uneasily. Did she really believe this? Did she really believe in ghosts at all, even though she was the honorary president of the society? Or had she chosen to become president because of what Tom had said about there being something amiss with it?

'Why would Tom do that, Lady Lendale?' Berowne asked gently. 'He had no reason to haunt us. His death was a natural one.'

'All the more reason for his ghost to be here,' her ladyship said brightly. 'There are good ghosts as well as horrific ones. You mark my words. Tom will be coming to protect us all. I've brought a photograph of him with his parents so that no one will be in any doubt when his ghost appears. Some people, including you, Cara, were never fortunate enough to have known dear Tom.'

She fished in her large handbag and produced a colour print of a group of three people, which Cara dutifully studied and passed on to Berowne. Tom looked serious, learned, and clearly the pride of his family. There would be no doubt as to who he was, should he turn up in ghostly form.

Cara gave three silent cheers for the Happy Huffkin. She was safely back. Sanity was regained. When she went inside, she found Sammy hard at work in his kitchen, food and sandwiches and cutlery all in place for the afternoon's visitors. He'd even been kind to her and overlooked the lemon biskets she'd smuggled in, made by her own fair hand from the eighteenth-century recipe. Since she was the owner of the Happy Huffkin, she occasionally wondered why she cared what Sammy approved or disapproved of, but such thoughts were dismissed for the greater good of keeping his goodwill.

Nevertheless, she did want to try Elizabeth Raffald's recipe, Solomon's Temple in Flummery, one day. The risk was too great, however. Sammy would undoubtedly have no truck with such oddities, and Virginia would not be interested in recipes from Sir Jeffry's time in the 1780s. With less than a week to go before the big celebration, it was better to play for safety. Flummery – what a wonderful word. As for Solomon's Temple, that surely implied the Knights Templar, who had passed on their way close to Tanton Towers, just as her own home, Knights Cottage, did.

To work, she reminded herself firmly. She should put the world of ghost hunts and Greek gods aside, at least temporarily, so that she could concentrate on the celebration. The feast would go ahead as planned with Virginia, and even the ghost tour afterwards could be a success. At least she wouldn't be involved with that, Cara thought thankfully. Sorry as she was for Lady Izzy and her late nephew Tom, there was nothing she could contribute to what happened after his ghost hunt. Surely Lady Izzy herself was now satisfied that she had done all she could for Tom? Was she really hoping his ghost would reappear after Tuesday's feast and she would find out what had led to his death?

Perhaps, Cara thought, it was merely that Tom had been frightened by something he thought was a paranormal experience. Or could Lady Izzy be fearing that something worse than that had happened? The words heart attack had a broad canvas and Lady Izzy's imagination could be far-ranging. As was her own, Cara thought uneasily, grateful that if Lady Izzy raised more doubts, they would be for Berowne to wrestle with.

Cara forced herself once again to bear in mind that this was not her job. The feast was. It was going to be a triumph for the Happy Huffkin. Daughter Kate had designed nameplates for her featuring a smiling Kentish huffkin with delicate garlands of cherries around it, and Cara envisioned next week's guests marching in like the Saints, one after the other taking up their places at this sumptuous celebration. First to come marching in would be Berowne with his wife, the as yet unknown Rachel, then perhaps Oliver Bright, patriarch of the society, thrilled that his grandson Harry would be present at tonight's feast, then Pete Brandon, the publican – whom Cara was used to seeing behind the bar. According to village gossip, his wife Charlotte kept a low profile. Luke Claxton might be stomping after her in the group, the practical one amongst them, whom she only knew by sight. Then would come the representatives of the youth of the village, Jamie and Emily, neither of whom would have been present ten years ago. In their wake would be young Harry Bright himself who, according to gossip, always had his eye on attractive young women.

They were all the society's guests for the dinner, together with Max, Alison and Lady Izzy, and therefore it was her responsibility that they should enjoy it. No qualms about that. But how glad she was that her duties ended with the dinner and not with the following hours dedicated to ghosts.

THREE

The day was here. Tuesday 20 June had arrived. True, daylight would soon be preparing to vanish, but the sun had apparently graciously decided to remain active for the celebration. The weather worry was out of the way, and ticked off Cara's mental list of 'what ifs'. Temporarily she could relax, she told herself. All was more or less ready as far as the Happy Huffkin's role in the evening was concerned, and even Sammy had declared that there was no more to be done.

On the lawn nearest to the Italian garden, she could see the field kitchens already in place, courtesy of quad bikes and trailers. Their progress over the grass must have been a nail-biting journey for Len Redman, who had been watching every movement with an eagle eye, ready to rush to their aid should it be needed, and his wife was doing the same. Josie, so Virginia had told her, had needed no urging to be part of the team tonight. Indeed, she had taken it for granted that she would be involved. Berowne, she had pointed out, would expect it. She'd worked part-time for him until recently, and so she knew all about the ghost society and had been eager to be part of the celebration.

The Towers' outside toilets had been given extra signposting in view of the sleepover in the grotto, and all seemed to be well there too as far as Cara could judge. Len and Harry were still rushing to and fro with bedding and cushions since the guests could hardly lug them into the Italian garden, and extra fire buckets (just in case needed) had been placed in the grotto, together with a small cupboard or two for nighttime water and refreshments for the brave souls who were taking the hunt very seriously. One of them would in due course be Harry in his role as a ghost hunter, not his daytime job as gardener. According to Len, the society members all had brought sturdy sleeping bags to await their arrival, but the cold floor would have easily made itself felt through those despite the mattresses, so protection had been necessary. Fortunately, Alison had dissuaded Lady Izzy from her sudden desire to sleep here herself overnight. That had been difficult, but the argument that it might affect her nephew's spirit from lingering there won the day.

'Presences,' she had then explained gravely to Cara, 'make their own decisions.'

Len had reported the arrival of the society members' equipment. It had been a struggle, he told her with pride, but their EMF meters, voice recorders and digital cameras were now safely stowed away in the grotto's side passages, which were also fully equipped with thermometers, notepads and so on. He said he'd heard the old lady jabbering on in the Italian garden and, no worries, there'd be plenty of stuff around to record the paranormal, with or without the ghost of Tom Chalcott.

Cara glanced at her watch. Half past six. Another half an hour and the company would be gathering for aperitifs and Virginia's delicious marinated olives. Yes, with a sigh of satisfaction, she could truly say that *the time had come.*

The time had come. No help for it. Jamie Dickens yawned. He had to get moving, and hopefully this ghost performance would be worth the effort. He wouldn't have joined this club if it hadn't been for its link with Rachel's property firm. Could be useful now he'd graduated and, anyway, ghosts were more interesting than he'd thought. He'd persuaded Emily to join too. He'd thought it was all a laugh at first, but he was coming round to the idea that there might be something in this ghost game. The Tanton Ghost and Phantom Society seemed keen on its technology, for a start. Might be a problem tonight though, as Emily was dead set on seeing her first ghost at this do and he wasn't going to risk her bedding down with anyone else but him. Harry Bright had his eye on her, so he'd have to take care of that. Maybe Harry could take up with Lucy. He pondered this idea. He was tired of her still hanging around him now he'd made it clear they were no longer an item. As for the rest of those ghost hunters, the old folk would soon be ghosts themselves, and tonight they were getting the practice in. He was beginning to look forward to it, he realized to his surprise. Nothing like a ghost or two to liven up proceedings.

* * *

The time had come. Luke Claxton was all too aware of that, and he had to be ready for it. It was ten years since Tom Chalcott had got his comeuppance, and had anyone in Tanton's Ghost and Phantom Society seen sense since then? No. They were miles behind the times. They couldn't even make up their minds as to which were phantoms and which were ghosts. That was easy. They were the same. It took technology to tell you that, yet old chaps like Oliver Bright wouldn't have it. To him phantoms were invisibly dancing around so they could pop up anywhere and whisper boo in your ear. They knew who you were all right, and targeted you. He claimed ghosts were a different matter because they knew what they were about, where they were and why they wanted to be there. Fair enough up to a point, Luke granted. Look at those Roman centurion ghosts who went marching along with their legs a couple of feet below floor level because they were on the old road and not the modern one. They didn't care about you, they just wanted to march on like they used to in the good old days. But where was the evidence that phantoms were any different?

He'd stick to ghosts, thanks. Something real to catch on to. No place like home for a ghost. Technology and science were the answer to ghost hunting. Ghosts came when they liked and went when they decided, like that old witch who was still protesting her innocence for a while. She'd given up – and that's what this society was doing. He'd expected Berowne Dyer to knock some sense into them, but he hadn't. Sometimes, Luke thought, he was treating it all as a game, a game that he was preparing to throw open to all and sundry with this new idea that non-members could come on hunts. And that would be Berowne's undoing. The society deserved more than that. It needed leadership – quickly, Luke decided. Not the ghost of a chance they'd ever elect him though. He'd have to do something about that.

The time had come. In the Farran Arms, Pete Brandon was sure of his ground now. There had to be a reckoning. He'd joined the society for good reason and where had it got him? Nowhere. At first Tom Chalcott had been the chair and that was bad enough, but since then they'd been landed with Berowne, his landlord, to whom he was still drowning in debt. He was doing OK but his show of joking with the villagers over the counter every evening was a waste of time. As was his belonging to this society. He'd hoped that they would see sense. That phantoms were shadows of yourself and nothing to do with ghosts. Ghosts – who needed them when real-life phantoms were the problem? Fear. Fear taunted him with his debts – and with his darling wife Charlotte. *Whose* darling, though? What a laugh, eh? Berowne Dyer was the one laughing. Pete couldn't take it much longer. He'd had enough of him.

The time had come. Charlotte carefully combed her hair just in the way Pete liked it. But probably he wouldn't even notice. He was too fixated on whether she was chatting up other men. She was all too aware of that. They'd been married a long time and the tenth anniversary of the last time they'd had a ghost hunt in the Towers' grotto was an uncomfortable reminder of that. She'd been engaged to Pete then, but even so she couldn't help being smitten by Tom Chalcott – who wouldn't be? Serious, good-looking, rich, and destined to inherit a baronetcy. Unfortunately, Pete had noticed. Just as he watched her all the time with Berowne. Poor Tom had died ten years ago, and after that awful time she had seen sense. Her future lay with Pete. She loved him. Didn't he realize that? Perhaps this evening would help. She'd pretend for his sake that phantoms were different to ghosts, though she didn't believe they were. And she would go nowhere near Berowne. Well, she'd try not to anyway.

The time had come. Oliver Bright was, he acknowledged, getting on in years, and seeing his grandson, young Harry, bouncing around so importantly made him all too aware of it. He was heading for trouble was Harry, in his view. He could always tell. He'd been chair of this society up until twenty years ago and nothing had improved since then. He had half a mind to run for chair again, but it never seemed to go the right way. He had a duty to the society to rectify that, despite Berowne Dyer's tendency to behave as though the supernatural was something to be taken lightly. And it wasn't. Far from it. It needed a leader, a leader who knew the difference between phantoms and ghosts. A leader who wasn't going to allow non-members to come on ghost hunts without knowing what they were doing. A leader like him.

The time had come. Harry Bright decided the time had come to stop lugging stuff around for Len, even though Len was the boss. Tonight, Harry had other fish to fry, and one of them was Emily. He'd spotted her a week or two ago and his path was clear, now that the fling he'd had with Ava at the Towers had come to an end with a bang. He'd heard Emily had taken up with Jamie, but he could have a shot at her. And then there was Lucy, Virginia Harding's niece. She was a looker too, and she had something to do with the catering tonight. Which to go for? Difficult.

Grandad, or Gramps as Harry liked to call him, was always nagging him to join this weird society, and so he had. It had started off as a joke, but on the other hand there were really such things as ghosts. Plenty of them around if you searched, though why complicate matters by claiming phantoms were different from ghosts? They were all out there somewhere. The Towers itself had a few ghosts, so did lots of places in Kent. Pluckley was roughly the same size as Tanton and it was supposed to be the most haunted place in Kent, or maybe in Britain. Whichever, Tanton was going to give them a run for its money – even if he had to help that along. Besides, he'd been joking around with Emily at the last meeting and she'd be there tonight. That would help the time pass if Jamie was in hot pursuit. It was going to be an interesting night. After all, Gramps had said that the last time they'd held a meeting here, some chap had died of fright. He wouldn't wish that on anyone, but things happen. Like this new idea Berowne had of charging non-members a fee for joining the hunt. Good plan, though the old crew didn't see it that way.

The time had come. Cara's adrenalin surged. Yes, it was time for her to join Victoria at the field kitchen marquee. She'd finished everything she needed to do here in the Happy Huffkin and, as she set off for the field of action, she could see guests already at the entrance to the Italian garden. By the time she reached the marquee, she could see Max and Alison in their evening attire arriving there together with Lady Izzy. Lady Izzy seemed to be wearing pyjamas at first glance, but a second look made Cara realize that she was clad in sparkly silver lamé wide-legged trousers and jacket – plus a crimson hat with a peacock perched on top, looking almost large enough to be real. It passed through her mind that peacocks were often thought to be symbols of bad luck. Sheer superstition, she reassured herself.

Not far behind was Berowne with his wife Rachel, whom Cara now remembered from last year's summer fête. Then Rachel had been in jeans but now, in full splendid evening dress, she looked a different person: tall, stately, self-confident – and good-looking, Cara conceded. She fitted the role of Berowne's wife admirably. None of the guests seemed to be lugging suitcases, so presumably all their personal gear had now joined their ghost-hunting equipment in their rooms at the grotto, courtesy of Len and Harry. Len would probably be lurking somewhere in case someone decided to light candles – which he had strictly forbidden. Lanterns were acceptable, and otherwise the Towers' estate lighting would have to do. Behind Berowne and Rachel, she recognized Jamie; the pretty girl with him, wearing a ghastly pink dress that didn't suit her, was presumably Emily. A sudden thought struck her. Virginia had chatted about her niece Lucy Parkin, who had had a boyfriend called Jamie who had dropped her, but Virginia had assured her that there would be no trouble tonight. All looked good so far, as there was Lucy calmly taking round platefuls of delicious-looking nibbles while the said Jamie seemed to be more interested in Emily. Anyway, Cara reasoned, she wouldn't pick an evening like this to start a row. All would be well – but she crossed her fingers just in case.

'A toast!' Lady Izzy was on her feet, waving her wine glass in the air.

What was this sudden move about? Alarm bells rang like crazy in Cara's mind. She had edged her way to the arbour once her duties had been fulfilled in the field kitchen and the dinner was under way. Apart from a hitch when a dish of black olives was somehow tipped over Emily's pink dress, courtesy of an apparently remorseful Lucy, all had so far gone well with the first and main courses, and there seemed to be a table full of satisfied customers.

Lady Izzy, however, was breaking new ground. Here she was on her feet again and they hadn't yet had the dessert course, let alone cheese. Cara had noticed that Lady Izzy had drunk not one but two negronis even before the wine began circulating for the feast itself, so hopefully this was mere exuberance rather than something she'd planned. But those alarm bells were still ringing. Lady Izzy, looking majestic in her glittering silver outfit, seemed almost a prophetess of doom. Nonsense, Cara told herself, she was foreseeing problems where none existed. And yet . . .

'Ghosts,' Lady Izzy shouted out. 'We're all here for that, aren't we? We're the Tanton ghost hunters. *And* phantoms. I'm your honorary president and I'm going to make a speech.' She shook off a restraining arm from Rachel. 'It's been ten years since you all last popped into the grotto to see what was going on in the spirit world. Now you're all here again. I heard about you pinning down your twentieth ghost. Must have been busy with those ghosts since then. What's been happening? Seances? Table turning? Ouija whatsits? Met any mediums? Run into any fully fledged spectres? Tell us your stories one by one and I hope you're ready for another one. Tom's. Maybe he'll join us tonight. Any objections?'

There was a stunned silence, which Lady Izzy took for a negative. 'Right then. On second thoughts I'll spare you. You can start, Berowne. You're the boss. How many ghosts and phantoms have you run into?'

He took it in his stride. 'A difficult question to answer, especially before we eat what promises to be a delicious dessert,' he said good-humouredly. 'But let me try to reply. The number we run into is nowhere near the number we can't because nothing appears to our human eye. There are presences where, even though nothing materializes, the spirit world is clearly at hand; there are strange noises, creepy feelings, all sorts of phenomena.'

Lady Izzy grinned. 'Nicely put, but suppose it's balderdash?'

Berowne laughed. 'To you perhaps, but to someone whose dog refuses to enter a perfectly innocuous wood, or barks at an apparently empty field, it's far from balderdash. Nor is it balderdash if there's the sound of someone singing in an empty room. And then there are seances, of course. Our members attend those if called on.'

'Mediums can be fakes,' Lady Izzy said gleefully.

'But what if they're not?' Berowne countered. 'That's where the Tanton Ghost and Phantom Society comes in.'

'Good for you,' she crowed. 'Let's drink to it.' Another sip and then: 'Rachel, when did you last see a ghost?'

Rachel answered promptly. 'Last see one? About a year ago. He makes a routine appearance in one of our bedrooms. He used to own our house and still thinks he does.'

'He likes to see we're looking after it properly,' Berowne contributed.

Cara wondered whether Sir Jeffry had ever had the same idea. She noted that Alison and Max were doing their best to keep out of this discussion, but she knew that Max would make short shrift of any ghost that dared to haunt him.

'It's no joking matter,' Oliver growled. 'We know that this grotto's haunted. That's why we came here ten years ago. And a phantom must have killed Thomas Chalcott. He must have died of fright.'

What would Lady Izzy make of that? Cara held her breath. This was new to her.

Luke got in first. 'Rubbish. Too short a stay to expect much of a result and there was no evidence of the phantoms inside or outside,' he grumbled.

Cara didn't know him well but, being well primed by Berowne, she gathered that grumbling was natural with him. He was divorced, so Berowne had said, and probably had a grudge against the world. And, it seemed, against phantoms. 'Only here till one o'clock or so. At least we're doing the thing properly tonight.'

'Yeah,' said Jamie. 'Snug as bugs we'll be, eh?' An arm went round Emily's shoulder, perhaps to make it clear that ghost hunting was not at the top of his agenda.

The arm hadn't gone unnoticed. The minute it was withdrawn, Harry promptly put his arm round the other shoulder, which made Emily squeal, then he withdrew it as Jamie glared at him. Lucy, Cara noticed, was glowering in the background. Josie and Virginia were hovering to step in should back-up be needed anywhere. Lady Izzy was still standing but rocking on her feet. Len was no doubt discreetly keeping an eye on the whole proceedings on behalf of his beloved gardens, as were one or two others from Virginia's team who were keeping a watchful eye on her domain.

'It will be fun sleeping in the grotto,' Charlotte Brandon piped up. (Somewhat unconvincingly, Cara thought. Did she have fun with her work at the Farran Arms? Unlikely.) 'Well done for arranging all these self-contained luxury quarters, Berowne,' Charlotte continued.

That brought forth laughter and cheers from all except her husband, Cara noticed. Pete Brandon scowled, but he at least made an effort: 'Good dinner, Berowne.'

'Hear, hear,' Lady Izzy said approvingly. 'The ghosts are shivering in their boots.'

She was definitely tipsy – as Cara's grandmother used to say. Rachel was now having another go at taking her arm to steady her, but once again Lady Izzy defiantly removed it.

'We're in for a great night,' she yelled, as she clutched her wine glass, realized it was empty and reached out for the bottle.

'We're already having it,' said Max politely as he quickly removed it before she could seize it.

She was not quelled. 'Ghosts. That's what we're here for. Ghost hunters. Waiting to see who turns up.'

A sudden chill in the air. The mood was changing. Cara shivered.

'Shakespeare.' Lady Izzy was in full flow again now. 'He liked a nice murder. Hamlet, Macbeth, Othello, all that lot. That's why I hope my Tom's popping back tonight. Not as a presence this time. As himself. He'll want to have a word about his murderer.'

A silence. An audible intake of breath. Cara froze. *Murderer?* Was that what this was all about? Not a heart attack but murder? Of course, she realized with horror, it was obvious now. This is what Lady Izzy had been leading up to all this time.

Lady Izzy chuckled. 'That shook you, didn't it? Well, you never know, do you?'

An uncertain laugh of relief all around the table. It had all been a joke – hadn't it? Cara realized she was trembling.

'Who might this murderer be?' Berowne politely asked.

'A ghost of course.' Another chuckle from Lady Izzy.

FOUR

The sky was darkening now and so was the mood of this hitherto successful evening party. Even Josie's hasty refilling of glasses failed to reignite the early congenial chatter. Cara watched almost in disbelief at how quickly this had happened after Lady Izzy's mischievous speech. Joke or no joke, it had left its mark. Even the raspberry compote had not been greeted with zest, and the array of Kentish cheeses failed to raise much enthusiasm.

Berowne was clearly aware of the changed atmosphere, for he very shortly rose to his feet and donned his now familiar inscrutable smile. Was that assumed or real? Cara wondered. She could play no part in these proceedings, and in any case she doubted that anything he said could gloss over the effect of Lady Izzy's words.

'The time has come,' he announced in his usual easy manner, 'to begin the most important ghost hunt for the society in the last ten years.'

'Hear, hear!' cried Lady Izzy, removing the peacock hat and waving it in the air as rumbles of relief came from the members. Even Max and Alison joined in the applause, probably mightily relieved, Cara thought, because they would now be able to depart, bearing Lady Izzy with them – if they were lucky.

What lasting effect had Lady Izzy's dramatic words had on her audience? Joking or not, they might have cast a shadow over the hunt that was shortly to begin, Cara reasoned. Perhaps she was judging too quickly, but to her some of the assembly looked as though they wanted to crawl away and forget the whole evening. Was that her imagination working too hard? Did the manner of Tom Chalcott's death come into this? Almost certainly, she thought, even though he'd collapsed not in the grotto but on his way home. Surely that wouldn't affect tonight's ghost hunt? Not unless, of course, she reluctantly considered, there had been some truth behind Lady Izzy's outburst. But *murder*? Surely that couldn't have happened. Not at Tanton – but then she had thought that before.

Could Tom have been murdered? In theory, yes, as he had left the grotto alone with the rest of the team having already left. Was one of them waiting in the car park for him? His car must have been parked there. Did something scare him to death there? Unlikely. It could have been sheer coincidence that he died that night as he suffered from a weak heart. Asphyxia? No, that would leave evidence on the face – bruising, finger marks, discolouration and other dreadful signs – and a big struggle would have taken place.

Nothing to cause such a ghastly ending seemed to have occurred during the ghost hunt that Tom had superintended, where at least some of the society's members here tonight had also been present. Not Jamie and Emily, though, because they were too young to have been involved. They were sitting with arms entwined, spending more time gazing at each other than listening to Berowne's speech. Pete Brandon, the pub landlord, was scowling at him – he would have been here ten years ago, and presumably his wife Charlotte too. She recognized Pete, of course. He had always struck her as though he found it hard to fulfil his role as 'mine host of ye olde village pub'. Apart from that, he was likeable enough, even if he looked somewhat overcome by the difficulties of life. Charlotte wasn't cut out to be a pub landlady either. In her late thirties, she gave the impression that her role didn't come easily to her. At the moment she was listening intently to Berowne. So was Rachel, his wife, whose elegance, flawless make-up and expression of great interest clearly indicated her role as consort to the leader. Was she present there ten years ago? Cara wondered. Who else would have been there?

Oliver Bright, the elderly chap giving the impression of being the elder statesman of the group, would certainly have been present as former chair of the society before Tom Chalcott's reign. His grandson, Harry, would obviously not have been there ten years ago. Who else? Well, there was Luke, who in Cara's view was one of those people who adorn many groups. He was doing his Mr He Who Does Things Best act, and making little secret of it, judging by the way she had noticed him haranguing his neighbours this evening. Perhaps, she conceded, he did know best. From visits to his handyman shop in the village, she sensed that he was very knowledgeable about everything in the technology line.

'And now,' Berowne continued, clearly reaching a high point in his speech, judging by his tone and body language, 'ahead of us lies the excitement of the as yet unknown. What we are hoping to see, hear or sense throughout the night is unexplored territory. There's always the hope that our former chair, Tom Chalcott, will visit us at least as a presence, as he may already have done.'

A pause as he looked round his audience, now very still. 'There's the Laughing Lady who has come to haunt the grotto in quite recent times but awaits verification,' he continued, 'and there are others that in the past have been reported and are worth investigation, such as the witch who hid in the woodland that in her time had preceded the grotto and was evading the search party. She's said to crow with pleasure because they never found her. And there's a village legend of an eighteenth-century naval captain, who rushed over here from Chatham in defiance of orders to sail; he came to meet his lover, who never turned up, and he calls out for her still. According to Len Redman, who knows this grotto like the palm of his hand, other weird noises and cold spots have been reported to him over the years.'

This all seemed to be going down well with his audience. Berowne had obviously done his homework, and some of it was new to Cara. From their looks of surprise, she suspected it was new to Alison and Max too. Could the stories just have been manufactured for the day? She dismissed this tempting thought. The records would prove Berowne wrong, surely, and his flock wouldn't like that.

'And,' he continued, 'it's often thought that ghosts are drawn to water, so they might be attracted to the stream that runs underground by the side of the grotto. What we're lacking is a sufficient number of ghost hunters for all the great opportunities that await us. This little group of ours does splendidly but, as we've discussed, we need to make our hunts open to non-members as well, so that we can investigate much further afield. I've plans afoot for that.'

'Cheers,' yelled someone – Jamie, Cara thought. He was the only one, she noted, and indeed Jamie looked quite amazed at himself. There were no other signs of enthusiasm from the rest of the audience.

Berowne had not yet finished. 'But as a swansong to our present ghost-hunt methods, we shall remember our former leader, Tom Chalcott, who – as his aunt and advocate Lady Lendale reminded us – died on his way home from here ten years ago. He achieved so much for this society, and his memory needs no ghost to remind us of what he meant to us. A toast,' he said, reaching for his glass, as his listeners scrambled to their feet with their drinks in hand. 'To Thomas Chalcott, the respected master of the paranormal.'

For a moment Cara thought that Lady Izzy wasn't going to join in but, true to form, she did it her way. She remained seated until the very last moment as the guests raised their glasses and got to their feet.

Then she stood up, raised her own glass and yelled out: 'Tom! Get ready to make your appearance. Give these folk a show tonight like you've never done before.'

She was losing her audience now, Cara could see that, and there seemed to be some reluctance to move on to the grotto. It was still quite light, and though Virginia's team was clearing the tables, the guests were still chatting, with some taking the opportunity for toilet visits and others just finishing their drinks or wandering round the Italian garden.

It was clear that Lady Izzy hadn't finished what was obviously her mission for the evening, and Cara decided to make her way over to her.

'I'm getting too old for this job,' Lady Izzy informed her. 'Max is right. No prancing around in pyjamas for me. You can tell me if my Tom comes back tonight, won't you?' A keen look told Cara that the Dizzy Izzy she'd seemed earlier might have been manufactured. 'Something's going to happen, Cara,' she continued. 'I wasn't joking. But Max and Alison are ordering me to leave now with them, so it's over to you. You can tell me about it tomorrow.'

Whoops! This wasn't what she had bargained for. 'How?' Cara asked blankly. 'I won't be here tonight. I'm not on the hunt.'

'You'll find a way to discover what happens, I'm sure, even if you have to wait until tomorrow,' Lady Izzy assured her, not a whit dismayed. 'Tom will help you. You'll see. I've what they call second sight, Cara. You come along with me while I have a word with dear Berowne. At least we've got someone sensible in charge of the hunt. Just pop along until they're all dispersed to their little rooms.'

She patted Cara on the arm, smiled happily, hooked her own arm inside Cara's like the Duchess in *Alice in Wonderland*, and marched her off to join Berowne who was now making his way to the grotto entrance.

This did not bode well at all, Cara decided. What did Lady Izzy mean by having second sight? In what way was Tom designated to help her, Cara? She sincerely hoped he wasn't. The last thing she wanted was a ghost nipping down to her own cottage irrespective of whether he wanted to help or not. Knights Cottage was her private realm, and not a hotel for ghosts.

'Do you *really* believe in ghosts?' Lady Izzy shouted happily at Berowne as they reached him.

Here we go again, Cara thought. How was dear Berowne going to deal with this? What was Lady Izzy's game now?

'I've run the Tanton Ghost and Phantom Society for ten years, Lady Lendale,' he said equably.

'You could be running it and thinking everyone but you is loopy,' she pointed out.

He smiled. 'Whether I believe in the ghosts is immaterial. They are part of the atmosphere. Ghosts form a presence. That's why we need to enlarge the attendance at our hunts. Not too large to frighten them away, but enough of us there to welcome them.'

'Well said, young man,' Lady Izzy said approvingly.

Again, Berowne's reply sounded almost too plausible to Cara. Lady Izzy seemed intent on challenging her dear Berowne, whether he liked it or not. Still, it was important to keep Lady Izzy satisfied, which she certainly seemed to be at present. It didn't last.

'You go ahead with it,' Lady Izzy continued. 'Have fun. Of course, but don't forget dear Tom died here last time.'

'Not here,' Berowne reminded her. 'He died on his way to the car park after the hunt was over.'

'Did he?' Lady Izzy looked vacant, which put Cara instantly on guard. Lady Izzy had been told this before, so why was she so intent on hearing it again? Hoping for something new?

'Perhaps something appeared to him during the hunt,' Lady Izzy continued brightly. 'Frightened him, perhaps.'

Berowne looked concerned. 'I don't recall anything more than what you already know. We all left the grotto about midnight, more or less together except for Tom, who as leader would have checked everything here before he left. We don't know how long that took him. He wasn't found, as you know, until dawn the next day.'

'I knew it!' Lady Izzy said triumphantly. 'He was alone here – and murdered by a ghost who wanted him out of the grotto because he considered it his private domain.'

Cara held her breath, but Berowne took this in his stride. 'I'll check the records again, Lady Lendale,' he said politely, 'but I think I'll find that there was no activity while Tom was here alone.'

'Splendid. You're too kind, too kind.' Lady Izzy beamed. 'I'll be off now, thank you. And thank you, dear Cara. Did she tell you, Berowne, that although I have to leave you, I have persuaded Cara to watch the beginning of the hunt tonight so that she can describe it to me tomorrow. Such fun to picture where everyone is.' The now familiar giggle again.

Berowne looked as taken by surprise as Cara was. She was amused that she had been caught, despite the need to help Virginia and see that all was in order at the Happy Huffkin. Nevertheless, she would have to obey orders, however nicely put, because Lady Izzy must have good reason for giving them. Just what that reason was, she wasn't sure. Reporting anything about Tom Chalcott? Did the group expect to see him or was that all Lady Izzy's imagination? She certainly expected something out of the ordinary tonight, and Cara was thankful that her job would end before ghosts began to walk in.

If ghosts were going to get up to their shenanigans, then she was extremely glad she would be away from it. Perhaps it was because she was tired, but to her the evening had begun to take on a distinctly sinister aspect. From where she was standing, she could see the dark opening to the subterranean part of the grotto, but the fun element predicted by Lady Izzy was missing. Perhaps this always happened on ghost hunts? It was merely a sign that the professionals were getting down to work.

Guests were beginning to drift through the grotto entrance towards the slope down to the underground chamber as their after-dinner chat petered out. Adieux were paid to Lady Izzy, who was following Max and Alison back to the Towers' family wing. Some of those staying tonight were looking distinctly grim, so why was that? Cara wondered. Was it that the night ahead had lost its charm, or was it because of Berowne's plan for the society? Luckily the grotto garden itself still looked restful, so peaceful with the flowers growing amid the stones, with only the odd Cupid peeping out to aim a stone arrow in her direction. Fine job he did for her last time.

Cara laughed to herself as she remembered that night Cupid had visited her over twenty years ago. Her daughter rarely mentioned her father or cared about him. On the contrary, she considered it all a great joke that he'd scurried off to go round the world after what Cara had imagined was a blissful start to lifelong happiness. Now she blenched at the very thought of that night.

The group was growing now. Virginia was finishing the clearance of the Italian arbour dinner; Len Redman would have finished checking the toilets, putting any final equipment into the various side passages and ensuring guests hadn't strayed into his precious greenhouses. Harry Bright, despite his dual role as both guest and employee in the Towers' gardens, should be on his way to help out where help was needed. The last time she had glimpsed him, however, he had seemed more interested in chatting up Emily – to Jamie's all-too-obvious annoyance.

Cara was thankful that she could rush over to the Happy Huffkin and then shoot off down the hillside to her cottage once they were down below and Berowne had officially declared the hunt in progress. No problem. Then she remembered she had driven here today – and she hoped she wouldn't sense anything on her trail as she walked round the path leading to the car park, let alone Tom's ghost.

First, though, she had to fulfil Lady Izzy's commission – once she could figure out just what was expected of her. She was counting the minutes, aware that she was achieving little so far. She decided she would stay until the members had all been shown their accommodation for the night. They were welcome to it. It might be summertime, but she preferred her own bed.

She waited until the last of the members had entered the grotto and followed them down the steps. At least the lighting, although very dim, was twenty-first century, which was just as well for those poor souls for whom this was their overnight accommodation. Sooner them than me, she thought. It felt musty to her and distinctly damp. Still, she reasoned, these were all fanatical ghost hunters and must know what they were letting themselves in for. Now that she was down here, she was even more relieved that she would soon be creeping out again – after she had done her best at playing observer, with her antennae out.

What immediately struck her was that the atmosphere amongst the ghost hunters had changed again. Now it seemed indefinably tense – no, that wasn't quite it. It was *demanding*. Sheer imagination, she tried to tell herself, just because ghosts were on everybody's mind and the hunt would shortly begin. Without her, thankfully – and the sooner the better.

'I've appointed myself Zeus,' Berowne began cheerfully when everyone had gathered at the foot of the slope in this underworld. 'King of the gods. That's just because I'll be in charge of co-ordinating the results. The society's equipment has been distributed amongst your rooms, including notebooks, EMFs and voice recorders, together with your cameras and personal belongings, and of course the bedding. Tomorrow morning, you can go your own ways, but please leave everything as it is. At midnight we'll rendezvous here to share results and record your own experiences so far, and then you're free to doze off – and let those ghosts frolic around you.'

There was a general nervous laugh. Except, Cara noted, from Oliver. He was glaring in disapproval. 'Equipment? None needed. You'll frighten them off. They come to haunt us, not blinking machines,' he shouted.

'As you wish, Oliver. My room is at the end of the wide passage at the far end of the grotto, should you need anything.' Berowne pointed in that direction. 'It's the side passage with a majestic stone statue of His Majesty King Zeus outside. I'll have a trigger object in my room – it's an ornament of a cat looking pleased with itself. And as king of the gods, I shall be in control there. So come along with any queries. We're very democratic, though. Even though I'm king of the gods, there's no need to bow when you enter my room.'

Another nervous laugh.

'Now I see the plan.' Rachel sighed heavily. 'I get to be Hera, much-put-upon wife and cook to King Zeus.'

Cook? That sounded suspiciously like a real-life complaint rather than one plucked from mythology, Cara thought, then reproached herself for jumping to unwarranted conclusions about the Dyers' home life. Anyway, the gods on Olympus only drank mead and ate honey, as far as she recalled from her distant memories of books read long ago. Looking at Rachel's graceful figure and generally confident air, she didn't seem too put-upon to her.

'You do,' Berowne answered her cheerfully. 'But at home, not here. Hera adorns the quarters nearest to Zeus. I'll show you shortly. Now for who's where in this main passageway.' He pointed to a belligerent-looking statue first on the right of the entrance. 'Meet Ares, god of manly things like fighting and wars. You're in his territory, Pete.'

He gave a friendly nod to Pete, which wasn't, Cara noticed, returned. Instead, Pete was taking a brief detour over the narrow stream alongside the path to pop his head into his chamber for the night. He wasn't wearing his usual 'genial pub landlord' face.

'Next to Pete is yours, Luke,' Berowne announced. 'You're Hermes, crafty god of invention and on-the-spot thinking.'

Luke looked tight-lipped, eyeing the statue of a god that indeed looked very crafty, with his hand in the air, as though about to snatch any opportunity coming along. Cara wondered about that. Perhaps she was doing poor old Hermes an injustice. Luke didn't comment on his new status, but his arms were significantly folded, as though he was waiting for any opportunity to complain.

'Apollo, for our Harry,' Berowne laughed. 'You're next in line, lucky devil. Or rather god. You're the one with everything going for him, especially in the female line.' His statue outside had his lyre prominently in front of him, as if about to serenade every woman that crossed his path.

The joke was definitely not appreciated by Jamie, whose arm immediately shot around Emily, as though Harry was about to drag her off to his domain right away.

'Cool,' Harry said enthusiastically. The look of devotion he gave Emily might be put on for the occasion, but it looked to Cara all too real. The gods of Olympus were traditionally all at war with one another, and there could be one brewing up right now.

'And now for you, Oliver, keeping your eye on your grandson next door. No Olympus for you, Oliver. Sorry about that,' Berowne added, 'but for some reason Sir Jeffry's appointed you king of the Underworld. Hades.'

His statue was the tallest of all of them so far, looming over his onlookers. He looked smug, his arms folded, as though he was making up his mind who to drag off next, Cara thought.

'In other words, I'm Hell,' Oliver muttered. He did look rather pleased, Cara thought, even though Berowne was hardly going out of his way to gratify everyone. Perhaps she was reading far too much into this, however. She should shake off this feeling that Lady Izzy had been worried that trouble was brewing. It was all straightforward, wasn't it? Just a special club meeting.

'And now for the other side of the pathway,' Berowne said. 'You're by the entrance we came in, Jamie. Right by the door, you're Dionysus, god of wine and all the joys of life. And there's another trigger object in your room, Jamie. A china dog. The triggers are checked to see if their position has moved after a period of time; if they have, it's vital evidence of a presence.'

'That'll do me fine,' Jamie smirked, as Berowne pointed out the way.

'Good. Emily is next to you. You're Aphrodite, goddess of love.'

That was having interesting results, Cara thought, amused. Jamie was definitely gloating, with a protective arm round Emily, while Harry as Apollo was looking far from his usual happy-go-lucky self. A giggle from Emily was the only reaction so far.

'Where am I?' Charlotte asked uneasily.

'Next along. Wise and stately Athena. Rachel's on the end of the row, nearest to me as Hera, and you're between her and Emily. The goddess Athena, the favourite child of Zeus, and the cleverest.'

Husband Pete most definitely didn't like that, Cara noticed, and even Charlotte looked nervous. But this was all fun, wasn't it?

'And along the wide side passage past Hera's chamber is, as I said earlier, Zeus. His palace has only been there a year or two, after the old cottages above it were pulled down, and the Laughing Lady ghost came to haunt the grotto,' Berowne said.

'So you'll be well placed to have a laugh with her when she pops down tonight,' Rachel observed. 'Literally right up your street, darling.'

'She might shoot you like she shot her husband,' Luke pointed out.

'Far more likely to climb into bed with him,' Rachel added dispassionately.

Berowne didn't seem to notice these pleasantries. He ignored the comments and was still smiling. 'There's water provided in your chambers, you know where the toilets are, and you should have everything you need for a scientific hunt. Personally, I prefer the six senses with which our Lord provided us, plus good old pads and pencils. Only ghosts don't have to move with the times, but we do. So, my quarters are your HQ and we'll be gathering in the main passage to compare notes at midnight. Everything gets reported to me then. Anything occurring during sleeping hours will be studied tomorrow.'

It wasn't her imagination weighing in now, Cara realized from that snappy interchange between the king and queen of Olympus, Berowne and Rachel. Nor was the tenseness of the group her imagination. Why was she feeling so uneasy about this ghost hunt? It could be fun for the participants. Anyway, she was a mere observer, thankfully. Certainly something seemed to be in the air, however, something strange. Is that what sixth sense meant? If so, what was it telling her? That something was very much amiss? Something she could not grasp?

Berowne was *still* smiling. 'Settle down,' he continued, 'and we'll meet here at midnight to hear what's happening – and let's hope a lot is.'

Good, Cara thought with relief. She could quietly slip away now without even being noticed. The group began to move away to their various rooms, and here was she at the rear entrance door through which she could quietly disappear. This was nearer to the car park where her car awaited her – and where ten years ago Tom Chalcott would have been heading. She wasn't sure why it seemed important to be taking the same route, but – who knows? – she might meet Tom's ghost coming down to haunt the gathering. There was a presence of some sort here, she thought uneasily. Fortunately, whatever sixth sense she possessed didn't seem to be sending out warning signals as she pushed open the exit door and came out into the darkness of the night, torch in hand.

FIVE

In the early morning sunshine, climbing the hillside from her cottage to the Happy Huffkin should have been a pleasure. Why wasn't it today? Last night's festivities had passed off reasonably well and a night's sleep had reassured Cara that her misgivings over the evening were ill-founded. Climbing the hill, however, usually such a pleasure, today lacked its usual charm.

The woodland was studded with mainly deciduous trees that shared their space with all the wildflowers that Kent could boast. In the autumn the trees provided a feast of colour that enchanted the valley below and now, in summer, they were basking in their green glory. Halfway up the path, she had passed the track that had once led to the now demolished old cottages, the home of the Laughing Lady. Had she been laughing last night? Cara wondered. One of the still remaining cottages had been used as a smugglers' storage den, because it was close to the secret tunnel leading to the Towers itself. Its contents of brandy had greatly pleased the lord of this manor, and his wife was no doubt ecstatic over the supply of tea. Had any smugglers' ghosts appeared last night?

She had now reached the path branching off to the grotto and she stood there undecided for a moment or two. Should she have a peep at the grotto to see that all was well or go straight on to the Happy Huffkin? It was eight o'clock and the overnight sleepers would have left by now if they had jobs to go to. Even if they didn't, they would likely have already scurried home for breakfast, no doubt in dire need of a shower after what must have been an uncomfortable night, even if productive in ghostly phenomena. There had never been any suggestion of breakfasting in the grotto, she supposed, because home would have far superior charm than the grotto first thing in the morning.

Berowne might still be here though, she reasoned, and possibly Harry Bright too, with his dual role as society member and gardener. She was still irresolute. One half of her was telling herself there was no problem about a brief visit to the grotto in the hope of finding out if any ghosts had appeared, but the other half was telling her to run like hell back to the Happy Huffkin. Ridiculous! She took the path leading to the grotto.

She had only gone a few yards before she stopped short. There was a yell, almost a scream. A man's. Was it in fear? No, but there were more shouts. Urgent ones. Desperate. She had no choice now, despite her sixth sense telling her to run back to safety. Cara rushed, heart pounding, towards the grotto, from where the noise was coming.

There it was. The grotto. Harry was stumbling towards her, clutching his phone. Normally he would be peaceably obeying orders as Len's underling. Not today. Something awful must have happened.

'I've called them,' he yelled at her, white-faced.

'Who?' Cara cried out. What was wrong? Roof caved in? Alarm bells were ringing loud and clear in her ears.

'Ambulance, police. He's dead. The ghost. Just like they said.'

Ghost, dead? He wasn't making sense. Ghost? It couldn't be Tom Chalcott. Ghosts can't be dead. What was Harry talking about? Crazy thoughts careered through her mind as she rushed towards him.

He clutched at her arm as she reached him. 'Don't go in, Cara. It's a bloody nightmare in there.' He was screaming at her. 'He's dead.'

Her stomach lurched. 'Who?'

'*Berowne.*'

Berowne? No, that didn't make sense at all. A whirligig was whizzing in her head and she knew she had to go inside the grotto. Something had happened. Neither police nor ambulance would be here as quickly as she could get in there, and that might be important. Why call the police? Suppose he was still alive? He might have had a heart attack or stroke and be recovering. But what if he *were* dead? Frightened to death by a ghost? Cara forced herself to think rationally. There are no such things as ghosts, she told herself, and even if there were, they couldn't take physical revenge. She had to act *now.*

'I'm going in,' she said, pulling away from him. 'I'm trained in CPR.' The official trained staff from the Towers wouldn't be here yet so there was no point in calling them.

'I'll come with you,' Harry told her bravely.

He looked completely shattered, and Cara wished she had the strength to prevent him having to go through it all again, but she hadn't. She needed company.

'Len will be here soon,' Harry blurted out, half choking. 'I've left a message. He and Josie were going to deal with all the bedding stuff.'

'Is anyone else still there? Berowne's wife?' She realized, appalled and belatedly, that she might be here, and so might the other members.

'No one. His equipment is still here and the notes and so on. Got to get them out.' Harry must have realized how crazy this sounded at the moment. 'Later,' he muttered.

Cara braced herself to pull the grotto door open. Perhaps it wouldn't be the ordeal she feared. Every minute might count though. Thankfully the dim lighting was still on. 'He's in his chamber, Zeus?' she asked.

'Yes. but don't—'

She couldn't wait. She had to get to Berowne's room as soon as possible. His life might yet be saved. Even as she ran down the slope into the grotto, she felt the gloom closing in on her. The door to Hera where Rachel had been sleeping – at the far left end of the corridor where it branched off to Zeus – was wide open but there was no sign of her here now. Cara ran along the short corridor to Berowne's quarters, straight into the chamber.

She saw nothing at first. Then blood, blood, blood – everywhere on the mattress, over the sleeping bag, and on what she could see of Berowne's body inside it. Clad in pyjamas, he lay sprawled on his back. The staring eyes, no heartbeat when she forced herself to pick up an arm. Drying blood everywhere. No heart attack, no stroke, no natural death. Cara was rigid with shock. Take it step by step, she tried to tell herself. There'll be time to collapse later. This must surely be murder and she had no place here.

'I told you. I told you,' Harry screamed. 'Let's get out of here.'

He was right. Berowne, whom everybody liked, was dead. No CPR could help. Harry clutched at her, dragging her away. 'Get out. Let's get out.'

This felt like home. With enormous relief, Cara had retreated to the family wing where Max and Alison had led her and Harry. She had done her best to clean the blood off herself, but it didn't clear her memory of the horror that had met her such a short time ago. Len and Josie had been notified not to go near the grotto, and thankfully Max had gone to meet the police. Alison's tea was acting like smelling salts, to Cara's relief. At least she might be making sense when the police arrived. Alison's company alone calmed her down.

'Lady Izzy,' Cara managed to ask Alison. 'Have you told her yet? And Rachel?'

'Max will go to see her with the police as soon as possible. As for Izzy, yes, we've told her. She listened without saying a word and then announced she'd have breakfast. Typical Izzy,' Alison said wryly. 'It sounds harsh, but she's taking it on board in her own way. She likes preparing her own breakfast when she stays here, because we never know what time she's getting up. Sometimes she's not up until twelve.'

Having breakfast – such an ordinary thing to do in the midst of a crisis. It was almost comforting, Cara thought. Typical Lady Izzy. This would be a frightening blow to her.

'This is all unbelievable,' Alison continued soberly. 'Yet it's happened. We weren't close chums with Berowne, but it's going to be a terrible shock for Rachel. And to you, too, Cara. Tanton Towers is pulling you into another disaster. Is talking about it going to help?'

'Perhaps.' Cara would have loved to have dived under a mental blanket and pretend it had all gone away like a bad dream. Not possible. 'I'll have to talk to the police anyway.'

'You said that all the overnight sleepers had already left?' Alison queried.

'Harry said he'd checked and I did a quick whizz up and down too,' Cara said. 'Everyone had gone with their possessions and the notes that Berowne wanted. Even Rachel had gone.'

Had Rachel left without Berowne, or had she seen what had happened and then left? Cara wondered. Surely not. She would have raised the alarm out of sheer shock. Unless . . . No, she told herself firmly. Don't start thinking that way. It was too soon.

'Whenever he was killed, someone must have heard something,' Alison said. 'There must have been noise and that could have been recorded.'

'His quarters were tucked away from the others, though,' Cara said, 'and I suppose weird noises might have been taken as being ghosts up to their tricks.' What about Berowne's equipment? She forced herself to think back to the terrible sight she'd faced earlier. Did she remember seeing the recorders? No. Nothing but that blood.

Alison sighed. 'Berowne of all people. Everybody liked him.'

Cara grimaced. 'Clearly not everybody. Someone must have been paying lip service to that sentiment.'

Alison was silent for a moment, then said diffidently, 'Is it likely we'll have the same DCI and team as last year?'

It was inevitable, Cara supposed, that this might crop up. She braced herself. 'Detective Chief Inspector Andrew Mitchem is still on official police business somewhere in France or the Netherlands or Spain,' she managed to answer. That sounded so formal, so distancing – and probably so correct.

Occasionally he kindly sent her a postcard conveying what a wonderful life he was having away from these shores, and one or two emails had informed her of some film she might enjoy or book that was worth reading. There had been no hint of when he might return. She had thought that he was an issue safely parked to deal with in the future, not *now.* And so he probably was, she comforted herself. His arrival would be the last straw.

When they had first met a year ago here at the Towers, their relationship had been far from smooth. It had ranged – at least on her side – from stormy to something she had barely recognized after she had managed for so many years without it. Her daughter Kate's father, full of great ambitions at university, had set off to save the world after their brief bonding there and vanished from their lives. The creep. The world hadn't been saved but no doubt he was busy doing his best in some bar or other. And now Kate was at university in Cambridge and she, Cara, was happily installed at Tanton Towers running her own business.

So what was making her so edgy about Andrew Mitchem's possible return? Sex poking itself up again? Love? Passion? Or, she realized, fear? If so, of what? If he marched in, now of all times, how could she possibly cope? The Happy Huffkin would be a haven once the police arrived. Cara decided to take refuge there until the furore really began. For a start, the police would need somewhere to work, although that, hopefully, would not mean their taking over the Happy Huffkin. It was far more likely that they would choose somewhere in the former servants' wing or elsewhere in the main house.

She stumbled into the Happy Huffkin with relief, then realized that the door had been unlocked, although it wasn't yet nine thirty. That meant Sammy was already here – and out he came to meet her. An honour indeed. Normally he was far too busy with preparing huffkin dough to actively seek her company, but today it was otherwise.

He emerged from the kitchen immediately. 'Murder, eh?'

So he had heard the news already. Grapevines operate fast in a village and Sammy had a masterly touch in picking up the latest information although not necessarily passing it onwards. Today, thankfully, she wouldn't have to tell him.

'Told you. Trouble,' he added.

'You were right,' she admitted. 'Does Virginia know?'

'Yer. Everyone.'

Ramifications and theories rushed through Cara's mind. She seized on one of them. 'No casual killer would know the layout of the caves and who was where. Even Virginia's team wouldn't know that, so that means Berowne was targeted – and by someone who knew where he was sleeping. Getting close to home, isn't it?'

Sammy agreed. 'Yer. All want to be boss.'

'Boss of the society? That wouldn't lead to murder, would it?' Cara replied, her mind trying to grapple with this thought but failing. The memory of what she had seen today was beginning to overwhelm her.

Sammy retreated to the kitchen again with a murmured, 'Things to do.'

He was right and that was another problem, Cara realized.

Should they prepare for visitors or police or no one at all? It seemed unlikely that the Towers would be opening today, but that was in Alison's and Max's court – and the police would have the final say. Whatever that was, the Happy Huffkin would need to know. She desperately hoped the Towers would remain closed. Could she face customers today? No.

'Cara!'

A shout from the garden. When she looked out of the window she saw Lady Izzy, making her very determined way up the slope, and hurried out to help her into the Happy Huffkin. The prospect ahead of her was daunting. Not again. Could she face more discussion?

'We need to talk, Cara,' Lady Izzy said briskly. 'How are you feeling? Over the shock? No, of course not. Takes time.'

She plumped herself down at the nearest table, and with a sinking heart Cara joined her. Lady Izzy was right. Shocks can't just be dismissed or conquered at will. Was she up to this?

'No,' Cara answered honestly. Her stomach was churning, her brain was buzzing, and all she wanted was to crawl back home. Instead, she had to talk to Lady Izzy and then the police – who were already here and at work. She could now see a cordon going up around the grotto and Italian garden. The hunt had begun, not for ghosts but for a killer.

She made an enormous effort. 'I'm so sorry, Lady Izzy. You were very fond of Berowne.'

'Everyone liked him.' Lady Izzy reiterated the familiar phrase. 'That was the trouble.'

'Why trouble?' Cara managed to ask.

Lady Izzy considered this, her head cocked thoughtfully on one side. 'Dear Berowne liked being king of the castle. Publicity and finance were his role in Rachel's property firm, which is why he became head of this ghost-hunting society. He was eager to find ghosts at Tanton Towers – and I suppose to attract people to the hunts. And of course, I'm always hoping that Tom's ghost will bless us with his appearance.' She smiled sadly. 'Dear Tom. Dear Berowne. Such dreadful deaths.' She paused. 'Cara dear, I thought you might like to know that as I left the police arrived. That nice Inspector Mitchem is with them.'

* * *

'I'm back.'

Detective Chief Inspector Andrew Mitchem's abrupt acknowledgement of her presence disconcerted her, as did the sight of his familiar figure. Cara had managed to pull herself together after Lady Izzy's tactful warning, but now that she was with him she felt back to square one.

Andrew was standing at the window, gazing out onto the gardens. Alison and Max had allotted the police incident rooms in the servants' wing, which would temporarily be closed to the public. On the guided tours of Tanton Towers, this room was on show as the housekeeper's domain, which had been hastily converted by the general manager to accommodate the police.

The kitchen, larders and several other rooms were shut, but much of the rest of the servants' wing was at the disposal of the police, including the housekeeper's room in which she was now sitting. Placed at the end of the wing it had the advantage that you could see the garden and the grotto through its windows. Cara particularly liked the room's fascinating bookshelves, full of cookery books from past centuries. Not only did weighty nineteenth-century recipe books adorn it, but earlier treasures such as Sir Hugh Plat's *Delightes for Ladies* could be found and enjoyed. Elegant seventeenth-century ladies all over the country must have had a whale of a time working their way through it.

At the moment such delights seemed a long way away, and probably from Andrew Mitchem too. This, his demeanour suggested, was police territory. The usual display cupboards, shelves and photos on the walls looked somewhat at odds with police personnel and paraphernalia, although the sergeant sitting at one end of the table was ostentatiously busying himself with notepads, recorders and computer. Awaiting her statement, no doubt.

Seeing Andrew, even though she'd been warned, was another shock piled on the first of the day. How to respond? How to act? Was he back in the UK for good or by chance or – a wild guess – merely here at Max's request because Andrew had handled the case here a year ago.

Cara struggled to make sense of her situation. This just wasn't fair. The call had come and she had duly accompanied the police officer over here. And now she had this blow to absorb. She had tried to comfort herself that there was no way Andrew could be here, but here he was. The last postcard she had received from him was at least a month ago and had made no mention of a return to Britain, but then he'd never bothered to tell her last year that he was going away. The shock of seeing him here was mixed with anger. He must have kept the sergeant here on purpose so that she could make a formal statement without the need for anything more personal. Very well. If that was his attitude, she'd deal with it. The tragic death of Berowne Dyer was the focus of this interview, not her.

'You're back from choice?' she nevertheless asked politely. That would fox him.

It did. No reply. He was clearly avoiding anything at all personal. Cara was fully aware, however, that with the murder looming so strongly over them, her stomach was churning once again with the effort of controlling her private thoughts. This morning's gruesome discovery was quite enough to wrestle with, without adding the remembrance of her last meeting with Andrew. Yet that had been a *happy* meeting, hadn't it? At her request there had been loving intent between them, but no more than that until she felt ready. She was aware that she had no idea whether he still remembered that, but *it didn't matter.* Not at the moment, even if he had engineered this way of announcing he had returned. All that mattered – *should* matter – was dealing with the horror of today.

Concentrate, she told herself. Go back to what you found this morning. She was a vital witness – surely not a suspect – and Harry had first discovered Berowne's body. She'd have to cope with DNA and fingerprint tests, but otherwise she would have little connection with the case. Nevertheless, she thought uneasily, in theory she could have committed the murder and hidden in the bushes to wait until someone else came along in order that she wouldn't be automatically suspected of guilt by being first on the scene. No, that wouldn't have worked anyway, as she would have been covered in blood. The mere thought of that made her feel sick.

'The first estimate of the time of death is about three o'clock in the morning,' DCI Mitchem (as she must think of him here) began abruptly. 'Harry Bright came rushing out as you reached the grotto entrance at about eight o'clock. Is that right?'

Concentrate. She couldn't think of him as Andrew in this context. 'Yes, although technically it is the rear exit door,' she replied matter-of-factly. 'I'd walked up from the village and decided to go to the grotto to see what was happening. Then I heard a scream – well, more of a yell really – and Harry came running up to meet me. He told me what had happened and we went in together.' How bland that sounded, she thought, as the horror of the scene rushed back to her.

'That took courage. And, as far as you could see, all the other people sleeping over for the night had left?'

'Yes. No one else appeared, and before I left I did look around at the sleeping quarters. Rachel, Berowne's wife, had been assigned the quarters nearest to him, but she too had already left.'

'What did you do then?' he asked.

'I left too. I'd thought I might be able to give CPR, so I went into Berowne's quarters but when we . . .' She swallowed as the memory of what had faced her when she entered that room came vividly back to her. 'I could see there would be no point, and Harry had already called for an ambulance and the police.'

He nodded. 'I'll need to speak to you again, but I'd be grateful if you could give my sergeant here a full statement. I'm afraid your tearoom must be closed today, as is Tanton Towers.'

'How long until it can open?' she blurted out, then mentally kicked herself for sounding so mercenary.

'I can't guarantee it, but I hope tomorrow for the Towers and therefore you too.' He seemed to hesitate, but if something had crossed his mind, he dismissed it.

'Thank *you,* chum,' she muttered under her breath as he left. Point taken. It was clear that he was here for only one purpose, and it didn't include Cara Shelley. His purpose was to find out who had murdered Berowne Dyer. That brought it all back to her again. Her chats with Berowne. She'd liked him. *Everyone* had liked him – and yet he'd been murdered.

Cara hurried back to the Happy Huffkin, her refuge. Having to go over in detail with the sergeant every step of what had happened earlier had left her longing even more for time simply to collapse.

On a sunny Wednesday in late June, she would normally be preparing for afternoon guests, as they enjoyed their tea and cakes before leaving or walking round the extensive gardens. Not today, with the Towers closed, and even if the press managed to get by the gatehouse into the grounds, they wouldn't know that she had played any part in the story they would be so eager to report. Dealing with the press was a horror she really didn't want to face. Alison would probably be in the gatehouse, fielding them off and explaining to other hopeful visitors what had happened, and so she and Sammy would be left in peace, Cara thought gratefully.

Wrong. Peace? That she should be so lucky.

There was no sign of Sammy, who must have already left on his bike. Sitting on one of the few outside tables that he must have put out was Lady Izzy again, enthroned with her walking stick clutched in her hand. She looked like a very determined monarch as she awaited Cara's arrival. There was nothing she could do to escape, so Cara summoned up all her fragments of strength. She'd already had one bout of Lady Izzy today. Now she would have to face another.

'Can I fetch you some tea?' she asked.

'Thank you, but no. Brass tacks is what we need to get down to. Agreed?'

'Yes, but . . .' With foreboding, Cara knew she was going to lose this battle.

'Now dear Berowne has been murdered, it's up to us. We're going to find out what happened, aren't we?'

'We?' Cara asked very warily indeed.

'*We.* I can't do it on my own. I'm a dotty old lady,' Lady Izzy informed her earnestly.

'Do what?' Cara waited in trepidation. It was obvious what would come next, and it did, but at least she had time to prepare.

'Tom's ghost is going to help us find out who murdered dear Berowne.'

This was too much. Was Lady Izzy serious? Cara was getting even more confused, but she forced herself to struggle onwards. 'But why should he? Your nephew didn't die in the grotto, so why would he haunt it?' she asked reasonably. 'And,' she added, wondering whether she could risk it, 'it doesn't add up because we can't be sure Tom was murdered.'

Stupid of her, she thought. She was getting into dangerous waters here. Too dangerous. She had enough to focus on with Berowne's death.

'My dear, Tom is, I'm quite sure, appearing as a ghost and one with a mission because you don't become a ghost for nothing. He is most concerned about Berowne.'

At this upside-down logic, Cara gave in. She tried to take command, difficult though that was. 'Has anybody yet claimed seeing him as a ghost?'

Ghosts usually appeared with a message of injustice, and unless last night's recordings showed anything to the contrary, she'd heard nothing that suggested Tom's ghost had been spotted. It could be entirely a figment of Lady Izzy's imagination, Cara reasoned.

'Yesterday was the first hunt here since poor Tom became a ghost ten years ago,' Lady Izzy retorted. 'No one has been looking out for him since.'

Cara tried again. 'There must some people besides the society who have walked through the grotto in the dusk or at night, Lady Izzy. Has anyone put in a report of his haunting the grotto?'

'No, but he has no message for casual visitors, only for the society,' she replied complacently. 'What did they discover last night? Who's checking all that paraphernalia? Are the police posting someone to ghost watch tonight? There might be a valuable witness.'

Laugh or cry? Cara could have done either or both. The idea of Andrew Mitchem hauling in ghosts to take their statements or waiting for them to reappear and declare their guilt was a wonderful fantasy, but she had to take this logically – if she could.

'I'm sure the police will be checking all the equipment left in the grotto. The arrangement was for Berowne to deal with it all this morning.' Cara's confidence returned. 'Whoever killed Berowne might have left some trace on the electromagnetic field even if he or she wasn't paranormal. Or odd things might have been disarranged or removed.'

'What time did he die?' Lady Izzy asked.

'About three o'clock, so the police say.'

'Good time for ghosts,' Lady Izzy said approvingly. 'Not for human murderers. Did it strike you as cold when you went into his sleeping quarters?'

Careful here, Cara warned herself. She could feel her stomach heave again as she remembered that moment all too clearly. Furthermore, she was getting too far into ghost territory. 'Everywhere felt chilly that early in the morning especially underground.'

'There could well have been a cold spot if Tom's ghost was around,' Lady Izzy persisted, 'because he would have wanted to protect Berowne.'

There was no dealing with this diagnosis, Cara realized. It was a case of a theory twisted in knots, but unfortunately it was one that Lady Izzy was clearly expecting her to follow up, although the look of satisfaction on her face suggested this could be a ploy.

'So that's settled then.' Lady Izzy was watching her closely. 'Together you and I will find out who killed poor Berowne because Tom would have wanted that, just as he wants his own murderer found. He's doing his best to help.'

His own murderer. Cara realized what this was all about. It had indeed been a ploy on Lady Izzy's part, and so perhaps for her to investigate her protégé Berowne's murder was a way to atone for her absence when her nephew had died. Cara still had doubts, though. Did Lady Izzy really think that Tom Chalcott's ghost not only existed – if she thought in those terms – but had been eager to save Berowne from his fate? Was there more to it? Lady Izzy had said, 'You don't become a ghost for nothing.' Why was she so set on Tom being a ghost? Perhaps because Lady Izzy believed that he too had been murdered?

'You're really convinced that Tom haunts the grotto because someone murdered him that night, aren't you?' she said gently.

A beam from Lady Izzy. 'Oh yes. It's obvious.'

Not obvious, at all, given that there was no evidence of any ghost appearance by Tom Chalcott, or that he had been murdered. Was she, Cara, therefore going to get involved in this chaos of fact and possible fiction? She knew she couldn't avoid it, if only for Alison and Max's sake, but she would go very, very carefully.

'I can't step on the police's territory,' Cara told Lady Izzy, 'but I'll do my best to find out if there's anything in Berowne's dreadful murder that links up to your nephew's death' – she braced herself – 'or to his ghost.'

What was she getting into? Cara had a momentary qualm. All her fingers were mentally crossed.

'Deal done,' Lady Izzy announced triumphantly.

SIX

By the late afternoon she had had enough. She had stayed on to clear away all the preparations for an open day that never happened, but now Cara longed for the comforts of home. Too late she remembered she'd walked up the hillside to the Towers this morning, so there was no car awaiting her. She would have to walk the long way home with the woodland exit cordoned off. It was the last straw after all that had happened today. Not only had she found herself in the middle of a murder scene again, but had managed to get involved as well, albeit to a minor extent. At least Sammy's appearance had been a blessing, despite the Happy Huffkin having turned into a comfort zone for tired policemen, but even he had now left.

If only she could just vanish too, Cara mourned. At least home, blissful home, now beckoned. All the warm June evenings in the world couldn't compensate for staying any longer here, despite the walk she was now having to take.

There's always a 'but'. Her heart sank. Guess who had spotted her and was strolling towards her as she reached the gatehouse. It was *him.* Another problem. She couldn't even turn and run, much as she'd like to. He was standing by the exit door of Sir Jeffry's masterpiece building. Sir Jeffry had actually restrained himself here in order to permit the greater glory of the Towers itself to be appreciated, judging by the comparatively modest number of carvings adorning it. Even so, why did they all seem to be leering at her?

'I'll drive you home,' Andrew Mitchem informed her, nodding to the two police officers guarding the gatehouse. 'My car's parked a few yards down the road.'

She could have declined the offer, but she hesitated. Mistake.

'I'm not planning to cross your threshold,' he added dispassionately, 'if that's what's worrying you.'

She'd no choice. To refuse now would be petty and pointless. 'Thank you,' she said stiffly. She was aware that it was her who had set the pace at that crucial point of their relationship, and that the occasional postcards he had sent were merely a reminder that it was still ongoing as far as he was concerned. Nevertheless, his sudden reappearance in her life had thrown her.

They walked in silence to his car, a classic BMW, she noted. No mere police car for him. It was, to her surprise, a fairly companionable silence. Finally he remarked, 'My Amsterdam assignment ended early. I was only back in harness here two days ago. Now this has happened.'

She was too drained to reply and, anyway, what could she say? I'm glad? Or, why should I care? This was not the time or the place for either.

'I've only one question,' he added, 'off the record.'

So that was it, she realized. He was offering her a lift to suit his own purposes. Very well. Silence from her would be the best and easiest reply.

He continued anyway. 'You're on good terms with Lady Lendale. I saw her talking to you.'

Still she said nothing, but she was cautious. She needed to be alone to think through the day in peace.

Again he continued, 'Did she by any chance ask you to do what you can to find out who murdered Berowne Dyer?'

She was caught. She could tell him the plain truth or she could explain further. It had to be the latter, she decided, and nerved herself to begin. She would normally have no problem, but today it was a challenge. A challenge she had to face *now.*

'No,' she began. 'What I did agree with her was to the effect that I'd try to find out anything about the death of her nephew, Tom Chalcott, ten years ago that might have a connection to Berowne's murder. In other words, if they are linked.' She toyed with the next hurdle and decided to take it. 'That includes Tom's ghost.'

She'd expected at least a grin, but it didn't come. She'd been a fool to mention it. He and his team would be intent on fact, not the paranormal. First there was silence, then at last he spoke. 'I can't stop you looking into the death of Tom Chalcott, or indeed his ghost, but usual rules apply where last night's events are involved.'

A step into dangerous territory, but at least some of this territory must surely be as new to the police as it was to her.

'Over Berowne's death, of course,' she agreed, 'but could there be an exception? You must already have all the recording equipment and cameras from last night. Lady Izzy had expected the ghost of Tom Chalcott to appear. May I see what's on them? She'd want to know the results,' Cara added hopefully.

'Exception refused,' he said, reasonably gently.

'You should reconsider,' Cara replied firmly. She was on stronger ground now. 'I agree that the recordings are vital for you because they might record movements, people moving around and even shots of his killer. Suppose there is something that suggests a ghostly presence last night?'

Quite what that would be, she had no idea, but it seemed valid to ask. 'I'm asking for Lady Lendale's sake, especially since some of those people here last night were also present the night that Tom Chalcott died. Even though he wasn't murdered, as far as we know, I do need to rule out anything that could have been his ghost being present last night – I have to do it, for Lady Izzy's sake.'

Even as she said it, she realized how crazy this sounded. She supposed that if – and it was a mighty big if – Tom's death had been murder, there could indeed be a link. Berowne could have been probing into it and discovered who or what had killed him. It didn't add up to a tenable theory, she realized. How could it?

His poker face didn't react, but the split-second silence spoke for him. 'There's nothing to suggest that one has bearing on the other,' he said at last. 'It's supposition – and so are the ghosts.'

Fair enough. She actually agreed with him, but she wasn't going to give up this fight easily. 'Have you looked at any of the recordings yet?'

'Yes.' A pause. 'I suggest a compromise. You'll be invited at our discretion to watch any suspected ghosts on the recordings.'

It was the best she could hope for, and it was, she admitted, quite a concession on his part.

'Other than that,' he continued, 'usual rules apply, as I said earlier.'

She knew what that meant. He'd tell her nothing about his case. Don't tread on his territory, and she must tell him anything relevant. Plus, if she made a hash of it, she was on her own.

Where had her suggestion of a link between the two deaths come from? She had no idea, but it had done the trick.

He drove the rest of the way to her home in silence. Even though she – and perhaps he too – felt the air was at least partially cleared, the outside lights of her cottage looked very welcoming indeed. She'd be going in alone and that was good. As for the next time they were alone together, perhaps it would be different. Or perhaps not. Just at the moment she couldn't tell the difference between her head and something called her heart.

At least Thursday morning looked brighter, to Cara's relief. Nightmarish dreams had punctuated her sleep. She'd woken up briefly after a dream of playing tennis at Wimbledon with Andrew Mitchem, which was really rather pleasant, but before that the nightmares had rocketed around her. Ghosts leered, the ghouls on the folly growled at her, horned monsters galloped up but refused to rescue her. Dreams were all very well if one could understand their purport. Anyway, this was a new day – a day in which she had to face another murder, she remembered, as it all came rushing back to her. A year ago she had faced the same horror, murder at Tanton Towers. She had thought then that it could never come again to such a peaceful place. But now it had.

On arrival at the Towers, Alison guessed immediately why Cara had come to see her so comparatively early. 'If you're looking for Izzy she's still in bed,' she said, 'which is not surprising after yesterday's shocks. Did she talk you into this mad idea of hers about her nephew's death and Berowne's murder?' she continued anxiously. 'It could bring trouble, and there's no earthly reason you need to do Izzy's bidding.'

Cara thought about this. 'No *earthly* reason, I agree. But maybe those ghosts are playing a part. Seriously,' she added.

Alison stared at her. 'You've fallen for Izzy's crazy notions, haven't you?'

'No, but you must admit that Berowne's death following from Tom's – possibly both murders, both leaders of the same society and dying more or less in the same place – is quite a coincidence. All the people who are best placed to be suspects were together. They could have personal reasons for wanting poor Berowne out of the way.'

'Take care,' Alison said soberly. 'Whoever killed that poor man is dangerous. And where and how do you begin, for a start?'

'I've no idea,' Cara said honestly.

Even as she said it, ideas began to spring up in her mind. The grotto was the key to this murder. If that was planned, why there? She would need to talk to everyone who had been there earlier in the evening to see what they had noticed, if anything. That included Virginia and her team, including Lucy, Josie Redman, Len, Sammy at the Happy Huffkin and even Alison, Max and Lady Izzy herself, who had been present at the celebration dinner. Or should she begin at the heart of the matter: with Harry Bright and the others who had slept – or at least tried to sleep – at the grotto on Tuesday night? Eight of them, any of whom could in theory have murdered Berowne.

And then the doorbell rang.

'That must be Rachel.' Alison leapt up from her chair. 'She rang earlier. She wanted to get away from the house because the press were gathering and she couldn't take it anymore. Amazingly she asked to talk to me, even though we barely know each other.'

She hurried to answer the door and Cara debated whether to stay or withdraw. Whatever the circumstances, the poor woman must be in no state to talk to a comparative stranger. She rose to her feet to leave as Alison returned with the tall, elegant Rachel, looking weary but in complete command of herself. That must be camouflage surely.

'Please stay.' Rachel managed a smile, obviously interpreting Cara's instinctive move correctly. 'I couldn't stay behind closed doors pretending nothing has happened and that it's just a nightmare that will soon be over. Does that make sense?'

'Yes, but it's brave of you to come out,' Cara said, meaning it, as she watched Rachel move with swanlike grace towards the Chesterfield, dark hair swinging around her shoulders. It felt like a filmset, she thought, then reproved herself. Whether she liked Rachel or not, she was a woman who had just lost her husband in appalling circumstances.

'Berowne told me about you, Cara,' Rachel continued, as Alison disappeared to fetch coffee. 'He said you were quirky – and that's a compliment,' she added hastily.

Cara wasn't too sure about that but murmured a reply.

'I'm here,' Rachel added, 'because I needed to talk to somebody. Almost anybody, bar the press. Then I thought of Alison and Lady Lendale. She tells me you're looking into the death of her nephew ten years ago. I remember that because it was the year Berowne and I moved into Ellum Place. We'd only been married a few months. He came to work for the family firm. Power without responsibility.'

Cara blinked. There didn't seem to be any rancour in Rachel's voice, but it seemed very odd to criticize him today of all days.

Rachel must have interpreted her reaction correctly. 'A wife has no illusions,' she added, as Alison appeared with a tray of coffee cups, 'but they have little relevance to love since they are immaterial. And I loved Berowne.'

A pause and Cara murmured a reply.

'I'm glad you're here, Cara,' Rachel assured her. 'You're interested in Tom Chalcott's death, and Berowne was too. So if I can help, do ask me. It would take my mind off what happened yesterday.'

Did she mean it? Apparently yes, but Cara decided to go softly, making it seem of no great consequence. 'Were you there the night Tom died?' she began. If so, last night must have been even worse for her, she thought.

'No, Berowne talked about it of course, but I was at home in the flush of a young bride's love and affection. Rule one, brides do not interfere with their husband's hobbies.' Rachel grimaced.

Whoops! Cara decided she should avoid any reference to Berowne if she could. Tom Chalcott was safer ground. 'Lady Lendale seems to think that Tom's ghost haunts the grotto. Do you believe in ghosts?'

'I believe our sins come back to haunt us,' Rachel replied – seriously, Cara thought. 'I say that because paranormal activities do seem to take place, judging by the numbers of ghost hunts and seances in this country. Berowne was looking forward to activating his new plan to let non-members attend our ghost hunts. Not that that was going down well with the members. Far from it.'

Cara was taken aback. She couldn't avoid the subject of Berowne, it seemed. She'd go very carefully though. 'No ghosts came along on Tuesday, did they?'

'Certainly not. I don't know what the equipment will reveal for that night, but it won't be that. I'd already told Berowne I'd be going straight back home in the morning, and that I'd leave my gear in the grotto as requested, and the police will have pounced on it. I was sound asleep at the time the police called me to say that Berowne died and I left to go back home without – as I thought – disturbing him.' Rachel paused. 'But I think I heard odd murmurs of voices or people moving around at various times of the night. Probably Jamie and Emily getting together. Anyway, midnight had been the time for Berowne to gather all the results up till then. I reported precious little. No ghosts came tramping through my quarters, not even a drop in temperature, which is significant in ghost terms. Ghost hunts are all too likely to end with a letdown, and it was chilly enough in those side rooms anyway without ghosts adding to it.'

Rachel's voice was so dispassionate that it was hard to think of all the emotions she must be going through. All the more need to tread very gently, Cara thought. This was a lady who might *pounce* despite her outward calm.

'No sign of Tom Chalcott's ghost?' she asked lightly.

'Alas no. I was hoping I'd hear the Laughing Lady, the one who shot her husband. Very apt. But if you think I advanced into Berowne's quarters, do knock me off your list of suspects,' Rachel said languidly. 'If I'd had any intention of seeking freedom from my husband, I'd have chosen a far easier route than murder.'

She had indeed pounced – and Cara caught a distinct warning note. Nevertheless she was beginning to see a path ahead, if she moved gingerly. 'Your husband was obviously very popular with the society members—'

'With the women perhaps.'

Four words. Four words and the whole picture kaleidoscoped. Had she misunderstood the implication? Cara wondered. No. Alison looked as shell-shocked as Cara felt. Surely all Rachel meant was that women liked him, not that Berowne chased every skirt in town?

Rachel was looking at them both with amusement. 'Didn't you realize what a womanizer Berowne was? He cherry-picked every one he fancied.'

'I knew everybody liked him . . .' Alison began weakly.

'Every woman perhaps,' Rachel replied calmly. 'Have a word with dear Charlotte or even Emily, or of course my staff. That's why I told Berowne I'd go straight home in the morning. I'd hate to interrupt his overnight frolics and find one of them installed with him.'

This was over the top. Cara pulled herself together. It had to be the stress and shock of Berowne's murder leading to this diatribe. It surely couldn't be fact. Berowne hadn't made the slightest pass at her, she reasoned, although granted she might not be in his age range. Anyway, he wouldn't have risked it, perhaps relying on charm alone.

Cara caught herself immediately. What the blazes was she thinking of? Here she was, over forty, a businesswoman working in Tanton Towers. Surely not anyone's cup of tea now, except . . . no, don't go there, she disciplined herself. Not with Berowne's murder so recent or with Lady Izzy's mission to carry out. No way should she let her private thoughts roam to sex.

Back to Berowne. Rachel had clearly decided to leave on a high note as she rose to her feet, Cara thought, then reproved herself. In the circumstances she should make no judgements. Nevertheless, there was plenty for her to talk to Alison about.

'Goodness gracious me.' Alison sank down on the Chesterfield as soon as she returned from escorting Rachel to the door. 'What do you make of that?'

'Quite a lot. Did Berowne make a pass at you?' Cara asked, still struggling with the whole concept of Berowne the predatory male. 'He missed me out.'

'And me,' Alison replied. 'Bear in mind, though, that if he had his eye on the social ladder, seducing Max's wife wouldn't be the best way of climbing it.'

'He was surely high enough on it anyway, as the owner of Ellum Place; or, if not owner, then married to her. They must have been well off.'

'Nowt so queer as folks when it comes to a name or two in *Who's Who*,' Alison said practically.

'Are we in it?' Max had appeared at the doorway and looked mildly interested.

'Probably. Anyway, we've more important things to talk about. Berowne. Rachel's informed us that he gobbled up every woman he saw – except us two present here.'

'Jealous?' He ducked as a cushion came his way. 'It doesn't surprise me,' he added soberly after tossing it back to Alison.

That was a surprise. 'Why not?' Cara asked curiously.

Max looked perplexed. 'I'm not sure. Lavinia—'

Groan from Alison, and Cara couldn't blame her. Lavinia Fontana, Max's passion, was displayed to everyone who climbed to the second floor of Tanton Towers and walked into the gallery of her paintings and drawings, grandly referred to as La Galleria. It was to there he retreated daily, and particularly when problems had to be solved – preferably by other people. If those other people failed him, then through the agency of Lavinia herself, who to him had the answer to life itself.

'Take her self-portrait at the spinet in the Accademia Nazionale in Rome, for example,' Max began firmly. 'It holds the mirror up to nature – exactly how she wanted herself portrayed; the reason being that this portrait was a gift to her prospective in-laws and yet it was the truth. However, I have a similar portrait we can study—'

'Yes, let's do that,' Alison muttered ironically. She was not a Lavinia devotee although, as she would describe it, she did her duty by them, commenting and admiring as required. Her own academic passion was Jane Austen, a different kettle of fish.

Max took her words as encouragement. 'Now Berowne, it seemed to me, on the few occasions we met, was also consciously conveying an image of himself. Not all of it succeeded. It sometimes fails when the subject tries too hard.' A pause. 'I wonder what Izzy would make of this story of his womanizing.'

That worried Cara. 'She was so fond of Berowne. Don't tell her – or certainly not until there's more evidence. Rachel's word alone isn't enough to assume it's true. She looked very calm, but she could still be a fantasizer, or trying to create a different image for her own ends.'

'Are you suggesting she might have killed Berowne herself?' Alison asked, looking appalled.

'It's been known,' Max stepped in drily. 'There were nine people sleeping there on Tuesday night and one of them must have committed murder. Izzy's theory that a ghost was guilty, whether Tom Chalcott's or anyone else's, is unlikely to carry much weight, I fear.'

'One or more of them could have had good reason to want Berowne out of the way.' Cara hesitated. 'If Rachel's right about his chasing other women, that could provide one motive for a start. She actually named one. Charlotte.'

'Oh yes. The publican's wife? Do you know her?' Alison asked incredulously. 'I can't believe it.'

'I only know her as the person who is occasionally behind the bar. She looks rather nice, but I suppose everyone said that about Lucrezia Borgia, who gaily murdered half of Italy,' Cara said rashly.

And then the whirlwind blew in. 'No proof of that, no proof.' Lady Izzy had appeared, clad in a bright green smock and purple trousers. 'Her murders have never been proven except by rotters. I'd have her to tea any day. Is that coffee in that jug? Enough for me?'

Alison leapt up to attend to this while Lady Izzy seated herself in a rocking chair.

'What's this about Rachel and that Charlotte? Tearing Berowne to bits, is she?' Lady Izzy asked briskly.

'I'm afraid she was,' Max replied.

'I always thought he was a womanizer.'

This seemed a turnabout, Cara thought with resignation. She should have been suspicious, when for Lady Izzy it had always been 'dear Berowne'. Somehow, however, she didn't think this was a turnabout.

'You've always spoken highly of him,' Max pointed out.

'Hush, Max. Who would dare mention this little peccadillo while our Berowne was out seducing all those ladies?' Lady Izzy carolled. 'At least he was a good sort, bar that. My Tom never told me otherwise; he deemed Berowne a remarkable fellow or he wouldn't have sanctioned him as his successor. I thought Tom would be there last night looking out for him. Unfortunately, he failed.' She pondered this for a moment, then added, 'He was certainly there, but maybe being a ghost he couldn't do much. But you mark my words, he'll go on haunting Berowne's murderer. Tom will be back. You can count on that.'

'Of course, Izzy,' Max said amiably.

'And,' Lady Izzy continued, 'he'll be hunting his own killer. Our Cara's helping him there, aren't you?'

It was now or never, Cara knew. 'Only by looking into the circumstances of *his* death.' That sounded ponderous even to her. 'But not Berowne's death too,' she added. 'Do you think there's a link between the two?'

'Oh, there's a link all right,' Lady Izzy replied brightly. 'Tom's ghost is telling us that. The same person involved, you see. Cara, dear, Tom's giving me an idea that you and I can put into effect. It would most certainly assist us all in finding out what happened. We won't bother that nice policeman, Detective Chief Inspector Mitchem, yet.'

Cara steeled herself. The same person involved? And what was this other scheme she had in mind? That sounded ominous. What had she let herself in for? She could follow her own path, but working with Lady Izzy would undoubtedly throw up problems. She could see Alison and Max looking alarmed – perhaps with good reason? She remembered some awful visitor once yelling at Sammy in fury when he found a dead fly in his mug: 'It's time for you to do your job.' Well, Cara, it was now time to do hers. Stand by, troops. She owed a lot to Lady Izzy, and whatever reason Lady Izzy had for wanting something done, she would do it.

Nice policeman indeed. Cara ruminated over those words as she returned to the Happy Huffkin. True, she had come to some kind of arrangement with Andrew Mitchem, but sooner or later there might be trouble as to where their dividing lines came between his case and the path she would follow. That was when their private relationship (or lack of it) might crop up. It hadn't yet, and perhaps he preferred it that way. For him, it might provide an escape route from that time a year ago when a far different relationship had unexpectedly appeared on the cards, from which she had been the first to back away. Was he relieved and had he moved on since then? There'd been no hint otherwise. Very well, she'd play along with that. She could play professional too, without yearnings about what might have been. It hadn't happened and so what? She too had moved on – or so she told herself.

Back to the challenge. Basic facts: leaving out Jamie, Emily and Harry, four society members had been present both on the night Tom died and on Tuesday night, excluding Berowne, of course. That would be Pete and Charlotte, Luke and Oliver. Did any of them have reason to want both Tom and Berowne dead? What if Berowne had discovered that Tom had been murdered and who had killed him? She might have a clear path ahead, starting with those four. As regards Berowne's frightful death, no outsiders could have stolen into the grounds that night without their presence being detected by staff or safety cameras.

As for the smugglers' tunnel which ran from the woodland to the Towers' cellars, its own safety cameras would have ensured that there had been no intruders using it. Andrew Mitchem's team would be checking all that out. Taking all this into account, suspicion lay on those who had slept peacefully or otherwise in the grotto. That, of course, applied to Berowne's murder. If Tom Chalcott had been murdered, a far different situation would have applied.

Groundwork first, though. Was anyone else present? Virginia was unlikely to have been at the Towers the night Tom died, but she was a fount of village information on any background that needed filling in. That could be useful, as Max and Alison hadn't been resident at the Towers when he died, as Max only inherited the Towers from his father a year or so afterwards. Yes, Virginia – and her tempting cakes – were the next step.

Virginia's bakery was in the centre of Tanton village. Like many Kent villages, it sprawled along one main road running past the river, which at present had shrunk to a narrow stream. The bakery was always a comforting sight. When Cara arrived the next morning, freshly baked loaves, huge eclairs and buns were temptingly displayed in the windows. The queues outside at midday proved how popular its sandwiches and pies were for speedy lunches. Virginia had run the bakery for some years after inheriting it from her father, but her initiative had expanded into her appointing a manager for it while she achieved her heart's desire of running an event service around a very wide area. Before Cara had arrived, she'd catered for several events at the Towers too, so Virginia had told her.

Virginia's views on life and the village and everything that went on there were therefore wide and profound and, having no children of her own, she was pinning her hopes on her niece Lucy to continue Harding's Bakery. Unlikely to happen, Cara guessed. Youngsters spread their wings and flew now, before deciding if they wanted to return and take over home territory.

'Tom Chalcott?' Virginia repeated when Cara explained her mission. 'I thought you'd come about Lucy. I never knew what she'd done down there in the grotto on Tuesday till she told me. A right giggler, she is. Know what she did? She only put a frog in young Emily's sleeping bag. Lucky for her that I guessed something was up, so I made her tell me and went down myself to hoick it out. I told Lucy it wasn't Emily's fault that Jamie had dumped her. What Lucy didn't tell me,' she added grimly, 'is what she dropped down Emily's dress at the table, so I—'

Cara seized the opportunity. Sooner or later, she could lead Virginia back to Tom. Meanwhile, what she had to say might be helpful. 'Was Berowne in the grotto preparing for the hunt by then?' she asked.

'Not officially. People were drifting down to the grotto and I had to ask him something as he was following them. Someone was complaining that their ghost detector thingumajig wasn't working; someone was shouting about wanting a spirit box and all that stuff. The society's having a meeting Saturday morning at the pub. There'll be fireworks there, you can be sure of that.'

A meeting indeed. That was an opportunity not to miss, Cara thought. She could legitimately be present, with Lady Izzy's blessing. She'd make sure to discuss it with her tomorrow. Time for Tom, though. 'I know it was ten years ago,' she began, 'but were you up at Tanton Towers the night Tom Chalcott died?'

Virginia looked surprised. 'Nowhere near, Cara. Just heard the news in the morning when they found the poor fellow. Tom was a good 'un, if you know what I mean. At least he'd pass the time of day with you. Shame he died like that.'

'Like what?' Cara asked cautiously.

Virginia grinned. 'Sudden like. The way her ladyship is carrying on about ghosts, she probably thinks he was done in, murdered. A proper Miss Marple she is. Who's she got her eye on for Poirot?' And before Cara could reply, she added: 'Don't tell me. You're Poirot. Watch it, Cara.'

Cara had every intention of watching it and of bearing Virginia's words of wisdom in mind, even if she disappointingly had nothing much to offer on Tom Chalcott. There were indeed dangerous waters ahead. She needed the stalwarts of the Towers for back-up. Virginia was one, but Len and Josie were too, together with Sammy and Max, plus Alison. Josie worked, or had worked, at Ellum Place, and so for any light to be shone on Berowne's story, she would be a prime candidate for information. Len was closer at hand to start with, however, and he was easy to track down since his workshop was on the hillside on the far side of the Italian garden. From there he could control this side of the grounds, plus the gardens in front of the Towers, including the glorious rose garden.

A call to his mobile established that he was 'at home'. With its earthy smell and wheelbarrows, cut flowers, sacks of earth and manure, the workshop was a comfortable place to visit – once she had worked her way through the jumble of tools and plants to the chair he dragged over for her. He even doffed his cap, which was so much an integral part of his personal image that she sometimes wondered whether it was glued to his head. She felt honoured, even though she realized he'd only done it to scratch his head.

'Mr Berowne you're here for,' Len pronounced. 'Not only the police, now you're here too. Mrs Alison send you, did she? Or her ladyship?'

His grumpy side was to the fore this morning, but Cara was used to dealing with that. It was only a guarded warning that she shouldn't take up too much of his time. Fair enough, as the police presence must still be restricting what he would normally be doing in the gardens on a June day. Although the house was now open, the gardens in this area of the grounds were still closed to the public, but nevertheless some gardening work had to go on.

'Let's say the Towers sent me,' she answered him. 'Lady Lendale wants me to find out more about Tom Chalcott's death ten years ago; the Farran Prydes and staff all want to find out what happened to Berowne Dyer; the ghost society members want to find out about both.' Slight exaggeration on her part, but true in a way. 'Plus the police,' she added. 'I can't help them, but I can help Lady Lendale over Tom Chalcott and how he fitted in with the Tanton Ghost and Phantom Society.'

She gave herself a mental pat on the back, and it must have succeeded because he nodded. 'Fair enough, but I can't see what Mr Chalcott's got to do with Mr Berowne's passing, whatever her ladyship says. Had enough with the police round here about that. Josie's real upset about it all, what with Mrs Rachel carrying on about losing her husband, poor woman.'

'Did Josie get on well with them?'

'It's a job, isn't it? Course she did,' he growled in typical Len style. 'Given in her notice, though. Freelance she worked for them, but no more. Popular is Josie, and life has to go on. Now you come in here about something that happened ten years ago. Waste of time for you and me.'

Looking at it from his point of view it certainly was, and even from hers: she was beginning to have doubts about there being a link between the two deaths. Coincidences happen all the time, and the fact that both Berowne and Tom Calcott had been chair of the ghost society could be exactly that. Already she felt she was hanging on to this case – if case this proved to be – by its coattails while it was steadily marching away from her.

Start with safe ground, she decided. 'What do you remember about Tom Chalcott?'

Len considered this. 'Remember seeing him around a few times, that's all. I wasn't on duty that evening. Heard about it all later. Junior gardener I was then, and lived down in the village. Old Percy Trimmer was head gardener. He's long gone. Anyway it were Oliver Bright found the body, Harry's grandad. Don't know what he was doing up round the car park early in the morning, but there he was. I remember that 'cos Josie and I had young Harry staying with us while his mum and dad were abroad, and we had young'uns of our own.' A pause. 'That the lot? I got work to do.'

We all have, she thought privately. At the Happy Huffkin she would normally be working with Sammy, getting ready for the afternoon. With the publicity, it was going to be a full house.

'Come on, Len,' she urged. 'Bear with me. We've all been going through the mill with the police, but this won't take long. It's good to get it out of the way just in case there's anything that could have a bearing on Mr Chalcott's death.' She drew a deep breath. Full speed ahead, Cara. 'Lady Izzy seems to have got it in her head that her nephew was murdered and that the two deaths could be connected, and that his ghost is around to tell us that.'

Another Len grunt. 'What's she on about? Had too much to drink,' he pronounced. 'I heard she was yelling about that on Tuesday. It were a joke, weren't it?'

'No. She's serious about it. It's probably a molehill, not a mountain, but you never know. In case these two deaths *are* connected, what I need to know, Len, is what you remember of the night Tom Chalcott died if you were on duty then.'

He brooded on this. 'Back in those days, no one was on duty at night. I was only an under-gardener then but, far as I remember, Mr Tom had left everything nice and tidy in the grotto. I can tell you what *weren't* happening on this Tuesday night, though. That do you?'

'It would.' If there was a link between the two deaths, then the more she learned the better, Cara thought, whether it trespassed on Andrew Mitchem's case or not.

'It were like this. I'd one chap watching the front entrance to the Towers and all round that side, so I was doing the same round this side of the Towers and the back entrance. See?'

She did. 'That included both the Italian garden and the grotto.'

'Yup. Never saw no one, except for a few of the gents nipping out for the toilets and one or two of the ladies the same.'

'You're sure they were all guests? No strangers. It must have been dark.'

A glare from him. 'I'm sure and I never nodded off either. Took time off during the day knowing I was on duty that night. The grotto entrances were lit and so was the path to the toilets. I told the rozzers all this,' he added. 'I remember who I saw and all. There was Pete's wife Charlotte from the pub, and the two gents were old Mr Bright and that bad-tempered chap Luke Claxton from the handyman's store. None of them had daggers in their hands.' Len even grinned. 'And no one nipped in later that night, no one. That was my job. To watch out for trespassers. And watch I did. All night. Like a blooming hawk.'

So that was that. Not helpful, Cara thought ruefully as she left. If there was a link between the two deaths, then she seemed no further forward on it. Was she downhearted? she enquired of herself. If so, so what? She'd only just begun, and the big challenge lay ahead. The Tanton Ghost and Phantom Society Extraordinary Meeting would be taking place, a gathering at which all those who had been sleeping in the grotto on Tuesday night would be present, four of whom at least had also been present when Tom Chalcott had met his death. Saturday's meeting was going to be interesting, to say the least.

SEVEN

Go, Cara, *go*, she told herself on Saturday morning as she marched up the stairs of the Farran Arms, and pushed open the door to the meeting room where the Tanton Ghost and Phantom Society was, she presumed, to sort out its differences and leadership problems in the light of Berowne's death. This major step towards Lady Izzy's mission was not going to be an easy path to steer, while at the same time avoiding DCI Andrew Mitchem's wrath. There was no evidence at all that Tom Chalcott had been murdered, and not even a whiff of a motive for it had emerged either. Looking for it was going to be part of her job. She'd discussed this with Lady Izzy yesterday – who appeared to have taken up permanent residence in the family wing guest suite. Alison and Max seemed patiently resigned to it. Whether that would still be the case when Lady Izzy's great scheme for a step forward had been shared with them was extremely doubtful, Cara had thought.

'They'll be happy as larks,' Lady Izzy had assured her. Larks, Cara thought, were much rarer in Kent nowadays, but she kept her misgivings to herself. Her job was merely to break the news to the society.

There wasn't much doubt as to where the meeting was taking place, owing to the racket she could hear. The sound of angry voices raised in argument had greeted her as soon as she had entered the pub. Ah, well, now for it. She'd won bigger battles than this. Onwards!

Seven hostile faces faced her, although with any luck the hostility was towards each other and not to her, even though she would seem an interloper in their affairs. It might be a different matter once she'd launched Lady Izzy's bright plan. There was – not surprisingly – no sign of Rachel, but Pete and Charlotte were sitting beside each other, with Pete looking far from genial and Charlotte distinctly upset. Oliver Bright had commandeered the position of head of table but didn't look happy at his conquest.

Even Harry was looking cross – a possible ally, though? Luke Claxton was looking at her with deep suspicion, as if she had some dark plan for a smash-and-grab raid on his shop, and even Jamie and Emily looked heated to say the least. She would have to work hard to get their support for Lady Izzy's plan.

'What do you want?' It wasn't quite a snarl from Oliver but getting on that way. The shouting stopped, however. Temporarily, anyway.

Off we go! Cara braced herself, as she stood at Oliver's side to address her unhappy audience. 'I'm here formally on a mission from your honorary president, Lady Lendale,' she announced amicably, adopting her 'how to deal with unruly customers' tone.

This achieved nothing except sullen silence, which was broken by Oliver. 'I'm the chairman now,' he declared gruffly, 'so I'm in charge. We're in the middle of debating the situation, so kindly wait outside and—'

'Rot,' yelled Luke. 'You haven't been elected—'

At that the 'debate' broke out again. Far from being an unwelcome interloper, Cara decided to take over. 'Lady Lendale,' she shouted, as she pulled up a chair for herself, 'as honorary president of this society, is duty-bound to ensure its rules and regulations are maintained, and is stepping in today after the loss of its chair. I have her authority to proceed on her behalf.' Well, that was true enough; amazingly, this worked, and they calmed down. True, that might be in the hope of getting rid of her more quickly.

Then an objection was raised. 'Why not come herself?' That was Pete, who was displaying his usual preference for a snarl not a smile.

'Because she has asked me to represent her,' Cara said patiently.

That brought silence again, rather to her surprise. 'Kindly proceed then,' Oliver graciously growled.

It was all or nothing now. Keep on an even keel, she disciplined herself.

'Lady Lendale sends her great sympathy for the loss of your chair, Berowne Dyer,' she began formally. Murmurs sprang up but they were easily dealt with.

'As you know, Lady Lendale has the best interests of the society at heart,' she continued in her best official voice. 'In the circumstances until the police investigations have finished, she suggests she continues to stand in as chair and authorizes me to speak on her behalf. Any objections?'

From the initial silence, Cara began to think she had hidden diplomatic skills.

Then the objections began. 'I'm chairman now,' Oliver cried indignantly, seconded by Pete and Luke.

To Cara's relief, Harry winked at her and calmed them down. She took another deep breath. The next step would be just as tricky. 'Lady Lendale has asked me to tell you that she wishes to honour Berowne by sponsoring an event in honour of both him and Thomas Chalcott.' Pause for audience reaction. It was, as she expected, caution.

'What's her ladyship up to now?' Luke asked suspiciously.

'She would sponsor a major ghost tour of the Towers itself, the first time such an event has taken place.'

Cara had had doubts about this plan when Lady Izzy had blithely announced it, even though it was for a tour and very definitely not a hunt. The latter had been vetoed by Max and she could see his point. The likelihood was that Berowne's murderer would be in this group, and since the group would be split up for a hunt, that would not be a welcome thought.

Now she could see its value. Whatever hidden reason Lady Izzy had for this, it did mean that she, Cara, would be a familiar face to this group and there might lie a chance of getting to the root of Tom Chalcott's death and its possible link to Berowne's. The drawback was that though she had offered her services to Lady Izzy for the tour and had been accepted, it wasn't clear exactly what that would entail. General helpmate, she had presumed, but she was doing some reading in the Archives Room so that she was au fait with all the Towers' ghost stories. That way she could answer questions about them on the tour. The reaction to Cara's announcement of the tour was even greater and louder than she had expected.

'No!' Charlotte cried out. Pete was looking furious, Jamie burst out laughing, and reactions were loudly expressed by everyone else.

'Hey,' Jamie shouted, 'we can invite the whole village, just like Berowne wanted.'

'I'm afraid not,' Cara said firmly. 'This is a very special tour just for the society, and there'll be a champagne reception to remember Berowne and Tom.'

Still the dissent grew. Press on regardless, she decided. 'It's planned for two weeks' time from today,' she concluded.

Suddenly, to her relief, she had their full attention. That wasn't too surprising. After all, there had never been a ghost tour of any kind in the Towers. (And from the look on Max and Alison's faces when they had thrashed the subject out, there wouldn't be again.)

'Mr and Mrs Farran Pryde,' she continued with her best attempt at an official-sounding voice, 'are sanctioning the essential research into their records of ghosts, sensed in the past and recent times, for you to study before the tour. One or two we already know about, but,' she added brightly, looking round the table, 'perhaps we'll be lucky and any old ghost around-about might get interested and turn up for the tour as well.' False step. Too light-hearted. She'd better turn serious again. 'It can't happen until there's police permission, of course.'

'It's miscalculated,' Pete immediately threw at her. 'We're serious ghost hunters not tourists.'

Oliver was also clearly against it. 'I shall have to consider the suggestion,' he said crossly.

Cara was not surprised. He had to establish his supremacy in the society.

'And,' Oliver continued, 'I must insist that both phantoms and ghosts are represented on the tour.'

'Not that old chestnut,' Luke said wearily. 'Insist all you like, Oliver, but they're both the same to any sane person.'

'They are not.' Pete glared at him.

'Scared Berowne will turn up as a ghost and spill the beans, both of you?' Luke jeered.

'There are no beans to spill,' Oliver yelled. 'How—'

Cara interrupted what was clearly going to be a long wrangling match, despite another part of her mind wondering what the spilled beans might have been. 'The Towers will be closed to the public, of course, but there's going to be wide interest from the press with the ghost society being involved.'

The argument was only half won. 'All Lady Lendale wants,' Charlotte said wearily, 'is for her nephew to be honoured on this tour. We were talking about Tom's death earlier, and we've agreed there's been nothing to suggest his spirit being active to any degree at all, whether as a ghost or a presence, or just through odd sounds or movements. Berowne never talked about it as a possibility, and the nearest I got to any paranormal reaction on Tuesday night was a chilly blast of air. Which,' she added, 'was probably someone slipping over to someone else's quarters.' She looked meaningfully at Emily.

It was high time this stopped, Cara thought with alarm, noting that Harry Bright had suddenly decided to give Emily his full attention. Discretion would be the better part of valour. Still, everybody's whereabouts on Tuesday night were most certainly relevant.

'Lady Lendale is naturally very shaken by Berowne's death,' she continued evenly, 'and she believes there's every possibility that it's linked to Tom Chalcott's.'

'Linked? How?' Pete barked. 'The old woman's lost her marbles.'

'Perhaps Berowne will appear with Tom on this tour that Lady Lendale wants to organize for us,' Charlotte suggested meekly. 'He was so wonderfully dedicated to his job.'

Was she serious? Cara wondered. It was hard to tell. It sent a ripple round the table anyway. An uneasy one, it seemed to her. The look on Pete's face suggested that Charlotte's husband didn't seem to think Berowne was wonderfully dedicated to anything. Nevertheless, Charlotte had pointed out the obvious. If the grotto was haunted and there was indeed paranormal activity taking place there – a big if, in her view – then Berowne could theoretically appear in ghostly form either there or indeed in the Towers. He might just be there as a presence – or a phantom (for those who saw a distinction between the two). He could be here, *now,* watching them . . . No, back to basics, she told herself quickly, otherwise she might become a believer herself. Not a good idea.

Back to Lady Izzy's mission. So far she wasn't doing well, Cara sensed, probably because she had doubts about its success. 'Lady Lendale wants to provide every chance for both her nephew and Berowne to visit either the grotto or the Towers in paranormal form, or both as they choose. There's a lot of ground to cover in the Towers, and so we'll be preparing a guide to the best rooms and corridors for the tour to concentrate on.'

Cara already knew where would most definitely be out of bounds. Max's main concern had been that no ghosts could be tracked down to his Lavinia Fontana gallery. Distinctly no entry. 'Lady Lendale,' Cara continued, 'wants each of you to remember everything you can about what happened to Tom, both on that night and during the lead-up to it, *and* anything you can recall that might have been recorded on the society's equipment.'

'Ask the cops. They took it all. Berowne's and Chalcott's too,' Luke muttered.

'All the more essential to have your memories then. So I'd like to talk to each of you individually so that we have a full record of activity both of the night that Tom Chalcott died and Berowne's. We all want Berowne's killer to be found, just as we want to be sure of what happened to Tom Chalcott.'

Somewhat to her surprise, no one objected – not yet, anyway. With the recent police presence, they might have become used to answering questions, though she doubted if Andrew Mitchem's force would be delving back ten years. The only comment was from Emily, who had her mind on other matters. 'Are we having another sleepover on this tour?' she asked eagerly, winning a look of interest from Jamie.

'I'm afraid not,' Cara said patiently. The very idea of those mattresses being slung down in the Towers' corridors would be enough for Max to veto the whole project. What, she wondered, were her own views on Lady Izzy's plan, given the reactions today? Looking at it rationally, there was a murderer in their ranks. If the proposed tour led to a link between the two deaths, would it be a help or hindrance to solving them? And what was Andrew's view on this going to be? Not a happy one, she guessed. But he could hardly forbid Max and Alison from holding the tour in their home, much less persuade Lady Izzy to give the idea up.

'Who's going to be in charge of this tour?' Pete demanded.

Here we go! Cara plunged in. She'd been saving this titbit until last. 'Lady Lendale will be leading it, with my assistance.'

How that would work, she hadn't the slightest idea. She'd do it somehow though, and what better way to play her part in fulfilling Lady Izzy's hopes? As well as visiting the Towers'

Archives Room and devouring every relevant document there, she had been reading all she could about other ghosts that might have chosen to haunt other reasonably nearby places – such as Biggin Hill, for example, with Spitfires and Hurricanes still keeping a ghostly presence, the murderess in Canterbury Cathedral's Dark Entry, the coach drawn by horses that gallop through the village of Grafty Green, or Pluckley, which claimed to be one of the most haunted villages in England.

Cara looked around the table. All suspects for Berowne's murder, and some in theory for Tom Chalcott's murder too, if Lady Izzy was right.

The next step beckoned, though Cara wasn't at all sure how this would be received. As she made her way back to the Happy Huffkin, she considered the people she'd just left sitting round that table. Pete, the sullen landlord of the Farran Arms; Charlotte his wife – could she possibly be one of Berowne's 'women', in Rachel's use of the word?; Luke, the embittered handyman, convinced the technological methods of ghost hunting were the one-and-only path to tracking paranormal activity; Jamie, the happy-go-lucky (apparently) young man with the whole world (normal and paranormal) before him; Emily, the attractive young flirt; Oliver the former chair, who seemed all too keen on reappropriating the role; Harry, the bright gardening student, who seemed to think it his right to breeze through life and the paranormal without a hitch; and then there was the absent Rachel, married to a man whom she knew to have an eye (and probably more) on other women. All seemingly harmless, and yet one of them may have brutally murdered Berowne Dyer and possibly Tom Chalcott – if he had indeed been murdered, she reminded herself.

The sooner she began to find out more about Tom Chalcott and the night he had died, the better. Who present that night could have benefited from that death? Did his heart attack come out of the blue? Could he have been frightened to death? Possible, but if so, how? Would he have had an expression of terror on his face when found? Could he have been smothered? He would have resisted, of course. Were there any signs of that? Coroner's reports would be closed to her, but Lady Izzy could get access as a member of his family. As a last resort, could she, Cara, approach Andrew for help on that? she wondered glumly. Not yet, but Tom Chalcott must be lurking in the background for him as possibly relevant to Berowne's awful fate. That link must be tantalizingly close for Andrew, just as it was for her.

For some people, Saturday was a day of rest or fun. For the Happy Huffkin in high season, it was neither of these. When Cara reached it after hurrying back from the village, snatching half a sandwich for lunch on the way, it was nearly opening time and the slightly reprehensive look from Sammy indicated he was well aware of it – even though Lucy and Virginia were working at full throttle. Tables were laid, display cabinets were full and the urns were ready. It was going to be a busy mid-season afternoon, and Cara quickly reassembled her wits from detective to café owner. It was not to be.

'Shall we walk?'

The voice came from behind her, and she spun round. Whom did she most not want to see? And whom did she see? Andrew, of course. It was the worst possible time after this morning's ordeal, and the knowledge that dozens of thirsty sightseers would shortly be marching towards the Happy Huffkin didn't help. Even though it was an opportunity to focus Andrew's attention on Tom Chalcott's death, she quailed at the thought.

'It's opening time,' she said pleadingly. 'I need to be here.'

'Police business. I've had a word with your staff,' Andrew said firmly.

Did she believe him? Not judging by the smug look on his face. She felt a traitor as she departed with him.

'Where are we going?' she asked crossly.

'I suggest down to the valley through the woods. We can find a bench there or wander over to the pub.'

If he thought she would suggest her cottage, he was wrong. 'OK,' she said. 'What's this about?'

'The recordings from the ghost-hunting equipment. We agreed on that, you may remember. Anyway, it's a nice day for a stroll.'

'That's cheating,' she muttered as he unlatched the gate. 'But I do want to know. Do they reveal anything helpful to Lady Lendale or you?'

'Nothing much – but that's revealing in itself.' He held the gate open for her; several sniffs of the woodland air made her feel more at ease. This was something she could cope with, whatever he might throw at her in her currently unwelcome role as witness – or indeed, technically, suspect.

'We took the record of the meeting in the main passageway at midnight, which was written up by Berowne Dyer. In most cases, each society member had also written a very short record for Berowne, and we took those too. In theory everyone retired to their rooms to sleep after midnight and the equipment in their rooms either went merrily and silently onwards or was turned off. As I expect you saw, in Berowne's case it was smashed. Nothing could be salvaged from it.'

'And?' she asked when he paused, looked at her, seized her hand and continued the walk. This clearly wasn't the time to ask him about Tom Chalcott.

'The voice recorders and the EMF detectors produced very little,' he continued, 'which isn't surprising since the other rooms were a long way from Berowne Dyer's, which shot off at an angle. There was only the odd grunt or two recorded.'

A large puddle then presented itself, and he let go of her hand to jump over it. The hand was then seized to assist her. All done very ceremoniously.

'There was a decrease in temperature in one or two rooms, which I gather is a hopeful sign of paranormal activity. And two reports of the movement of a trigger piece, which I'm told is an object that signals a ghost who intends to leave his calling card.'

Cara laughed. 'So, you are no further forward.'

'We are. Why don't we take a seat on this convenient bench overlooking a river that I understand used to be there, and I'll explain as much as I can in my position?'

She obediently took her place, and he continued. 'Any of the occupants of those rooms would know how to avoid being caught on the society's equipment, and the nearer they were to the passage that led to Berowne Dyer's room, the easier it would be for his murderer to escape notice on his or her way there. Of course it would have been dark, but individual torches could be used.'

'Were there no clues at all in Berowne's room?' Cara asked, shuddering at her memory of it as she had seen it then.

'Nothing at all to give any indication of who the intruder was. But I can assure you that he or she was not paranormal.'

He paused. 'I can't go any further, though I can tell you the case is progressing fast.' Another pause. 'Do you like ice-cream? I think we deserve one.'

'No time. I've a business to run.' She rethought this premature reply. 'OK, let's have one.'

'Done. There's a newspaper shop along there sells them. Ice-cream is very good for assisting hill climbing.'

Pete Brandon, pub landlord, should be top of her list to meet, Cara decided, possibly because the Farran Arms was automatically a meeting place for all the villagers, and so in a way it symbolized the village, and Pete was in charge there. He was unlikely to be a welcoming landlord today, however. She reached the pub on Monday morning to be faced with a sign on the closed door that announced it opened at eleven a.m. It was now ten thirty, the time she had arranged with Pete, but there was no apparent means of summoning the owner, as there was no sign of a bell of any kind. The side gate to the gardens, and presumably to the private entrance, was also locked. Was this a ploy on Pete's part, perhaps, designed to reduce her to insignificance? Too bad. It wouldn't work. Anyway, she shouldn't get paranoid, Cara warned herself.

The pub was much older than either Tanton Towers or Ellum Place, and perhaps had been serving the village since the early seventeenth century, judging by its beamed architecture. Sir Jeffry himself might have nipped down here for a drink or two while the Towers was being built. His beady eye would have been on every weird tower, turret and gargoyle, the pride and joy of his achievement.

When she finally gained access, thanks to her mobile, she favoured Pete with a cheery greeting. It was not returned, and she was led in silence to the saloon bar. This, she reckoned, was the most attractive room in the pub, with its dark panelling, and engravings of the Towers and the Syn river in earlier years, plus some early *Punch* cartoons.

'Can't offer you a drink,' Pete said with great satisfaction. 'Opening hours. Have to wait.'

'That's fine,' Cara assured him with the best imitation of a sweet smile she could give. There was no offer of coffee either, she noted. She took her place on the old leather sofa by the window and watched as he deliberately sat himself on an upright wooden chair, perhaps in order to dominate the proceedings. He would be a good-looking man if it wasn't for the wary look of suspicion that seemed to be his standby expression.

She laid her iPad on one side, hoping that they could chat rather than have a formal interview. One look at that angry guarded face made her realize that chat wasn't likely. Truculence and aggression conveyed themselves from his movements and expression. She'd noticed at the society meeting that when he relaxed, he had an interesting face, but he wasn't relaxed now and she was thankful she wasn't in Charlotte's shoes. She'd arranged to talk to Charlotte later, and Charlotte was an entirely different kettle of fish from her possessive husband.

'As you know, I'm trying to find out all I can about Tom Chalcott,' she began. Keep it cool, she warned herself. It was all a long time ago and so her claim to lack of knowledge was justified. 'Were you at that hunt in the grotto on the day he died?'

'What of it?' Aggression was turning to defensiveness. 'We all were. We'd had the annual club meeting a week or two earlier, when he stood down as chair and Berowne grabbed it, so this was going to be Tom's last hunt. Good riddance, we all thought. Time for change. Nice chap but no leader. So we had the hunt for several hours and then he died on the way home. Pure chance he died when he did. He could well have pitched over here in this pub because we had had a meal on the way to the grotto.' Pete sat back, looking satisfied that he had done his duty.

'What happened at the grotto?' she prompted him. 'Just the hunt?'

He shrugged. 'Like I said. We had the hunt for a few hours, spreading around a bit as usual. Tom stayed behind to gather the notes and equipment, and when he left he must just have conked out. No use her ladyship blaming us. Apart from him we all left and walked back to the car park together. He stayed behind to scribble a report and bring back some of the equipment, so we were well away by the time he dropped dead. We heard about it the next day.'

'Did you like him?'

Pete looked surprised, as though liking wasn't an issue with him. 'OK in his own way. Bit of a toff and he couldn't help that, could he?'

'Was Charlotte with you that evening?'

'You'll have to ask her about that.' He folded his arms, as if daring her to argue the point.

Press on regardless. 'Berowne must have been a good chair,' Cara persevered. 'He seemed to get on with people so well.' Nothing like being deliberately provocative.

He grew red in the face. 'Good chair? He was a chancer, that man. One of them blokes who go round sucking up the lifeblood of decent workers. Chalcott too, he was one of them, but at least he had the guts not to put on a show of being otherwise. The Great Berowne let everyone else do the work and then took the credit for it.'

'Why did you remain a member?' Cara asked curiously.

She thought he'd explode with rage, but he simply shrugged. 'Just mind your own business, Cara, or whatever your name is. You're here to find out about Chalcott, not Berowne the grabber. OK was Tom. Couldn't help being born with a silver spoon in his mouth, but he didn't pretend otherwise. Didn't live in the village, but came marching in for the meetings, regular as clock-work. Ten years later, and here we were cursed with bloody Berowne, living in that big mansion house, all thanks to his wife's money. I reckon he didn't give a damn about ghosts. Just wanted to rule the village, he did.'

'What about you, Pete? Do you believe in ghosts?' Cara asked curiously.

Taken aback, he actually laughed, to her surprise. 'They're like Father Christmas, aren't they? Useful on occasion for getting what you want. But some of the members are believers. Know how this society works, do you? Us doing all the work setting it up and then Berowne gets the glory. Forget what us society members wanted, let's have every Tom, Dick and Harry on the hunt and make sure they cough up a pile of money.'

'But Berowne hadn't passed that motion yet, had he?'

'No way. He'd have been lynched if he'd forced it through – and then he was. Murdered. So there we were, just us happy bunnies on Tuesday evening, sleeping it off down there like rats at the end of a rat run.'

'Did any ghosts materialize before you slept or during it?'

Another shrug. 'Can't say.'

Can't or don't want to? Cara wondered.

Then he continued. 'Look, we all reported to his majesty at midnight, then we went to our respective beds. His majesty collected the reports, such as they were at that time, and we settled down for the night. Tom Chalcott's ghost could have been flitting around chasing the bastard, but I never saw him nor any other ghosts. Others say they did? Well, usual murmurs and that sort of thing. If we were away and heard anything more after midnight, then we were to leave notes in our rooms for his majesty to collect after we'd gone in the morning. So off we trotted to bed, leaving the field wide open for his majesty to do what he damn well liked *with* who he liked.'

A clear hint at the 'women' Rachel had referred to, so Berowne's habits were more widely known than Cara had thought. However, Berowne would surely not have gone prowling on Tuesday night with his wife so close at hand, she reasoned, so there was no point pursuing that line. If Charlotte had by any chance been involved, Cara reasoned, she wasn't going to learn that from Pete. Moreover, she wasn't supposed to be trespassing on Andrew Mitchem's domain. Not on purpose, anyway.

'Did you hear afterwards from anybody about any evidence for ghosts after midnight? I gather the police took the equipment to check.'

'Not much – no phantom blew in and said he was Tom Chalcott,' Pete sniggered. 'You could pop down there one night and see if he turns up for you, Cara. That would be a treat. His ghost could give evidence as to who did Berowne in. Unless old Tom did it himself.'

Cara laughed. 'Seriously,' she said firmly, 'did you like Tom?'

'Like I said, he was OK. Wasn't the sort you could ask to lend you a tenner or down a pint in the pub, but each to his own. He was straight, if you know what I mean. Knew what you were getting. Berowne wasn't that sort.'

Everybody liked Berowne. That's what she had been told, but that clearly wasn't the case. Nor had Pete mentioned his having been in debt to Berowne. She ruminated on that as he stood up. The interview was clearly over as far as he was concerned, and he seemed extremely smug as she dutifully accompanied him as he led her to meet Charlotte. Bully for him if he felt triumphant, she thought crossly. It was clear he was no admirer of Berowne. Why? Was it just dislike, or disapproval of Berowne's leadership of the society, or, it occurred to her uneasily as she remembered her conversation with Rachel, could Charlotte really have been one of Berowne's 'women'? Sheer speculation, she told herself uneasily.

EIGHT

Charlotte looked startled when Pete ushered Cara into their first-floor living room with, it seemed to her, ironic courtesy. Her mind had clearly been somewhere else, as she leapt up from her chair as though royalty had entered the room, and left the computer she'd been using. Pete seemed to want to linger, but Cara thanked him so firmly for his 'help' that he had little choice but to retreat. She had already registered Pete as the controller in this marriage and she awarded him with a sweet smile as he left. Any ghosts thinking of haunting this pub would clearly have to be approved by Pete before they dared terrify Charlotte.

Once alone, Charlotte waved a hand towards an armchair. 'You're here about Tom Chalcott and Berowne, aren't you?'

Medium height, with beautifully tended long dark hair, she was a very attractive woman, Cara thought – or would be if she wasn't looking so anxious. It didn't seem the sort of anxious look that quickly vanishes when reassured, but the kind that settles into permanent grooves. Nor did she seem like a woman who would flourish as a publican's wife. She looked several years younger than Pete, but not the happier for it. Had she crossed Berowne's path? Cara wondered, remembering Rachel's outburst. From the few times she had met Charlotte, she seemed too devoted to Pete to fall for Berowne, but how on earth could she be a judge of that? Charlotte might be the greatest seductive temptress since Eve or the most doting wife in history.

'It's just awful,' Charlotte continued. 'Berowne was a wonderful man. He used to come here quite a lot to have a drink, and not always just to collect the rent. Pete took care of that anyway. I can't believe Berowne's dead. The society won't be able to function without him.'

So much for Charlotte having no interest in Berowne, Cara thought, although that could have been entirely platonic, of course.

'I didn't know Tom Chalcott well,' Charlotte continued. 'I remember his being very enthusiastic about Berowne taking over the leadership at first, but I think he might have regretted giving it up, especially to someone as gifted as Berowne. Tom didn't have his usual warmth that evening.'

Brief though her own contact with Berowne had been, Cara could understand how easy it would be for Charlotte – or anyone else that he decided to charm – to fall under his spell. But you're only going on Rachel's word that he had done that, she reminded herself, and Rachel might be completely deluded.

'Berowne was a great loss,' Cara murmured sympathetically, thinking that there could have been various reasons for Tom's reluctance to hand over the chair.

'And so was the loss of Tom Chalcott,' Cara added. 'Lady Lendale so much hoped that Tom's ghost would appear at Tuesday's celebration hunt. Were there any signs of that? Even just a presence or change of atmosphere?' The likelihood of that was remote, but she needed at least to sound knowledgeable on the subject. 'Was there *any* paranormal activity on the night Berowne died?'

'Nothing much,' Charlotte replied. 'If there was any indication that something paranormal was around it would have been recorded on the camcorder or EMF or our cameras as well as being written up in the society notes. The police took all of them, but Pete and I have talked a lot about the evening. I think there was a drop in temperature in my room, but it was so slight we didn't think it worth recording. After the midnight rendezvous I went to sleep like everyone else. There was nothing on either of our cameras either. With Berowne's awful death, Pete and I haven't talked to each other about the paranormal side of it.'

No help there then. 'Have you always been a member of the society?' Cara asked curiously. Charlotte didn't look the sort of person who would be interested in the supernatural. Though quite what such a person would look like, she wasn't sure.

She hesitated. 'No, I joined when Pete did. Initially, I wasn't sure I believed in the paranormal but gradually changed my mind. When Berowne joined the society, his knowledge was a great booster, and I began to feel their presence occasionally on our hunts. There were some odd occurrences, like things disappearing from where they were put. You leave trigger objects in a certain place to see if they remain there. Berowne explained that to me.'

'What about Tom? Was he popular?'

'Oh, yes, and he was always so polite. Lady Lendale must be disappointed that her nephew didn't appear at the celebration hunt,' Charlotte replied.

'Was Tom officially in charge that evening, or Berowne?' Cara asked. 'Did they fall out over that, if Berowne had taken over officially?'

Charlotte looked surprised. 'No. Tom wanted just one more hunt – that's what he told us. It seems awful now, but I left with everyone else that night, leaving him packing up and writing up the report. It would have been the last time he did that anyway, as Berowne was taking over. I don't remember anything paranormal happening, but that's quite usual. We think we're lucky if we can even report a sudden chill in the air or something moved. Certainly no one reported anything substantial that night.' A sudden giggle. 'Or not anything as substantial as a ghost.'

'And you're sure that everyone except Tom left together?'

'Yes. I remember that quite clearly.'

'Did you all reach the car park together? Was there any sign of Tom by then?' It was quite a long walk from the grotto, Cara thought, as the main path took one round the front of the house before branching off towards the car park at the Towers.

A pause while Charlotte thought about this. 'I don't remember,' she eventually said. 'It was such a long time ago. We did all leave together, save for Tom, but I've no idea whether any of us dashed over to the toilets or whether we all jumped into our cars together.'

Then she burst out, 'Why does Lady Lendale want to know so much about Tom? It's poor Berowne who's now died so awfully. Anyway, she treated Tom's ghost and death as a joke at the dinner. How could she do that?'

'It's her way of getting to the truth,' Cara said defensively. 'She does so because she does indeed believe that he might have been murdered.'

Charlotte shook her head. 'But that's impossible,' she said vehemently. 'She's barking up the wrong tree.'

Although sometimes, Cara reflected as she left, a barking dog is right.

It had been a busy day at the Towers, and a strange one. As it was a Wednesday, the Towers had been open to the public. It was odd to see visitors spilling out of the orangery after their guided tour, with the nearby servants' wing still mainly dedicated to the police. There had been no sign of Andrew, although his team had already disappeared from the Happy Huffkin after calling in for essential sandwiches and drinks. Perhaps he had given up the case? Cara wondered. True, he would be handling more than one case, but even so she'd expect he would be here some of the time. Or perhaps he was deliberately keeping his distance. No way. Reject that idea. Don't flatter yourself, Cara Shelley. Be thankful you're being left alone to do what you can for Lady Izzy *and* still run the Happy Huffkin.

Such platitudes were doomed. Talk of the devil. Or rather think of him. Here, strolling up to the folly was Andrew, just as she was closing up. Clad casually, it was hard to think of him as a DCI.

'Fancy a walk?' he asked.

She gaped at him, taken off guard. '*Walk?*' she repeated inanely. 'Another one? I'm just locking up to go home.'

'How about a wander through the woods? Different woods to the last time.'

How easy it would be to tell him to get lost and end the battle inside her. If she said 'no' that would be it. If she said 'yes', then that would be another matter. How easy and yet . . .

He seemed to sense the dilemma. 'Why the silence? Pride or prejudice?' he enquired.

That broke the ice. She glared at him. 'No to pride. Battling with prejudice,' she admitted. 'Is this evening work or leisure?'

'No idea. Lovely evening, though. We might see a rabbit or two prancing around.'

'Rabbits don't prance.'

'Perhaps they would if we ask them nicely.'

What was she doing, bantering with him like this? She should have said no right at the start. As it was . . . 'Let's ask them,' she heard herself say. The minute she'd said it, she regretted it. It seemed a momentous decision, but she could always make it a short walk and keep it strictly to business.

Andrew clearly had a particular route in mind. Although they set off on the path that led down to the river (she still thought of it that way, despite it being a mere trickling stream nowadays), he branched off in the other direction from Tanton village. She hadn't been consulted on this. No matter. Anywhere would be good on a June evening, rabbits or no rabbits.

Silence reigned. Someone had to break it. 'Do you often walk in the woods after work?' Cara asked.

'Or the fields. The flowers are all closing up then, getting ready for bed. Lucky flowers.' Sideways look.

'Andrew!'

A straight face. 'Yes, Cara?'

'Don't push it,' she said amiably.

He sighed. 'Work then. I've heard about this ghost tour of yours. Two weeks' time and you're involved? Sure you know what you're doing?' he added when she nodded.

'It's connected to Tom Chalcott, not Berowne,' she pointed out.

'In theory, maybe. Held in his memory, perhaps. But you can't convince me that the whole idea is simply to stroll along hoping for his ghost to grace the proceedings.'

'Even if not, it can't affect your case,' she said defensively.

'Who knows? You yourself think there's a link between the two deaths and you have a point there. The location and timing are too similar. By the way, I heard you were in the village earlier this week, chatting to Mr Brandon and his wife.'

'That's in the guidelines we agreed.'

'We may be following guidelines, but who else would? Murderers don't follow rules. Something that seems trivial to one person can be a nightmare to others. Jealousy and envy can be brushed aside by some, but consume others. End of lecture,' he said abruptly. 'Change of subject. What's Lady Lendale expecting out of this ghost tour?'

An easy one to answer. 'More about Tom Chalcott. The society will be focussing on any ghost territory, so that means good old Horace, and Sir Reginald and others. Sir Reginald was in the

Royal West Kent Regiment, but by a fluke his duties took him to both Isandlwana and Rorke's Drift during the Zulu War way back in 1879. Luckily for him, he had departed from both just before the battles began. I'm looking into the archives to see what other ghosts have been spotted over the centuries. But it might nudge memories about Tom, and that's what Lady Izzy is hoping for. A last spin of the dice.'

'And that's what worries me,' Andrew said grimly. 'You'll be the focus, especially as you're doing the rounds of the village.'

'I'll be fine,' Cara said stoutly. 'I'll be in a group, not wandering around on my own.'

'I'd like to be sure of that. I'll provide a police presence. Lady Lendale will have a new nephew or niece with her. And make sure you stick with them.'

'I am not, positively *not* a delicate flower.'

'Few flowers can survive snow and ice. Meanwhile, might I suggest the delicate flower and I have supper in the pub in Boxden, the George Inn? We can still get back before night falls.'

This was definitely getting out of her control. It was all a bit too pat. He must have had this plan in mind all along. Did that matter? Not really. 'Thank you,' Cara said primly. 'That would be fine.' She paused. 'Does this constitute work?' she asked, knowing the answer.

'On an evening like this? No.'

The quaint village of Boxden, close to an old quarry, was even smaller than Tanton. Tucked away by the river, it was off the beaten track and, although she knew the village, she'd rarely gone to the George. They weren't the only people who had decided to dine there and it was crowded. With its low, sixteenth-century beams, it was full of atmosphere – and noisy. It was warm enough to sit outside on a paved terrace, and just sitting and watching people come and go proved relaxing. It didn't escape Cara's notice, however, that Andrew was well known to the man behind the bar, clearly the owner or tenant. This visit, she realized, had been pre-planned – and she'd gone right along with it.

An hour and half later, after an admittedly enjoyable meal discussing everything from the state of the world to what books they had read as children, she realized that dusk was beginning to fall and the return walk along the footpath loomed ahead. It would not be easy. She was all too conscious that it was going to take two to manoeuvre its twists and turns in the semi-dark; she would be grabbing his arm for balance – and he hers. No choice – and anyway, why not? It might be fun – and it would also mean that they wouldn't be getting onto the stormy ground of their relationship. No decisions need be made tonight. Uneasily, it occurred to her that Andrew might be glad of that too. If this evening had been a Getting to Know You gimmick, it could work either way.

'Goodnight, Cara.' He watched as – once back on familiar ground at the Towers – she unlocked her car in the car park. Conversation had been limited while they negotiated muddy and slippery paths back to Tanton, but she'd gathered a few more interesting facts about Andrew Mitchem. One was that his father was a retired professor of English Literature, another that he, Detective Chief Inspector Mitchem, was scared of spiders.

'Goodnight, Andrew.' She slid into the driving seat. No kiss, no mutual banter, even if she did rather regret it. Anyway, it was her move: 'Where were those prancing rabbits you promised me?' She managed a light laugh.

'Next time,' he replied.

The mere existence of the Happy Huffkin was a good thing, Cara reflected the next day. In this wonderful world of Tanton Towers, the ghastliness of Berowne's murder, the uncertainty of what others wanted, what she wanted, and trying to do what she could to put the world to rights, the café was *there* in that weird, amazing folly. Sammy would probably already be here preparing the dough for the huffkins, the phone calls to Virginia for the day's orders had to be made, the china and cutlery checked, and the tables and chairs set out on the lawn. Routine, wonderful routine.

'No tomatoes.' Sammy appeared from his kitchen with this dire news.

'I'll ring round,' she assured him.

'Or strawberries.'

That was bad. What was June without strawberries? Maybe Wimbledon had snaffled the entire strawberry crop in Britain, now that tennis fortnight had arrived. Crisis, and yet she didn't give a damn. This was home. This was where she was meant to be, not rushing off to solve crimes that happened ten years earlier.

'I'll phone the farm shop right away,' she said.

What would the supreme cook Mrs Randall have done back in the eighteenth century? Cara asked herself. Whisked her very own preserved strawberries out of the pantry at the first sign of calamity? One of these days, Cara decided, she really would get round to some serious forward planning.

She took a second look outside. Change of plan. She made a hasty call to Sammy to take over the farm-shop call and prepared for the worst. She could see a very wrought-up elderly gentleman staggering up the steps to the café, furiously waving his walking stick at her. A side thought as she wondered why anyone would want to wave sticks and go up steps at the same time. Answer: Oliver Bright, would-be chair of the Tanton Ghost and Phantom Society, was on his way.

'I want a word with you, young lady,' he yelled, waving it even more vigorously.

Young lady indeed. Cara was flattered, but she'd sort that out some other time.

'Do sit down,' she said politely, drawing a chair by the window out for him. 'What's this word about?'

'Usurping my rightful place,' he thundered. 'I'm chairman and that's it.'

That's what? would be the tempting answer, but Cara refrained. She was in a surprisingly good mood this morning, and there were more important things to think about. How to be tactful about this?

'Lady Lendale is your honorary president,' she began her diplomatic reply, 'and it seems – while there is so much sadness over Berowne's death – the society needs a breathing space, with a relative outsider running it. I'm sure she – and I as her deputy – will be turning to you all the time for help and advice.'

'You won't get none from me,' he snorted.

'Why not?' she asked calmly. 'That would mean the police will be depending solely on Lady Lendale or me or other members of the society for information. And' – her diplomatic finale – 'the press will be too. You have the knowledge that they need.'

A silence. 'Right,' he said. 'I'll do it.'

She was just persuading him to have a coffee when his grandson Harry suddenly appeared through the doorway. 'Do what, Gramps?'

'I'll be the one the coppers ask for,' Oliver grunted. 'And them journalist fellows.'

Harry winked at Cara. 'There you are, Cara. Got yourself a willing little helper in Gramps. Mine's a cappuccino, thanks – no, make it two. One for Gramps.'

Oliver glared at him. 'None of that milky stuff for me. I'll have a real coffee.'

'Mine's to go,' Harry said promptly. 'We're working on the Italian garden. Got police clearance for that. The grotto's still blocked off, but the dear old general public can wander round everywhere else now.'

Cara seized the opportunity. 'Let me know when I can talk to you.'

'Can't this evening. Tomorrow maybe. Drop me a text.'

It was only last week that she had seen a very different Harry, Cara reflected. The one who reminded her of daughter Kate, so proud of her independence since she had graduated, and yet when something went wrong it was a different story. Kate was now somewhere in South America, or was when she last spoke to her. Nowhere near home, anyway. Cara was used to it now, but FaceTime calls didn't make up for the occasional hug. Maybe Andrew was into hugs . . . Her attention wandered, as she watched Harry leave, together with the cappuccino that Sammy had brought out.

Now to tackle Oliver. 'About Lady Lendale's ghost tour,' she began.

His belligerent face immediately darkened. Too bad. She'd press on.

'She's hoping that the ghost of Tom Chalcott will appear to cheer us along the way, and so she wants everyone to refresh themselves as to what they remember of him when he was such a popular chairman. I expect,' she added hastily, as she saw Oliver's expression, 'as you were once chairman yourself, she wants your thoughts on Berowne Dyer too.'

She'd misread him. 'Can't think why,' he grumbled.

'You must have known Berowne well,' Cara said.

'He pinched the chairmanship from me ten years back. I was going to take over from Tom. I was the obvious choice, still am. I know about ghosts, see? I know their little ways, when they want to appear and when they want to murder us.'

'Do you mean that literally?' she asked, aghast, taken aback. Did he really think that Tom or Berowne might appear and somehow get their own back on their assailant?

'Perhaps I do. I flaming well wish I could give that Tom Chalcott what he deserves. It was that Tom who pinched the society chair from me twenty years ago, after I'd run it like a dream in the Nineties. I would have been elected again like clockwork ten years later if it hadn't been for him. When he upped and died, that Berowne had already barged in and taken over. He'd done it again to me, though I was the obvious chap to run it, but did they listen? Oh no. That was him again, and that Rachel, egging her hubby on to grab my job. Fancied herself as the chairman's wife, see. Now Lady Lendale's waltzed in and started bossing us around. Don't even live in Tanton; how can she run the ghost society?'

Running the Tanton Ghost and Phantom Society didn't seem quite as glorious an honour to Cara, but each to his or her own.

'So,' Oliver swept on, 'Berowne said he'd take over. He's only been in the village a year, maybe two, and thinks he can rule the roost, knows everything. A few weeks back he appointed himself chairman for the next ten years. I'd said I'd take over, but Luke Claxton was up in arms about Berowne too, saying he'd stand for chairman. What happened? That idiot was outvoted and there we were, stuck with Berowne again. Done his best to ruin the society for ten years and he thought he was entitled to another ten. Wanted to open the hunts up to all and sundry. That idiot was dangerous too. He thought phantoms and ghosts were the same thing. Just like Tom Chalcott. Paved the way to murder, no doubt about that.'

A pause. Then he continued, 'Both of them maybe. All that modern stuff again. It's rubbish. You can't beat the old ways of ghosts – they all died in the days before they had all these gimmicks. They didn't have no EMF machines in old Sir Jeffry's time, did they? Just paper, pads and thermometers. That was enough. We saw some good ghosts in our early days too, we did.'

Here was one big motive for Berowne's murder and perhaps for Tom's too, Cara thought uneasily. In Berowne's case, he'd either appointed himself or been voted in to continue as chair, and that hadn't pleased Oliver – nor perhaps some others in the group. But murder? Thinking of the passion in Oliver's voice, was it possible that some might kill for such a reason? Yes, she told herself. Be wary.

'So, you and Tom were at daggers drawn. Didn't you have a vote?' she asked as casually as she could.

He glared at her. 'So-called vote. Back in his day, that Tom Chalcott bribed them, then Berowne barged in, and now ten years later he wouldn't budge.'

She couldn't believe any of this, but there might be a nugget of truth buried in it somewhere. 'I heard it was you who found Tom's body early the next morning. That must have been a dreadful shock.'

He stiffened. 'What about it? I get up early, see?'

Enough stonewalling, Cara decided. 'Lady Lendale thinks he was murdered. Is that possible, do you think?'

Another glare. 'How should I know? I just found him and that was that.'

'Did you have a mobile phone,' she persisted, 'so that you could call for help?'

'What do you want to know for, eh?'

'As I explained on Saturday, I need to fill in the picture,' she said amiably, 'so I can tell Lady Lendale and set her mind at rest.'

Another pause, a longer one this time. 'There he was, lying on the ground. Not in the car park, by the bushes near to it. Lying on his side.'

'Did he look peaceful?' If he'd been murdered, his face would surely reflect that.

She had struck a chord anyway – he half rose from his chair in anger, as though he was about to hit her. He didn't and he sank back. 'Peaceful? 'Course he wasn't peaceful, He was dead. He wasn't on the path itself, but at the edge of the woodland as far as I recall. Blood on him, dried of course. Fell over and hit his head on a stone, they said. But that's not what killed him. Heart attack. Poor chap,' he added hastily. 'I went to the cottages nearby, banged on a door and got them to ring for doctors, ambulances, police and the like. They all came. I did what I could and that's it.'

Oliver sat back, folding his arms, as if to indicate the subject was closed. He'd said all he knew on the subject.

Too bad, Cara thought. She'd push even further, much as he would dislike it. There could be something about this he wasn't telling her and that's why he was angry. Now was the time to get him talking.

'Was there anything else around? Any of his possessions – coats, papers, books? Was the ground damp, footprints—?'

She'd gone too far.

'I don't know,' he yelled. 'It was ten years back.'

That brought Sammy out with a rush. 'Calm down, Olly,' he ordered him.

Oliver glared. 'And you can belt up, Sammy. What's this lady on about? What's she want me to say? The fellow just tripped, hit his head on a stone and died of the shock. Weak heart. That's all I've got to say. There he was, lying down, briefcase, cushion, coat at his side.'

'Cushion?' Cara instantly picked up. 'What was that doing there? Was it to do with the ghost hunt, or had it come from his car? How close was it to him?'

'How should I know? I didn't have no yardstick with me, did I? Poor chap was dead.'

'How far was he from the car park? Was his car the last one left there?' Stupid question. Of course it was. Any others would have gone long before dawn when Oliver arrived.

He didn't even bother to answer her, but Cara went on thinking. Cushion? Did he bring it with him for some reason? Whether he carried it with him from his car or it had just been left there sometime earlier, it was more than interesting. It could be vital. Was it Tom's own cushion – or someone else's? That could be all the difference between tragic accident and murder by asphyxiation. If the official cause of death was heart failure, what had caused it and how could it be proven now? Oliver had been the first person on the scene that morning, always a factor to take into account, just as Harry had been on that recent terrible morning. One thing of which she was now sure was that, unusual though her methods were, Lady Izzy had good reason to be delving into the past in search of the truth about Tom's death.

NINE

Closed. Cara rapped even harder. Closed doors were beginning to be the norm, expected visit or not. She'd gathered that Luke Claxton's shop was prone to being shut, which she supposed for a one-man-band business was fair enough, given that his advert for the Handyman Store proclaimed that same-day home visits were available on request.

On the way home, she had been musing about the cushion Oliver had mentioned. This could be a vital clue. Why and how did that cushion get there? Pure chance? Had it been in poor condition, rain-soaked, dropped there accidentally, and whose was it? Answers came there none – yet – and now there was no answer from the doorbell.

She'd requested a visit, so where was Luke on this sunny Friday morning? She fished out her phone and called his number. The satisfaction in his voice was obvious as he informed her that he'd be 'right down'. Another one of the 'let the woman wait' brigade. He obviously lived over the shop, and she deduced as soon as he opened the side door that he probably lived alone. No partner, especially a female one, could live with a passageway quite so uninviting. A side door along it led into the shop, and she peered quickly inside. It had a dusty, workaday attraction. It looked old-fashioned, dark and long established, and in a curious way efficient. Boxes were neatly stacked, sample wires trailed over the edges of the shelves, household implements and ladders were resting by the wall shelves. A mahogany wood counter majestically reigned on the far side, together with what looked like very modern computer printers and accessories.

Quickly assessing the situation, Cara followed Luke as he stalked ahead. Another grumpy man – except this one wasn't as old as Oliver and was probably younger than he appeared. Thin and wiry, he must only be in his fifties, but not the sort of fifty-year-old who was satisfied with all he had achieved. This was a man who gave the impression that he'd been cheated of his due place in the world. Maybe that had more to do with his private life than with work. If so, why?

He was marching ahead of her into a rear room that had little to do with after-work relaxation and more to do with where to stuff such paperwork as was still necessary for work purposes. An unhappy-looking but modern computer sat on a small table. Could computers look unhappy? Cara silently asked herself. Yes, she decided, in this case simply from the way that this one, flanked with its monitor on its right and a printer on its left, was squeezed into a corner on one side and beside a sink and draining board that overlooked the garden on another. Clearly this had once been a kitchen proud of its status.

Why, she wondered, was Luke Claxton, who was now staring at her, arms folded, interested in ghosts? There was no answer to that . . . yet. Right. That would be her first question, she thought, as she sat on what looked the least uncomfortable chair available.

'What made you join the society?' she asked. 'Was it because ghosts seem drawn to old buildings?'

'Maybe. They like old wood, see? They can sniff it. It's like home to them. And water,' he added surprisingly. 'There's some likes that and some don't.'

Water? That was a lovely idea, Cara thought, picturing a group of Georgian-clad ghosts eagerly hurrying to have a paddle. She could understand Luke better now. He was a traditionalist at heart, she reasoned, despite his love of modern technology, and so she decided not to challenge him as she'd planned. 'Was Berowne modern in his approach to ghost hunts?' she asked. 'And how about Tom Chalcott? Was he a modernizer?'

A suspicious look from Luke. 'You've been talking to Pete. He sucked up to his lordship Mr Berowne just because he owes him a fortune in rent. And that wife of his, Charlotte . . . well, women are all the same. "Yes darling husband" to their faces and thinking the opposite. I had a wife once, just like that Charlotte. Pretends you're the best thing since sliced bread but keeps the carving knife behind her back. I reckon Pete doesn't know what's been going on there, her and her bloody Berowne.'

This, Cara decided, was one very unhappy man. She took note of his mention of Charlotte and Berowne, but it was difficult to fit her own impression of Charlotte in with this description.

'It's always hard to tell what's going on in a marriage because outsiders can only circle around it,' she replied as offhandedly as she could. 'You've known both chairs,' she added, 'Berowne and Tom Chalcott. Was Tom a good chair?'

'Suppose so.' Then Luke burst out again. 'Yeah,' he then said. 'Back ten years, Berowne grabbed the chair from Tom Chalcott and now he'd grabbed another ten. Old Oliver was raising the roof about it, saying it wasn't legal to be chairman twice. I was set on having a go at Oliver, because he'd been chairman himself before Tom Chalcott and here he was fluffing his feathers and wanting to stand again. Why shouldn't I have a go? I asked. Reasonable enough. He shouted me down, and the result was that Berowne grabbed a second term. Big surprise. He'd planned it all the time.'

Slight difference in stories here, Cara noticed, but the result was the same. At the time of his death, Berowne had just taken the chair for another ten-year period, leaving two discontented rivals with a grievance.

'Can't have an old man like Oliver in charge,' Luke raged. 'Berowne was always on about keeping up with the times, but that Oliver's the opposite. Doesn't want nothing to do with modern technology. That won't do, I told him. We've got to have a mix. Can't go so modern that the machines do all the work, but you can't do without them either. You need a bit of human input too. You want the spirits to know there's a person around who cares about them, not only machines. Bloody Berowne didn't care a tinker's cuss about getting to know the ghosts. He'd let the machines do everything. He just wanted the glory of being a power in the village. And then there's that wife of his. She was right at his side, she was. Had to be. An eye for the ladies, had good old Berowne. Eyes everywhere, from his gardener to the postwoman.'

Cara let him rant on. There's usually no smoke without fire and such smoke could be valuable for her. Nevertheless, she was here for a purpose. Back to her task.

'What was Tom Chalcott's stand on modern equipment?' she asked when he finally came to a halt. 'Was it an issue when he was the chair?'

Luke considered this. 'We're going back a bit here. Easy-going was Tom. A bit of everything from voice recorders to pads and biros. Shame he died like that. He was only young.'

Cara agreed. Luke might be fond of his rants, but nevertheless his feelings ran deep. 'What happened at the hunt before Tom died? Berowne had just taken over, so there was no official business to be sorted out.'

'Yeah, he made that clear. Not one for tact was bloody Berowne. Wanted to make it clear he was chairman – chair, you'd call it now,' he said grudgingly. 'You women get upset about details.'

Let that pass, Cara decided. A sweetish smile would suffice. It often had to do so.

'I heard that there wasn't much paranormal activity that night,' she said.

'Far as I remember, nothing had been recorded by the time we left. Berowne condescended to tell us later that the trigger object had moved from Apollo's bow and arrow to Hades, but Tom Chalcott had said there wasn't enough evidence to record that. Apart from it getting very chilly that night, there was nothing else special going on during the hunt. We were spaced out keeping a watch from the side-passages doorways, but nothing was picked up – nine times out of ten that happens. You'd expect at least a spooky presence, since Tom was going to be joining them out there an hour or two later.'

Cara struggled with this offhand comment. At least Luke seemed disposed to co-operate now. 'Why did the society choose to have the hunt in the grotto and not in the house?' she asked.

'Could have been because Mr Max wasn't in charge then. It was his dad owned the place and he wouldn't have wanted us in the Towers. It wasn't open to visitors so much then, only a day or two a year for special days, like.'

'So why did Tom want to come here, even if it was just to the grotto?'

'Dunno for sure. I reckon Tom found out there were a ghost or two there if we were lucky, and thought that was a better bet than persuading the snooty Farran Prydes into opening up the Towers. Mind you, the grotto wasn't so big then either. Those cottages were still standing, so the Laughing Lady wasn't haunting the place in Tom's time. There was some farmer he'd heard about who'd set his cap above his station in life and got his comeuppance when he fancied her ladyship.'

Fun perhaps, Cara thought, especially as she had begun looking up the records in the Archives Room for ghostly information in preparation for the ghost tour. Ghostly farmers could be helpful, but right now this was a side track. She tried again. 'Did Tom seem off-colour that night?'

'Don't remember his saying he felt ill.' Pause. 'Why are you asking all these questions? Does her ladyship reckon someone did him in? That why she reckons he's a ghost?'

Careful, Cara warned herself. 'Would anyone have wanted to?'

Luke shrugged. 'You never know, do you?'

End of that line. Now for the big question that might change the picture. 'Were there committee members there then who've since left the society?' If so, away with the theory of a link between the two deaths.

'One or two I reckon. Can't remember.' Luke seemed far more amenable, perhaps because she had moved off dangerous ground. 'Hang on a minute. Left the society? I'll have a look,' he said.

He disappeared up the stairs and returned with a framed photo that he handed over to her. 'There you are. It's the committee taken a few weeks before Tom Chalcott's death to celebrate our tenth sighting. That was taken at a fish-and-chip shop somewhere. Closed down now. One too many ghouls for the chap's missus to take. Look, there's Tom in the middle, with Berowne grinning at his side – squeezing himself into the better position.'

Cara peered closely at it. There was a younger Pete, looking happier than he did nowadays, and there was Charlotte, looking modestly down at the ground and clinging to Pete's arm. There was Luke himself, but he too looked a lot jollier than Pete did nowadays. She could pick out Oliver too, but there were more faces unknown to her.

'Who is this?' Cara pointed a finger at a jovial-looking man in suit and tie, with the suit bulging over a rounded stomach.

'That's the butcher, Eric Fowler. Died last year.'

'And her?' she asked, pointing to a stern-looking elderly lady.

'That's Gladys. You can count her out,' Luke said grimly. 'Left in a huff one day and passed away a month or two later. 'And that's Margie.' He pointed to a rather pleasant-looking middle-aged woman. 'Living in South Africa when last heard of. We fell out, her and me.'

So that is that, Cara told herself as she walked along Tanton High Street to return to the Towers. Was she relieved or sorry that she could continue to look for that missing link? So far she had learned some interesting information about Tom Chalcott, but nothing sufficiently significant to indicate Lady Izzy was right about Tom's death. That cushion was the only possible evidence for her theory that he had been murdered – and that would hardly convince Andrew Mitchem that there was a case to answer.

Was she downhearted? No. She still had a feeling that she was on the right road, but quite where that road was leading, or indeed how many side turnings she might still have to make, she had no idea. Cling to the link. That was the best route, despite the lack of proof. Excluding a teenage Harry or even younger teenage Jamie or Emily, the number of people who could have been involved with both deaths was growing smaller. And Andrew would undoubtedly say, more dangerous. Had Berowne strayed into this unknown territory and paid the price?

She was still ruminating on this when she reached the Happy Huffkin. Was there any point in discussing this theory with Andrew? Answer: still no. This huffkin might have its dough prepared but it wasn't yet sufficiently baked to offer him. What, after all, was her case? Only what he already knew – that there might be a link. There was more to be done. One swallow did not make a summer, and one cushion did not make a case.

Meanwhile she could swing into action and put the chairs out for customers, who would (hopefully) be swarming in here from two o'clock onwards.

'I'm back. I'll finish outside,' she called out to Sammy, who briefly appeared in the kitchen doorway.

'Her ladyship's here,' he informed her in return.

'Here?' What on earth did he mean? There was no sign of her unless . . .

Sammy's head jerked. Surely he didn't mean right there in the kitchen? Cara hurried over there, and sure enough Lady Izzy was at the sink, swathed in one of his all-encompassing aprons with her bright pink trousers peeping out below.

'Just doing the washing-up, Cara,' Lady Izzy called over to her. 'You sit down. I'll be out in a minute.'

Cara now knew better than to protest, so she busied herself with collecting the tablecloths and cutlery for the outside tables. The wait wouldn't be long as the washing-up could only be a few of Sammy's dishes used for preparing the huffkins. The display cabinets were already stocked with sandwiches and cakes. She was proud of the ones she had had a literal hand in when she adapted recipes from the past to modern tastes and products. There was a plateful of Maids of Honour, said to be Henry VIII's name for Anne Boleyn's favourite cheesecake, and there was her own invention, the Earl of Sandwiches, in honour of the traditional founder of this invaluable form of sustenance.

Lady Izzy duly appeared, plus a tray with two coffees on it, which she placed down on a table where Cara joined her.

'Such fun washing up here,' Lady Izzy remarked. 'I only have one of those dishwasher things. I can't even see the china bouncing around inside it. No job satisfaction at all. How are you getting on?' she finished all in one breath.

Cara duly obliged with as much detail as she could, and Lady Izzy nodded approvingly, especially at the mention of the cushion that had been found. 'Gathering the wool nicely,' Lady Izzy said. 'But the sheep aren't all shorn yet. Such a disaster that Tom didn't appear on the night dear Berowne died. But he will in due course, he will. He'll be wanting to tell us the truth about what happened then.'

Cara didn't have the same confidence. 'We only have that cushion so far to suggest he might have been murdered. I can't get access to the coroner's report, so all I have to go on is possible asphyxiation. Have you read it yet?'

Lady Izzy waved this aside. 'I have but it doesn't help. The coroner must have been new to the job. He hasn't realized that Tom was murdered.' She sat back in her chair and beamed.

Better not to pursue this point, Cara decided. As usual, she wasn't sure whether Lady Izzy was joking or not. There was one thing she had to get clear, though, and since Lady Izzy had arrived out of the blue, she might have the same thing on her mind.

'How are your plans going for the ghost tour, Lady Izzy?' she asked brightly. 'I'm deep into the archive records of ghosts. I hope that helps?'

'Undoubtedly,' was the prompt reply. 'Everyone will be there, alive or not. I shall do all I can to ensure Tom attends, and I would hope Berowne too, so that nice police inspector will have to be ready to arrest their murderer.' Another beam.

Cara froze. This did not sound convincing. Thankfully Max and Alice wouldn't blame her if the evening was a disaster. More to the point, it might be asking for trouble – and if Lady Izzy was serious about the police being present, it seemed she for one was expecting it.

Lady Izzy had clearly read her thoughts. 'Fear not, Cara. I shall conduct myself perfectly. I shall not point my own finger at the guilty party. I shall be far more interested in the ghosts themselves. At the very least one or two of them will surely take the opportunity to be a presence there, given that their murderer will be amongst them.'

Whether Lady Izzy was serious or not, Cara knew she must plough on with her role. She was sure of one thing: Andrew Mitchem was not going to approve of it.

'How do you want to plan the tour?' she asked. 'Do we divide into groups, go our separate ways or stay together?'

Lady Izzy answered decisively. 'Together, without a doubt. You and I will lead it, if possible one at the front, one at the rear. We have a duty to protect our guests.'

'From what though?' Her suspicions about this hunt looked well founded. 'So you think there will be danger?'

Lady Izzy laid her hand on top of Cara's. 'Yes. When I asked you to find out more about Tom's death, I had no idea that could be so dangerous. Tom had rested quietly until then. Berowne's death has changed that, so if you wish to withdraw from the tour then do. Tom would have been the first to agree that was sensible.'

'No. In any case, my leaving would make no difference,' Cara decided. 'We can be sure that there's a murderer at large in

Tanton. Being together might sharpen memories of what happened last Tuesday, or even on the night Tom died.'

'That's Max and Alison's hope too,' Lady Izzy said approvingly. 'And my own. I suspect Max will be armed with his shotgun ready to shoot any ghost that comes near his beloved Lavinia Fontana gallery.'

'I'll keep well out of the way of that,' Cara promised her, relieved that the mood had lightened. 'What role do I play? I've learned all I can about the ghosts.'

Lady Izzy looked surprised. 'Did I not mention that? Ah, perhaps not. Well, I've changed my mind. I'd like you to lead the group around so that you can tell them all about the ghosts and their history over the centuries.'

She must have seen Cara's look of horror, because she added smoothly, 'I'm sure the archivist will give you every possible guidance.'

'I've been reading as much as I can in the archives, but I'm not a historian,' Cara said feebly. 'Nor am I an expert in the paranormal.' She could see that this was a done deal. She was trapped.

'No matter. The ghosts will help you, as well as the archivist,' Lady Izzy said happily. 'And don't worry. I will be talking about Tom and his ghost.'

Cara's adrenalin level began to sink, to her relief. At least she didn't have to cope with that. 'But what do you hope to learn from the evening?' she asked. 'Even if it does jolt memories, they're unlikely to emerge immediately.'

'My dear Cara, I have no idea. But it's my last throw. We step into the unknown, you and I.'

TEN

The unknown indeed. Lady Izzy was right about that. As far as Cara could see, the only path to progressing any further with Tom Chalcott's death was relying on that link between the two deaths. The problem was that if she was wrong and there wasn't a link, then she would be floundering around and probably trespassing on the great DCI Mitchem's territory. Heaven forbid. One step that might help pull her out of the mud would be to talk to the three society members who had not been at the Chalcott hunt: Jamie, Harry and Emily. No matter what their private relationships might or might not be, they could have outsider views about Tom Chalcott simply picked up from conversations and meetings at the ghost society. None of them could have been members of the society for more than a year or two given their ages, but their opinions about the club or their fellow members could perhaps provide a feast of information or, failing that, at least a few relevant titbits.

Jamie Dickens lived on a farm, run by his parents, that had once been part of the Towers estate before the two world wars had deprived the Towers of finance. As far as Cara could make out, Jamie was living in one of the brick and ragstone cottages usually up for short-term lets. The track leading to it was further along the road from her cottage, and it was a pleasant walk from there in the early evening. She'd gathered from Alison and Josie that he had finished a management course with flying colours, and was working for a hotel chain based somewhere on the south coast. The image of himself that he had put over at the doomed celebration last Tuesday did not suggest management would be his role in life, but perhaps the tough, dominant male image he wore was a mask. He was a sturdy-looking young man, which was all the more noticeable as he wasn't that tall (maybe five foot seven, she estimated), and the mask – if it existed – was still in place.

A jerk of his head indicated she might enter after he answered the doorbell. A wave of the hand then permitted her to enter what must be his living room, which had a small kitchen area leading off it. The TV dominated the room, various machines were stacked under a table, a small bookcase was all that seemed allotted to the written word and a huge Taylor Swift poster adorned the walls along with several others. The bookcase showed every sign of its contents being in use, which suggested there was another side of Jamie that he kept tucked away. There were no indications that Emily shared the cottage with him, however, and Cara knew from Alison that her official home was with her parents in the village.

'Old Oliver says it's OK to talk to you. What about?' Jamie asked. 'Pete Brandon, is it?'

'Pete?' Cara repeated blankly. 'Why should I talk about him?'

A shrug. 'He's been marched off. Arrested. Didn't you know?'

She didn't and this was astonishing news. 'When?' she asked. 'Why? For murder? But . . .'

So many questions flew into her mind and she couldn't voice any of them. One was uppermost, though, and it had nothing to do with Jamie. Why hadn't Andrew told her? She tried to remind herself that she was here to talk about Tom Chalcott – officially – but she had to know more about Pete Brandon.

'Has he been charged?' she said.

'No idea.'

She could tell that whether the news was true or not, she would get no further about Pete, and tried to plunge back ten years and concentrate on Tom. 'Tom Chalcott, then,' she said. 'I need to know anything that might help Lady Lendale find out more about what happened to her nephew.'

He looked doubtful so she hastily added, 'I know that's long before your time with the society, but you must have gained a general impression of him and its history.'

'Can't think of anything.'

Try a different tack, she thought. 'Why did you join the society? Because of Emily?'

This worked. He grinned. 'No way. Other way round. Berowne gave a talk about the spirit world, so I got interested. He and Rachel had a good thing going.'

To Cara this sounded like a partial truth. With a course in management completed, could he have his eye on a job in Rachel's firm? She decided to break – or adjust – DCI Mitchem's rules again. 'The police will have talked to you, I'm sure, but is there anything else you can tell me about Berowne's death that you think might have some connection with Tom Chalcott? Little things that perhaps came to you afterwards and you thought weren't worth telling him?'

He stared at her. 'Can't help you there. Maybe he was another Berowne. Couldn't keep his paws off women. He had tried it on with Emily.'

Here we go again, she thought. The Berowne whom everybody had liked seemed far from the truth. This was not her territory, but coming on top of Rachel's accusations, it certainly should be of interest to Detective Chief Inspector Andrew Mitchem.

'There must have been talk about Tom amongst the members who remember him,' she persevered.

A shrug this time. 'Just his name. His ghost never popped down to see us, if that's what you're hoping for.'

'Didn't his name ever come up?' she persisted.

'Don't remember if it did.'

Abandon hope, she decided. 'You'll stay a member of the society now?' she asked, as she got up to leave.

'No problem with that.'

'Are you coming to the ghost tour? Will Emily come too?'

A distinct change of tone. Gone was his fairly affable response. 'Depends. Not if I say no.'

'Depends on what?'

'Whether that Harry Bright's going. If he is, she isn't.'

Was Emily as irresistible to men as Jamie implied? Cara wondered. Or did he just see it as his right to have control over the women in his life? She reminded herself that this was a sideline, not relevant to Tom Chalcott. Was the visit valuable otherwise? Apart from her learning the news about Pete Brandon? Yes, it was, since if by any chance Pete was Berowne's killer, her theory of a link between the two deaths was affected. If Tom had been murdered, either Pete might have been a double killer for whatever reason, or it knocked the link out of the picture. Anyway, every visit helped build up a background storehouse of information, even though it had done little to confirm or otherwise a link between Tom and Berowne. Was Andrew following up anything on the line she'd thought about, that Berowne had paid the penalty for having stumbled across Tom's murderer? Or was he digging deeper into the psyche of the Tanton Ghost and Phantom Society?

Her walk home along the banks of what had once been a thriving stream was a pleasant one, especially in twilight. The birds were out for their evening carolling, keen to point out that the day was fading away and they wanted their supper first. Wildflowers were closing their petals over their heads ready to sleep, and motor traffic had more or less abandoned its struggle to ruin the peace of this country road for the night. Cara turned the last corner, looking forward to supper, after which she might type notes – or, more likely, watch TV.

Her plans were doomed. Standing on the grass bank by the stream, opposite the gate into her garden, was a tall figure in an anorak, hands in pockets, surveying the scene. Could she handle this? Had he come to tell her about Pete's arrest? Even so, why had fate presented her with Andrew at this time of night? Much as she felt pleasure at seeing him, she was just too tired to cope if this was going to be about the Berowne case. She couldn't scuttle by him into her gateway unobserved though.

No decision was required from her. It was almost as if he thought his presence was expected. He simply took his hands out of his pockets and strolled up to her.

'I tried your doorbell. No reply.'

'I was out.' Hard to tell whose comment was the more inane. She felt hers won the day and, from the way he was grinning at her, he agreed.

'Time for a talk?' he enquired.

'Where?' She pulled herself together. That was nonsense. 'No, come inside.' Asking for trouble, she supposed, but why not?

He followed meekly at her side (or she liked to think it was meekly) into the cottage, even remembering to duck his head at the doorway into the conservatory. She liked her conservatory. It was the home of part of her collection of cookery books – those with bindings that would withstand the variations of the English climate without buckling in the sun. Mrs de Salis, Elizabeth

David, Mrs Raffald, Alexis Soyer, Signor Francatelli and several others all lived together in happy harmony with their recipes still valued. Tonight, their charms eluded her, though.

'Is this visit for work purposes?' she enquired.

'Yes and no.' He made for the cane chair that she was airily indicating. 'It has to be work at this stage of the investigation,' he continued, 'but on the other hand it isn't for work purposes that I feel impelled to talk to you.'

'Impelled?' she queried politely.

He laughed. 'You're a hedgehog today. All prickles.'

That made her laugh. 'Do I need them? And anyway,' she added, 'hedgehogs aren't *all* prickles, except when they roll themselves into a ball in justified self-defence.'

'Not needed. When this case is over and Berowne Dyer's killer is charged, it'll be a different matter,' he said casually.

Charged? Different matter? Three words and all she had to do was reply. But she couldn't.

She was both relieved and – her heart sank – slightly disappointed. She was uncomfortably aware that her body was taking another path than her brain and her brain wasn't too sure that it could control her emotions if tested. To have him sitting in that armchair was nearing a time when it might be all too easy to be a whole lot closer and in his arms. But not tonight.

'Cara?' he asked, when she said nothing. It was almost as if he were aware that some kind of milestone had been passed.

'I'll make sure I'm at home next time,' she managed to reply, as though mere banter was called for. Perhaps after all she should concentrate on work. She'd try. 'I heard you've arrested Pete Brandon.'

'Misinformation. Not arrested. Brought in for questioning. Now sent home with a caution not to leave town. We might need to question him again. Does that satisfy you?'

'Thank you,' she said humbly. She wasn't sure that humility was called for, but she was too tired to fight it. Concentrate on work. 'Are you here about the ghost tour again?' she asked brightly. 'It's only a week away now.'

'Not about the tour as such. I know you're pursuing your line about Tom Chalcott, and I'm still agreeable to that.' Piercing look. 'I've become more interested in that line and its possible murder, so we can talk about it within reason. We can't, of course, talk about Berowne Dyer's death, but there could be something in the Chalcott line to consider. I've spoken to Rachel.'

'Why? Rachel wasn't at the ghost hunt where he died.'

'No, but she was already married to Berowne, who was there and doubtless told her about it.'

'Did she tell you about Berowne chasing after other women?' she countered.

'Ah. So you have crossed our agreed boundaries.' He looked pleased, as though he'd scored a point.

'No, I have not,' she said crossly. 'But I can't help it if he's mentioned while I'm discussing Tom Chalcott, can I? The society members could hardly not mention Berowne. They all knew him, they all worked with him and, well, things just emerge. Rachel casually told me about Berowne and women.'

'Women aren't the only aspect,' he replied. 'Anyway, evidence about Tom's death is thin on the ground, so I'd like to know the gossip.'

'That cushion found with him is possible evidence,' Cara pointed out, still mutinous at his scoring this point. 'It was in such an odd place for a cushion. But I can't see any reason so far why anyone would want to murder him. Lady Lendale has said very little about Tom Chalcott's love life, only that he had nice girlfriends. Passion for power might be a valid motive for his murder, but that doesn't actually work as Tom had no objection to Berowne – or probably any of the other society members – taking over the leadership. After all, it's only a small club, even if it was highly regarded, and he didn't even live in the village. That's different from your Berowne Dyer case.'

'One of the others might have set their hopes on it, though; a mission that went wrong when Berowne grabbed the opportunity.'

'Grab?' Cara picked up. 'That's an emotive word. Do you have evidence to back up your implication that he was stepping out of turn in doing so?'

'My apologies. For Berowne, substitute Pete or Luke, or indeed one of the other committee members who I gather have now left the country but who might have fancied taking over from Tom Chalcott. Have you taken them into account?'

'No. Two of those who left the society have since died, and the third hasn't been heard of for yonks.' One point to her, she thought.

'The link between the two deaths is still weak,' Andrew replied. He paused. 'I'll leave now, but there's one more thing.'

'Which is?'

'It can wait.'

It did wait. Well, until he left, that is. She escorted him to the door and there had been no further mention of 'the thing'. Then he turned round, put his arm round her, and kissed her. She had realized in time to pull away, but why on earth should she? She was enjoying it. It was far too long since she'd felt lips on hers, and now that she did there was no way she wanted to stop. The glow had spread throughout her body. When she finally broke away, she looked at him aghast. Another minute or two and all vows that work had to come first would have been doomed, especially as she was theoretically a suspect in a murder case he was handling.

'Was that the matter that had to wait?' she asked him shakily.

He seemed as shaken as she was. 'Not all of it.'

Emily looked distinctly wary. She'd agreed to meet Cara for a brief chat the next day during her lunch hour at the florist's in the neighbouring village of Hemden. Cara was still battling with what had happened the night before. Such a small thing on one level, on another quite the contrary. The starting pistol had been fired. She had assumed that he had, as had she, been sticking to an unspoken agreement to postpone private life until this case was out of the way. Too bad – but she wasn't sorry it had happened.

To work, she told herself now. Sammy had not been best pleased at her need to abandon preparations for the Sunday afternoon visitors, even though she'd made arrangements with Virginia to step in and fill the gap. She'd have to make peace later. After all, she wasn't doing this just for Lady Izzy's benefit, but for the Towers. Tourist attraction or not, and quite apart from their tragic personal effects, the death of Berowne and possible question mark over Tom Chalcott's death should not lie as unsolved mysteries to scar the Towers' image.

She'd found Emily waiting on a bench outside the florist, an empty paper bag screwed up next to her, evidence that lunch had been concluded.

'It's nothing to do with me,' Emily said defensively, before Cara had said a word.

'That's what makes chatting to you so valuable,' Cara said diplomatically. 'The objective standpoint. Jamie—'

Emily was clearly not pleased. 'What's he been saying now?' she interrupted.

'Only that he doesn't know whether you'll be going on the ghost tour.' A slight slant to the story.

'Is he going?' Emily demanded.

'Pass,' Cara said promptly. 'You sort it out. But you should go. Lady Lendale needs support.'

'Yeah. All she really wants is that Tom Chalcott to pop down from above and say hello to us and we'll all clap . . .' She broke off. 'Sorry. Shouldn't make fun of her. It's all a bit difficult really.'

Cara decided to plunge in. 'Why's that? Because of Harry?'

Silence, then a reluctant 'Maybe.'

Cara quickly switched direction. To get entangled with Emily's love life was not going to help her mission – or Emily. 'What brought you to the Ghost and Phantom Society? Did you join because of Jamie?'

Immediate reaction from Emily. 'No way. I joined first.'

Time to stir things up. 'He says he did,' Cara shot back at her.

'Then he's wrong,' Emily said crossly. 'There was nothing much else to do round here and I saw a ghost once and got interested. I was in a drama club too, and we did that Scrooge play with ghosts popping up all over the place. And there was that woman who was done in at the Red Barn. That had a ghost in it. So I reckoned the society here was all like that. But it's not. It's just a lot of hanging around and hard work. Then Jamie joined so it was sort of fun too. Even more when Harry joined up. Now it's a bit awkward. You see, I—'

Whoops. Cara thought she'd better move fast or she'd turn into a mother figure, giving comfort and advice. 'Yes, it's tough, isn't it?' she said sympathetically, then: 'You wouldn't have known what it was like in Tom Chalcott's day, but I expect the others chatted about him. That's what I'm here to talk about.'

'Don't remember anyone saying anything about him.'

Another change of direction required. 'It must have been spooky sleeping in the grotto, even without the awful thing that happened to Berowne. Did you record anything before midnight, when I gather Berowne collected the first results?'

'Yes, but . . .' Emily glanced at Cara and giggled. 'I wasn't there all the time after that. I kind of made a mistake. Not much light, you see. I went the wrong way and thought it was Jamie at first, but it wasn't. It was Harry. So I' – a sideways look at Cara – 'sort of stayed.'

Keep away from this, Cara decided, a trifle reluctantly. Emily didn't seem to have suffered from the experience anyway. Would Andrew be following up this line? Too late she realized that she was automatically thinking of him as Andrew, whether he was in his official capacity or otherwise. Berowne had been murdered about three o'clock, and with room-switching in action, Emily's movements plus Jamie and Harry's might be relevant.

'You didn't see or sense anything odd during the night, nothing spooky?' Cara asked.

'No.' Emily seemed to be relieved that there were no signs of disapproval. 'I went back to my room quite early and it seemed a bit chilly. There were no ghosts, though, and I remember thinking about what Lady Lendale had said at that meal we had beforehand. It was a shame there wasn't a ghost around for her. I hope you can fix one for this tour we're going on.'

Cara wasn't too sure about this.

'Maybe Berowne will come along as a ghost as well as her nephew,' Emily continued brightly.

'Is it true that everyone liked Berowne?' Cara asked. That concept was getting out of date, but still the answer might be interesting.

'No. He was a creep.'

That was decisive enough. Emily was so offhand that Cara was startled.

'Did he make a pass at you?' she asked.

'Yes, but I don't think it was serious. I reckon he had something on the side though. Don't tell Rachel that.'

Rachel, Cara thought as she left Emily, probably knew all too well. She had Charlotte within her sights.

ELEVEN

Harry Bright was almost too bright, Cara decided, as she greeted him at the door of the Happy Huffkin on Monday morning. Gone was the Harry who on that never-to-be-forgotten morning had stumbled his way towards her, pale with shock at what he'd just discovered. Today he didn't exactly swagger into the Happy Huffkin, but there was no lack of confidence here. At nearly six foot in height and with his gingery-coloured hair and general aura of lazy awareness of his own charms, she could see why Emily had been wooed away from Jamie, whether temporarily or permanently.

He must surely be on the police suspect list, however, just as she would be in theory, irrespective of Andrew Mitchem's views. She and Harry had been first on the scene, and thence automatically suspect. Moreover, as a member of the Tanton Ghost and Phantom Society, Harry had been one of the nine who had slept overnight in the grotto. His work for the Towers meant he knew the woodland area well, together with all its entrances and exits. She hated having to consider cheerful, happy-go-lucky Harry as a possible murderer, but she couldn't rule him out, if only because there might be a link back to Tom Chalcott through his grandfather, Oliver. Andrew would undoubtedly have interrogated him both as a witness and a suspect, since no one else could have escaped Len's eagle eye and crept in during the night unobserved. Nevertheless, he was an odd fit for the ghost society, especially.

She duly escorted Harry up to the first floor, where she had set a table for him, plus the requested sandwiches, since he'd be missing out on elevenses. 'Is this your seduction suite?' he asked grinning, as he looked round the otherwise empty café. 'I'll bring Emily here.'

'I'll warn her,' Cara said amiably. 'That's fair, isn't it?' Emily was quite capable of looking after herself. In the interests of Lady Izzy's commission, she held back from mentioning Lucy.

She needed his co-operation. Harry was too young to have known Tom Chalcott but he might have picked up interesting information about him from the other members.

'I guess so,' he replied, equally amiably.

He had a way of making it seem that he was laughing at himself as much as putting over an act, Cara thought. Nevertheless, his current enthusiastic two-handed method of attack on the crab sandwich did rather diminish the 'I'm every woman's dream' effect.

'Tom Chalcott,' she began firmly. 'You wouldn't have met him.'

'Gramps filled me in. But I was only a lanky teenager then, without a ghostly thought in my head. He thought good old Tom was the cat's whiskers. Is Tom going to turn up and rattle his chains on this ghost tour?' Another bite at the sandwich. 'He's probably expecting Berowne to join him.'

'One can always hope.' Cara thought she might be getting the hang of Harry Bright. She'd try dabbling in forbidden waters, forbidden by Andrew anyway. After all, Harry's testimony about Berowne would be intertwined with hers. 'Finding Berowne like that was bad enough for me, but it must have been worse for you, Harry,' she continued bravely. 'You weren't prepared, when you went along to his quarters and found him. What made you go there? All the others must just have gone straight home.'

'That's right. That's what was arranged,' he said, after his last gulp of sandwich. 'But I was meant to be on garden duty that day, so I'd crept out of the grotto to have a shower at home double quick to get back for clocking on at eight. I'd told Berowne I'd look in to see if he needed a hand with getting the grotto straight.'

She had to ask. 'Were you alone there?'

He shot a look at her. 'You know I was. By the time I got there, everyone else had already disappeared. Never so glad to see anyone as I was you, Cara.'

'Your grandfather had left too? He seems very committed to the society.' Cara tried to put this delicately, remembering the 'raging bull' approach he'd taken with her.

'To the society. Not to Berowne.'

Another vote against Berowne. Didn't *anyone* like him? Yes, Charlotte did, and apparently Lady Izzy too. At least Harry was frank about his dislike. 'What made you interested enough in ghosts to join yourself?' she asked curiously.

He shrugged. 'They're a good crew.'

He wasn't going to get away with that. 'And the real reason?' she asked.

She thought he wasn't going to answer, but he did. He grinned. 'You have to keep grandfathers happy, don't you? Mine's backing me for my uni course, provided I support him over keeping to the old methods of ghost hunting. No problem. Anyway,' he added, 'I'd spotted Emily.'

'No comment,' Cara said drily. 'Back to Tom Chalcott. He seems to have been generally popular, unlike Berowne apparently. Is that your impression from what you've heard?'

'Yeah. And he didn't give a toss about Berowne either.'

'What?' Cara was taken aback. 'That's odd, because from what I've heard, he was quite happy with Berowne taking over from him ten years ago.'

'Gramps told me that. Doesn't matter much, does it?'

'It could.' She remembered Charlotte saying something about Tom not displaying his usual warmth at the hunt on the night he died, but then there could have been various reasons for that, perhaps because Tom regretted having handed over the reins, or perhaps he was just tired or beginning to feel off-colour – naturally enough as he had a heart attack later that evening.

'An Emily-type problem maybe?' Harry came back with a straight face. 'Pistols at dawn? Shouldn't think so. This Chalcott doesn't sound the sort. Gay, was he?'

'I've no idea,' Cara said honestly. 'He had girlfriends, though. And Berowne certainly wasn't gay. Nor,' she added, 'do I think Tom Chalcott sounds as though he would take part in an Emily-type situation.'

'Wait till this ghost tour,' Harry chortled. 'All their ghosts will pop along to see us. Or maybe they'll have a punch-up amongst themselves. Can't wait.'

Cara could wait, however. All these strands of information needed pulling together. Right now, she felt she was faced with a plate of spaghetti with so many strands that she couldn't get her fork round them. Perhaps that was because she didn't yet know what sauce was needed to bind them. It seemed to her despairingly that one by one the strands were falling off, only to have new ones quietly present themselves.

There was one last sauce to taste on this spaghetti plate. The one where it had begun: with Rachel. She was at the centre, the one who knew Berowne best, even if some of his secrets were unknown to her. And with luck Berowne, forbidden territory or not, could well prove the gateway to Tom Chalcott.

Ellum Place had never appealed to Cara, although it was hardly fair to compare it with the Towers. She had mentally christened it Bleak House. It was from a later period than the Towers, perhaps late Georgian, and it lacked the joie de vivre of Sir Jeffry Farran's masterpiece. He had had enormous pleasure in building the oddities of the Towers, with its turrets, towers and gargoyles, whereas whoever built Ellum Place had no aspirations to personality at all, as far as Cara could judge.

For some reason it was making her shiver today, though she couldn't tell why. It was just a house, a block of red brick with doors and windows dumped into an uninteresting park. Nevertheless, its trees seemed to be eyeing her with menace, throwing their shadows at her as though preparing to declare war.

The front door was answered by Rachel herself, who seemed far more welcoming than the house and gardens. She was clad in a black trouser suit, her dark hair flowing gracefully around her shoulders and, widowed or not, she appeared a model businesswoman of today. Appearances don't always reflect the inner self, Cara reminded herself.

How's your quest to discover more about Tom Chalcott going?' Rachel asked, once the courtesies of tea and where to sit in her huge conservatory were out of the way.

'Moving gradually. It's on its way though,' Cara replied lightly.

'Is Lady Lendale still on the trail herself?'

'She's left Tanton Towers for the moment.' To Alison and Max's relief, Cara mentally added. The relief was only temporary though, as Lady Izzy would be returning in plenty of time for the ghost tour evening. 'She's probably saving her strength for the ghost tour,' she added. 'That's less than a week away now.'

Cara was all too aware of the passing days – and that she still had plenty to do unearthing ghost stories in the Archives Room.

Was this passing of teacups and skirting round what must be on both their minds deliberate on Rachel's part? Cara wondered, or just her standard business practice? Rachel really was remarkably composed. 'I'm not sure you knew Tom Chalcott, but you knew of him, didn't you? Will you feel up to coming on the tour?' she asked.

'Considering that my late husband might be one of the ghosts of honour, I'll be present.' There was no bitterness in Rachel's voice; she was completely calm as she continued: 'I only met Tom the once, and that was when he called here to see Berowne one day. I wasn't a member of the society until later, so I wasn't there on the night he died at the ghost hunt.'

She took a sip of tea before she continued. 'As you probably know, Tom lived some way away from Tanton, so we didn't normally socialize with him. When he called that day to see Berowne, it was I who opened the door. He said he was from the ghost society. He'd brought a lot of paperwork with him, so I didn't join them.'

This interview was going rather too smoothly, Cara thought. It was almost as though Rachel had practised what she was going to say.

A glance at Cara, then Rachel continued, 'Berowne worked mostly for my family property business in publicity, and the rest of the time he looked after this house, its staff and its gardens, of which he was very fond. I'm in charge of the company now. Berowne was highly pleased when he was appointed leader of the society. That was a week or two before Tom died.' A pause, then she said, 'When he called here, Tom told me how delighted he was that Berowne was now in charge. No problem. Berowne was only too happy to take it on. He said running the society would be fun now that high-and-mighty Tom Chalcott had handed over the reins to him.'

'Your husband must have been shocked when he got the news of Tom's death,' Cara said.

'Indeed. I remember Berowne thought the heart attack had been brought on by Oliver Bright, who had been complaining that night about reliance on modern technology which had apparently failed to record a presence somewhere. He was forever airing the opinion that he should have been the next leader, not Berowne. That was something that was promptly opposed by Luke, who thought *he* should have been leader. Both of them then turned on Berowne. They were passion without the fruit,' she joked. 'He'd always tread carefully around them.'

Either Rachel had a remarkable memory, or she had rehearsed much of what she was saying, considering that she was talking about events of ten years ago. Interesting though her information was, Cara decided to be prudent and note it with a question mark.

'Lady Lendale will be interested in that,' she said. 'She was very fond of Berowne.'

'All ladies were very fond of Berowne,' Rachel said dispassionately.

Here we go once again. Andrew's territory or not, Cara's ears pricked up. After all, he could hardly complain if Berowne's name cropped up in conversation with other people.

'I suppose it's natural enough that those in the society appreciated him,' she replied diplomatically.

'Dear Charlotte certainly did,' Rachel said coolly. 'She certainly would have been in the running for Berowne's woman of the year. I take it you've heard that Pete Brandon was hauled in for questioning. Quite right too. He's a nasty piece of work. I suppose he has to be with that vixen wife of his.'

This was getting vindictive, but that was the time to forge ahead. Cara decided she needed to ferret further. 'She seems very fond of her husband.'

'I've no doubt she does now that Berowne is dead. Before that it was a different matter. It wouldn't have lasted, of course. It never did.'

It wasn't hard to detect the bitterness in her voice, so perhaps Rachel wasn't so detached from her husband's infidelity as she seemed. Nevertheless, Cara still could not believe that the anxious-looking Charlotte would have been capable of maintaining a passionate love affair on the side.

She decided to try another tack. 'Are you sure it was Charlotte and not Josie or Emily perhaps?' she asked.

'Berowne preferred mature women,' Rachel said casually. 'But short of catching him in bed with one of his flings, how could I be sure? I didn't stay up all night at the grotto in case Charlotte or anyone else tiptoed in to visit Berowne and, as it turned out, that was very sensible.'

This was getting unbelievably acidic. Was Rachel truly as offhand as she sounded? Cara struggled to remain calm and objective. 'And you slept well? You didn't hear anything outside your quarters?' She was trespassing on Andrew's ground with a vengeance, but she couldn't stop now.

'Not a whisper of a foot passing by. I slept like a log thanks to pills galore, so my evidence is nil on that score. And, before you ask,' Rachel added, 'I obeyed the rules. I woke up quite early, packed up as quickly as I could and scurried back to civilization to make myself presentable again. And no, I didn't pop along to kiss my husband good morning. I didn't want to risk the ignominy of finding Madame Charlotte in bed with him. Pete Brandon probably did that and look what happened. Murder.'

Whoa! Time to take a step back, Cara decided. She was way off her own territory with this kind of talk. 'Will you stay on as a member of the society?' she asked hastily.

'Why not? I even thought of standing as chair.'

As Alice in Wonderland remarked, curiouser and curiouser. The idea of Rachel running the society was hard to imagine. 'Would you want to?' Cara asked cautiously. 'Won't Luke or Oliver or Pete oppose you?'

'Pete at least wouldn't dare oppose me,' Rachel replied matter-of-factly. 'He owes my firm a fortune in rent. We own the pub's freehold, although Berowne preferred to think of that as his own. Anyway, it looks as though he'll be behind bars.'

Village life was always complex, apparently running smoothly on the surface but underneath punctuated with problems. Tanton was no exception. Did Andrew know about this? Almost certainly, Cara thought. Rachel certainly wasn't mincing her words with her.

Rachel laughingly continued. 'Don't look so surprised, Cara. Pete doesn't owe me a fortune by today's standards, but enough to put him and dear Charlotte out of business. Believe me, that tempts me. His rent is payable to our business, and Berowne helped himself to monies due. I doubt if Pete's gambling habits do much for the family fortunes either.'

Gambling habits? This was new, Cara thought. Did Andrew know about this? It could be very relevant for his case.

'Berowne liked his role of lord of the manor, twenty-first century style,' Rachel continued calmly. 'He looked after the house and gardens, hiring and firing staff, and pocketed any income that came his way, plus any other perks. Such as his women on the side,' she added. A pause. 'You look distressed, Cara. Don't be. I've worked out my future lifestyle here. The house and grounds will continue with myself as lady of the manor. In earlier times the lord of the manor had perks like sex on demand with his serfs and tenants, and of course obedience was essential. I'm afraid I intend to forget any perks like that. In return, staff and the one or two tenants can expect nothing from me.'

Cara left Ellum Place bemused. Rachel was a most unusual widow, and she found it hard to believe that all she had been told was true. Had she been outwitted, she wondered, or had she won on points? The latter, hopefully, in that she'd learned there was a new dimension to the case Andrew was investigating – money.

The drawback was that as far as Tom Chalcott was concerned, she had learned nothing here that would be of interest to Lady Izzy, save that he had called on Berowne the day before he had died. So? That seemed natural enough. But then there was Rachel herself. Was that the *real* Rachel talking, in which case she was a very hard nut to crack, or was that just a defence mechanism for a woman who had been deeply wounded? A woman who had slept in the chamber nearest to Berowne on the night he had met his death.

Cara was glad when she reached the outer gates of the Ellum estate, realizing that she was shivering again. Do houses and gardens take on the atmosphere of their owners? she wondered. Sometimes they do, she decided, and today had been a prime example, threatening in its intensity, as though the spirits of the wild woods had their eye on her, making note of her visit, waiting for their opportunity to strike. It was almost as though they were following her, waiting to pounce.

Don't be stupid, she told herself uneasily. There were no spirits, the woods weren't wild but carefully managed and, anyway, why would they have any grudge against her? All her imagination.

* * *

'Sammy,' Cara said, as she carefully placed the last huffkin on the baking tray for the afternoon visitors on Wednesday, 'I have a suspicion that I'm making very little headway where Tom Chalcott's concerned. It's like climbing a very steep hill.'

Sammy was adamant about the timing of his precious huffkins, and it was difficult to please him as they had to be eaten as soon as they emerged from the oven, which was tricky to arrange at the Happy Huffkin. Unlike him, Cara was all for a bit of flexibility over how long they remained on sale after their introduction to the display cabinets. Sammy, however, had been known to whisk a huffkin away from under a prospective buyer's nose if he deemed it to be stale.

Sammy stopped on his way to the rear door of the folly, putting down the disposable bag of leftover food items he'd chosen as suitable to throw out to the birds from the back terrace, which overlooked the village and river beneath. The birds had plenty of room to await their dinner as they gathered in the trees on the slope, ready for the great moment, which happened more or less at the same time every day the Happy Huffkin was open. What they did on non-opening days was a mystery to Cara, but she wouldn't put it past Sammy to creep in surreptitiously in order not to disappoint them.

'Right now,' she continued, 'Berowne keeps popping up and distracting me from the path.'

'Better than going nowhere,' he pronounced with typical Sammy wisdom.

'Huh!' Cara commented. 'True. I'll carry on climbing that hill then. I suspect Lady Izzy is expecting her ghost tour to provide answers, but I'm not so sure. I think there's trouble ahead, though I can't work out why. It's only a group tour round the Towers. And anyway, it's about Tom Chalcott. Berowne would be far more of a nightmare. What did you make of Berowne, by the way?'

Sammy considered this. 'Daft name.'

She couldn't see how this was relevant, but she did her best. 'His parents' choice. He didn't leap out of his cradle and demand to be called Berowne. He was named after a character in *Love's Labour's Lost*. Berowne later became the leading light of his parents' company for a short while.'

Sammy had already lost interest and disappeared back into his kitchen, leaving Cara contemplating Shakespeare. In the play, women lead the men a merry dance. The Berowne she'd known wouldn't like that. He had been fully in charge of his own love life. And Tom Chalcott, as far as was known, had little in the way of a love life. She came back to the as yet unanswered question. What links, if any, did his death have with Berowne's? So far she hadn't unravelled any, and yet . . . and yet . . .

'Where are you going to, my pretty maid?' She hummed the song. The only place Cara could see herself going was up a gum tree – and there she was stuck, she thought crossly. The ghost tour was getting closer, though that had nothing to do with Berowne, did it?

Sammy had trudged back to fulfil his mission in the kitchen, and his body language had very clearly indicated it was time she got on with her job. Such as putting the baking tray of huffkins into the oven.

The last of the dawdling visitors had left, the dishwasher had been stacked and the fridge and larders sorted out. Her hands were washed, her jacket was on, and the key to lock the folly door was in her hand. And then the landline rang. It was Alison, and Cara heard her sigh of relief as she answered it.

'Could you spare a minute or two to come over here?' Alison asked.

That was their shorthand for 'it's urgent', and Cara's heart sank. What now? Of course she could go. Perhaps it might help assuage that awful feeling she had that Alison and Max might think she was somehow to blame for having initiated this ghost tour, which was now beginning to loom large in her mind as a red herring to what was supposed to be her role. The last thing she would choose to do. For one thing, were any ghosts expected to appear?

On arriving at the Towers, at first she thought she was mistaken in thinking this was an urgent meeting, as Alison ushered her into the family living room. Max was already sitting there, although without his usual placid welcoming expression. Perhaps she was imagining that, though, because Alison began quite calmly after Cara was settled in one of their comfortable armchairs.

'I've browsed the archives,' Alison began, 'and had a peek at the ghost stories that you've been swotting up on. We're thinking that we could rush through a short booklet in time for the hunt, both for those taking part and for selling in the gatehouse bookshop afterwards.'

'That sounds like a good idea,' Cara said truthfully. Nevertheless, she was aware that there was an odd tone in Alison's voice. 'What can I do towards it, apart from going through the stories with you and sounding knowledgeable on the tour?' she asked. Was this the 'urgent' reason for the summons?

'Forget the booklet. Try crying about spilt milk,' Max said grimly.

Whoops. This did not augur well, Cara thought. What on earth had she done? 'Doesn't Lady Izzy like the idea?'

'She does. She's coming back here and she thinks that a ghost booklet is a great idea,' Alison said gloomily.

'Have I put a foot wrong somewhere?' Cara asked, really concerned now.

'Good grief, no,' Max said to her relief.

'The problem is that Izzy wants to put in a map of where the ghosts haunt,' Alison said. 'And one place is on the second floor.'

Cara looked from one to the other. She had not yet organized her stories, but she could manage that. It seemed a reasonable idea, but Max was getting rattled now. 'In the Archives Room area or the bedroom suites area?' she asked.

'One of them is in the long gallery—' Alison began.

Max exploded. 'It's the *Fontana* gallery,' he shouted, his face red with anger. 'And I am not, definitely *not*, having an army of feet trampling through La Galleria in the dark, bashing Lavinia's portraits under the impression that they are ghosts. Understood?'

'Perfectly,' Alison replied. 'I think the whole of Tanton village has understood.'

'My apologies.' Max calmed down a little. 'But you *must* see my point.'

Cara understood now. The Fontana gallery was hallowed ground. It housed most of Max's huge Lavinia Fontana art collection. 'But is there a ghost that haunts the gallery?' She hadn't come across any mention of it yet.

'There is one apparently,' Alison said. 'I'm sorry to say there was a letter from Thomas Farran in 1815, with a reference to a painting of an unknown nobleman in 1577, thought by Max to be by Lavinia and a friend of her husband, Giovanni Zappi. The nobleman had a high opinion of himself, and his ghost has been – apparently – coming to admire his portrait.'

Was she being blamed for this catastrophe? Cara wondered. She wasn't sure but, whether she was or not, there had to be a way out. 'Has his ghost been seen recently?'

Alison looked at the notes. 'Not since the 1980s. We weren't here then, of course – that was Max's parents' era. Max grew up here, but he doesn't recall any talk of it.'

Cara was thinking hard. 'We could cheat a little. La Galleria has only been on the second floor for the last few years, so we could truthfully say that the ghost follows the painting and haunts its former slot, which was then near your office on the first floor. The tour will be going along past where the portrait used to be.'

Max wasn't listening. He seemed engrossed with his own train of thought and then announced complacently, 'I have been studying the ways of ghosts. The painting of course was created in Italy. How did this ghost therefore come over with the portrait when Sir Thomas bought it? No respectable ghost ever crosses water.'

Cara desperately scrabbled for a way past this stumbling block. 'Perhaps the unknown nobleman was English?'

A silence. 'It doesn't work,' Max then pronounced. 'It still involves crossing water.'

This was getting serious. A few moments' hard thinking required. 'The ghost,' Cara began firmly, 'is surely the ghost of the sitter *not* the painter. Let's say that the nobleman lived in England, even though his portrait was painted in Italy, and his ghost spotted the painting hundreds of years later when Sir Thomas brought the portrait to the Towers. The unknown nobleman has haunted it ever since.'

'Brilliant,' Alison crowed.

'We don't know the nobleman lived in England,' Max repeated.

It was now or never. 'He must have done,' Cara said blandly. 'His ghost would have been around after the nobleman died, and it couldn't cross the Channel to see the painting because that involves water, and in any case Sir Thomas Farran had acquired the painting for the Towers by then. I can make all that clear in my commentary and in the booklet. Then all we have to do is move the painting safely down to the first floor. We could put it temporarily into a separate room and rope it off, which would satisfy both the Tanton Ghost and Phantom Society and Lady Izzy. Then we could stop La Galleria from being on the ghost route.'

A long silence. Then Max beamed. 'Accepted.'

That was a close one, Cara thought with relief.

'That's sheer genius, Cara. Thank you. This is the last time I let Izzy have her way over her crazy ideas,' Alison declared. 'After all, ghosts move around and change locations. There's our Horace for example. He goes everywhere.'

'You make it sound as if he still existed. He doesn't,' Max retorted.

'He might, darling,' Alison said. 'And ghosts come and go. Look at the Laughing Lady. She only emerged when the cottage was pulled down.'

'And look what happened.' Max glared at her. 'We've now got a murder on our hands.'

TWELVE

Two days to go. The day of the tour was coming closer. Should she go with her instinct or her common sense? Cara debated. Her research into ghost territory was coming along reasonably well, as was Alison's booklet on it, but nevertheless her doubts were still growing, even if she was probably busy building a mountain out of a molehill. Instinct, however, pointed out that there was a black cloud hanging over this ghost tour. She was musing on this when Sammy pointed out that the huffkins had been ready for baking ten minutes ago and Virginia would be here any minute with the sandwiches and cakes.

Cara sprang into action, but the cloud refused to go away. Max's outburst had not helped.

'It won't work,' she muttered to herself. Too loudly. 'Sorry,' she said, seeing Sammy's eye on her. 'The ghost tour. I'm worried it might get out of control.'

No comment from Sammy, who had returned to his rattling of the plates. The Towers would be opening in half an hour at two p.m., and for the next three hours she wouldn't have time for contemplation of the ghost-tour situation. The last of the Towers guided tours usually finished with customers enjoying a leisurely tea in the café, despite the passing of closing time.

Today was no exception. It was past six o'clock by the time the last groups of satisfied customers had departed and the clearing-up had been concluded. At last Cara was free to hurry across the lawn to the family wing. This time she had no apprehensions. All seemed normal. She'd been lucky and an idea had popped into her head. Simple, but it could be effective.

'Champagne afterwards?' Alison repeated when Cara had breathlessly spilled out the idea to her. 'Is there much point in that?'

'All the difference in the world,' Cara said. 'Otherwise the tour might end up with some people wandering off before it ends—'

'Max won't like that, and nor would I,' Alison interrupted in agreement. 'They might wander off to La Galleria or back to Lavinia's unknown gentleman now that he'll have a room to himself. Let's see how Izzy feels about it. She's returning tomorrow.'

For the next twenty-four hours, Cara waited impatiently, and was pleasantly surprised to see both Lady Izzy and Alison at last making their way over the lawn to the Happy Huffkin after closing time on Friday evening. Only one day to go now and Lady Izzy's stick was waving vigorously. That was a hopeful sign. If she was displeased, that stick would be firmly hitting the ground at each step. That was good – except that one could never be quite sure with Lady Izzy.

'It's a capital notion, Cara,' Lady Izzy carolled as she sat down at a window table, from which she could survey the world of Tanton Towers in comfort. 'A nice gathering beforehand at the Happy Huffkin with canapés and whatnot, and keep the champagne for after we've all had a good old march round the Towers peering into different rooms – that's if there's anyone left stable enough to enjoy it. I'll notify the guests – and the ghosts,' she added cheerfully.

Lady Izzy had an odd way of putting things, Cara thought, somewhat puzzled. Stable enough? What did she mean by that? Aha! Did Lady Izzy too have misgivings? That was highly unlikely. What would scare someone during a tour? She decided she was foreseeing difficulties that didn't exist.

As if reading her thoughts, Lady Izzy said cheerfully, 'Only joking, and we want this event to be a tribute to Tom, don't we? If his ghost turns up, we don't want him reporting to his mates that we were all gloomy. If Berowne's ghost materializes, we'll pay tribute to him as well at the reception. But as for the tour itself . . . what ghosts have you got in store for us, Cara? I'm told you and Alison have been foraging around.'

'Quite a few candidates,' Cara said brightly. 'There's dear old Horace, of course, Sir Jeffry's twin son, who causes all the mischief; Sir Reginald, who haunts the master bedroom in case his wife is entertaining a replacement; the sister of Lady Eleanor Pryde, who was a practising witch; and poor old Edward Smith, an eighteenth-century farmer who quietly sings Handel's "Did

You Not Hear My Lady?" as he climbs up a long-gone ash tree to Lady Farran Pryde's bedroom window where he was duly shot by her husband, Sir Gerald. The Towers shares him with the grotto, which is where he used to woo the lady if he wasn't up to climbing the tree at any time.'

Lady Izzy considered this. 'A good start,' she said approvingly.

What a relief. 'We'll winkle out one or two more with luck,' Cara concluded, 'and end the tour in the library where there's plenty of room for everyone to gather.'

'No, that won't suit,' Lady Izzy said sharply to Cara's surprise. 'It should end in the butler's pantry.'

The butler's pantry? Not a good idea. Cara was taken aback and so clearly was Alison.

'That's far too small, Izzy,' Alison objected.

Even though the eighteenth-century pantry at the Towers was large compared with modern pantries, it surely wasn't big enough for Lady Izzy's purpose, Cara thought. Not only were the society members coming, but some of the staff too.

'The tour should end there, regardless of that.' Lady Izzy grinned. 'The butler knows everything that's going on upstairs and downstairs, so if there are any ghosts of butlers or servants, they can make their appearance there and feel at home. Don't worry, Alison.' She waved a regal hand. 'We'll leave the door open and people can spill out into the great hall.'

Alison gave in. 'If that's what you want, Izzy, we'll do it that way.'

Why was Lady Izzy so keen on this? Cara wondered. It seemed odd, and would the twenty or so people who would be on the tour all manage to squeeze into the butler's pantry? It had, of course, been a major part of the Towers' life in previous centuries, in command – as Max had once put it – of the two worlds, the servants and the Farran Pryde family. The butler would also have had his own room in the servants' wing, but the one at the rear of the great hall by the entrance to the servants' wing was carefully positioned so that he was at hand for the family's convenience. To be a butler was, after all, a position of high importance. Much of the butler's work was carried out in the servants' wing, but his pantry was equipped for the management of the house, both practically and financially. A pantry's modern role was a far cry from the former grandeur of the butler's working abode. Nevertheless, its modern desk, shelving, tables, visitors' books, electronic devices, files and maps of the estate, did make for rather a dull room, in Cara's opinion. Still, whatever Lady Izzy wanted, Lady Izzy would get.

'Excellent!' Lady Izzy beamed. 'Roll on tomorrow.'

'You rang my office,' he said.

For Andrew to turn up at the Towers unexpectedly on Saturday morning took Cara by surprise. She had indeed rung his office first thing, only to be told that he was unavailable. Therefore the call to request her presence in the servants' wing, in the rooms still temporarily occupied by the police, came as quite a surprise. On her way, she had walked past the magnificent eighteenth-century kitchen, which was now open to the public again. Sir Jeffry had allowed his architects to be reasonably conventional over its design, and it was now once more aglow with its early roasting range, stoves, turning spit, and huge oak cupboards and tables.

At least this was on neutral ground, not at her home, she thought thankfully. Here in the housekeeper's room again, she could be objective and discuss other relevant matters – such as the ghost tour if he chose to raise that again.

He did.

'It's about the ghost tour tonight,' he began.

'We've changed our plans for it.' Cara tried to sound nonchalant. 'It might settle your reservations. As it's a tour not a hunt, everyone will stay together instead of shooting off in all directions. So your possible eagle eye won't be needed,' she added uncertainly as he didn't comment.

At last he spoke. 'It's still a tour with a probable murderer in your midst.'

'Who could hardly attack someone in a group,' she retaliated. He must be thinking of Pete Brandon. There had been no more word about him, but she had to go carefully. Reason told her that she was in no danger herself, and yet his insistence on it was beginning to have its effect. Every time she came to the Towers now, she imagined she was being followed by some unknown threat behind her. But that was just nonsense, of course.

'The tour is being held in honour of Berowne, but it will have nothing to do with your case on him,' Cara assured him. 'It's being held because Lady Lendale also wants to remember her nephew.' This sounded weak and she was well aware of it. 'It's an unusual way of doing so, particularly as it's so close to Berowne's murder, but that could be linked to Tom Chalcott's death.' Once again, she had put her foot into a delicately balanced situation.

He immediately picked up on it. 'Linked. One murder and a possible one. We're looking into the latter at your suggestion, which means that there's every reason for a police presence.'

Cara was trapped. Was she relieved to hear this or otherwise? 'But although this tour is truly dedicated to Tom Chalcott, it only features ghosts of the past, even though Lady Lendale is still expecting his ghost to appear.'

'You know what paves the path to hell, don't you?'

That riled her. 'Lady Lendale has the best of intentions, and so do I. Are you,' she said with dignity, 'planning to abolish all good intentions in the world just in case your own path takes a wrong turning?'

A pause. 'You win on points,' he replied. 'But practice is a different matter.' Another pause. 'You may be under the impression that the case of Berowne Dyer isn't advancing. I can't give you any more information, but it is.'

'All present and correct?' Lady Izzy shouted amiably at her flock, as they gathered at the Towers' front door for the tour after what turned out to be a very enjoyable drinks and nibbles reception at the Happy Huffkin. To Cara's relief, that had proved a big hit, and the champagne reception to take place afterwards would be a pleasant end to which to look forward. Not only were society members present, but also Alison and Max, Virginia, Lucy, Len, Josie, and several other staff members – or Cara presumed that's what they were. It belatedly occurred to her that they might be Andrew's team. Sammy had declined the invitation.

Once again Cara wondered whether they would all fit into the butler's pantry. If her fears were justified, then Andrew's team would be planning to reposition themselves as the tour progressed. Still, that could wait. The tour was about to begin, and the lighting was low enough to create the right mood. There was thankfully no need for darkness: that didn't always deter ghosts anyway, according to what she had been reading about the paranormal.

The general amiability of the group continued as they moved into the great hall. That was just as well, as Cara was beginning to get stage fright at the thought of what lay ahead for her as tour leader and historian of this merry band. Or was it more than that? Perhaps Andrew's insistence on there being a police guard was having the wrong effect on her. Instead of reassurance, she was beginning to have a sense of doom about this tour. Irrational, but definitely there.

For the moment Lady Izzy was leading it, however, with Alison anxiously at her side. Max had disappeared after they had left the Happy Huffkin, muttering that he already knew more than enough about the Towers and the paranormal. He had anxiously checked that La Galleria had been locked for Lavinia Fontana's safety, and most of the rest of the second floor was out of bounds too. Lavinia's unknown nobleman was established in his own room on the first floor, and at least ten feet from the reach of any onlookers who took a fancy to him.

Rachel, looking as elegant as ever, was close behind Lady Izzy and talking to Jamie, who was casually clad in anorak and jeans. To Cara's amusement he kept casting anxious looks behind him, while at the same time endeavouring to maintain his nonchalant attitude. Could that be because Harry Bright was shepherding Emily very possessively? Luke was striding along with Oliver, both seeming grimly determined to prove their worth as the elder statesmen of the group, each trying to outdo the other with their ghostly knowledge.

And there was Pete! So he'd been released. He and Charlotte were bringing up the rear, with Charlotte clinging on to his arm, which he had obviously ensured was as close as possible. Intentionally? Cara wondered. Did she fear he'd be snatched away from her by the police guard again – wherever that was? No sign of them yet, although there were one or two faces she didn't recognize. Concentrate on your own role, she told herself – whatever that was in view of what was happening. Shortly she would be taking centre stage.

Concentration was hard, however, especially as Dr Samuel

Johnson's eyes were benevolently staring down at her from his portrait hanging close by. He had died, so Max had informed her, in the same year that Sir Jeffry had built Tanton Towers. The artist was unknown, but it was a splendid portrait of this notable gentleman, who had paid several visits to Kent towards the end of his life. He had been much attached to the Malling area, not that far from Tanton, and so it was quite possible, so Max had pointed out, that he could have met Sir Jeffry in his travels. Now he looked benignly down at them as if wishing them well in their quest. Had he believed in ghosts? Cara wondered. She couldn't see Dr Johnson being perturbed by them. If he'd met one, he'd probably have tackled it with a polite request: 'Pray, sir, whose ghost are you?'

Keep to the point, Cara told herself. The time had come. Lady Izzy was climbing on to her dais. The show was about to begin – and her doubts about it flooded back.

'Ladies, Gentlemen, and Any Ghosts that are honouring us with their presence,' Lady Izzy began her introductory speech. She was waving her arms around so dramatically that Alison was having to cling on to her in case she lost her balance.

What was her true attitude to the paranormal? Cara tried to fix her thoughts on what Lady Izzy was saying and disregard the niggles of doubt about this tour and the reasons for it. At the moment her approach hardly seemed appropriate for a group consisting mainly of firm believers in the supernatural. Did Lady Izzy truly believe that Tom Chalcott was going to materialize, or at least make his ghostly presence felt? If so, surely that didn't make sense. From what little she knew about ghosts, they didn't respond to orders from this world. Nevertheless, there was no doubt that Lady Izzy was intent on finding out what had happened to Tom, although this was an elaborate way of doing so. In any case, Lady Izzy couldn't rely on Tom's ghost obligingly moving to the Towers for the evening, celebration or not.

As if reading her mind, Lady Izzy continued her introduction. 'I'd hoped that Tom would be with us at some point, but I've just received this letter.' She waved a piece of parchment in the air. 'It's an email from the afterlife.'

What on earth was this? Cara froze. This was a step out of the blue, and surely out of place with this audience.

'Ah,' Lady Izzy exclaimed. 'It's an apology from the Honourable Thomas Chalcott. It reads: Sorry not to be with you. Here's wishing you well for your tour.'

Cara looked cautiously at the group to see how they were taking this feeble joke. Many were whispering to each other, but whether in approval or distaste it was hard to tell. Who was in Andrew's team? What would they be looking for anyway? Danger obviously, but of what kind? The whispers were growing louder and it didn't take long before she could hear the name of Thomas Chalcott in the buzz of conversation around her with Oliver's, 'Him? He can stay where he is.'

At that, a short hush followed, until Oliver took over again, shouting, 'Before Mister Boss Berowne barged in, it was that Chalcott fellow who cheated me out of being leader.'

Then came Luke's contribution, which she strained to hear over the buzz of conversation. 'Didn't understand a thing about it, did he? I tried to tell him, but he wouldn't listen. Ruined this society, he did.'

Rachel seemed to be in earnest discussion with Charlotte, now separated from Pete, who was talking to Josie Redman. Emily was giggling, and Jamie was smouldering as he watched Harry whispering in her ear. Nevertheless, the mood seemed to have swung back to being reasonably cheerful as they moved on up the grand staircase to the first 'ghost' of the tour on the next floor.

It was a mood Cara didn't share. She braced herself. Her part in this drama was about to begin. On the first floor, the state bedroom seemed not to have attracted the ghost world, but further along the corridor was one of half a dozen bedrooms known to the staff as the 'second best beds', overlooking the gardens. The furthest along was the one picked by Lady Izzy for the group to enter.

Time for her to take the stage: 'Looks so innocent, doesn't it?' Cara began as the group assembled around the ornate bed with its heavy curtains fastened back. 'That's more than the Honourable Eleanor Pryde was in 1835,' she continued. 'You'd think that being the sister of Lady Jane Pryde, who married Sir Jonathan Farran, the grandson of the great Sir Jeffry who built the Towers, she would have more respect for her status. Instead, she's said to have stirred her potions on the dressing table and hidden scripted curses under the pillows.

'Our Eleanor was a witch,' she continued. She looked round. With that word she had gained their attention. Now to exploit it. 'Witchcraft was still popular in the early nineteenth century,' she explained. 'Even if witches weren't burned at the stake anymore, it wasn't wise to take it up as a profession, but Eleanor did so regardless of her status. Whether she jumped or whether she was pushed, she fell from this window on the thirtieth of May 1835. It's said that she laid a curse upon the house as she fell – but don't worry too much,' Cara reassured her audience. Given her fears over this tour, and her underlying stress, she thought she was coping reasonably well. 'Exorcists were brought in very shortly after her death,' she added. 'Nevertheless, occasionally on bitterly cold and rainy nights she can be heard and sensed in this room.'

Cara gave herself another mental pat on the back, despite the disapproving look from Oliver. Undeserved, she thought. She had only embroidered the story a little. 'Her ladyship's ghost was last seen at the end of the nineteenth century,' she continued. (According to the diaries she'd read in the Archives Room, that was true. Lady Izzy looked satisfied anyway.)

She looked round her flock. It seemed to be attentive, luckily. Lady Izzy was at the rear of the group, wearing her vague look. Cara had learned to beware of that. It usually meant that Lady Izzy had her inner eye on something or someone. Danger ahead, perhaps? That was beginning to feel all too possible, and she was managing to talk with a confidence that was merely external. Inside her tension level was rising again. 'This ghost,' she began confidently, having led the group across the corridor to a bedroom overlooking the front of the house and rose gardens, 'has been sensed much more recently – about the time of our late Queen Elizabeth's coronation. I'm sure most of you know the story of Sir Gerald Farran Pryde, who returned from the battlefield unexpectedly. As he galloped up the drive, he spotted a humble farmer climbing up to her ladyship's window – perhaps by invitation – and shot him point blank. Over here' – Cara indicated a portrait of a frosty-looking lady – 'is his wife. How did Sir Gerald break the news to her? Did he gloat? Relish the fact that he'd slaughtered her lover? Leave it to someone else to mention it? What would he do today? Just hope no one noticed that poor farmer's body? Or pray that it would never occur to the police to think that such a devoted husband would be behind such a fiendish act? Nothing much changes. That's what so interesting about ghosts. They transcend time. Their awful tragedies could have taken place last week or centuries ago.'

This gave rise to a fervent discussion, particularly between the society members, which had all the signs of turning heated. She should move on, Cara decided, feeling that tension level rising again. Lady Izzy was also indicating that it was time to break the discussion up, although she must be getting ready for her own address at the end of the tour. That would be good, Cara thought with relief. Her own role would be over then, and the group could return to the Happy Huffkin for the champagne celebration as satisfied customers.

Next step then. 'This bedroom,' she began, having moved the tour on to the last of the bedrooms on the first floor, 'is haunted by the ghost of another suspicious husband, Sir Reginald, of the Royal West Kent Regiment. He is the well-known ghost who while carrying out his duties in South Africa had fortunately left both Isandlwana and Rorke's Drift with his command of ox waggons just before the Zulus attacked the camp at Isandlwana in 1879. The South Wales Borderers, who were there, were not so lucky. He managed to return home safely, but as his army duties took him away after that for long periods, he was doubtful about the fidelity of his wife Emily. Was she unfaithful to him? That was never proven, but he haunted the bedroom after his death in 1887 just to be sure. He had just been promoted to captain and no doubt enjoyed showing off his medals to his fellow ghosts.'

A glare from Luke indicated to Cara that ghosts should not be a laughing matter.

'Ghost or phantom?' barked Oliver.

Cara had been prepared for this one. 'Sir Reginald has been recorded twice as a ghost and once as a phantom, affecting his son who also joined the Royal West Kents and was about to set off to the Punjab Frontier in 1897. Meanwhile,' she said hastily, seeing Luke about to explode with his opinions, 'we've another important ghost on this floor.'

She led her flock back along the corridor to the bedroom that had been hastily converted into a temporary art gallery. The door had been fastened back so that visitors could see the portrait displayed on an easel without entering the room, but with Max and Alison present in the group her tension level was still high.

'Here,' she declared with all her mental fingers crossed, 'is the portrait of an unknown nobleman thought to be English. Its painter was Lavinia Fontana, the famous artist from the Italian city of Bologna.'

It was, Cara agreed, an excellent portrait and she could understand Max's concern for it. From the knowing look on his face, this unknown gentleman had secrets of his own, with his hand resting on what looked like a Bible – risky in a seventeenth-century Catholic city, as the sitter came from Protestant England. The lady in the background looked equally enigmatic. Young, beautiful and coy. Did the unknown nobleman have his eye on her and – if so – as a bride or as an amusement? The portrait looked so interesting displayed on its own here that Cara thought if she were Max, she'd keep it here.

'Is it the ghost of Lavinia who haunts it?' Emily piped up.

'No, it's the nobleman's ghost, so fond of his appearance in the painting that he haunts it here.' Cara tried her best to sound confident.

'It was upstairs when I saw it last,' Oliver said suspiciously.

'True,' Cara explained as loftily as she could. 'But the portrait's original home was here on this floor. It was moved upstairs a few years ago, and has been brought down for this tour as this is the area that his ghost haunts.'

Her fingers were still crossed in case Oliver or Luke started probing further, but thankfully they didn't, and Cara pressed on with the rest of the tour. However, the mood of the tour had started to change from its initial joie de vivre. Was she too boring? Was her nagging feeling that something was wrong not sheer fantasy but real? She now longed for the tour to end and was glad when at last they reached the ground floor again.

If only they could stop now, Cara found herself thinking. But there was no way of cutting the tour short, because Lady Izzy was firmly set on making her speech so as to end the tour on a high point. Cara fervently hoped it would do just that, despite Lady Izzy being so set on ending the tour in the butler's pantry; but once Lady Izzy had made up her mind, there was no chance she would be talked out of it.

Once there on the ground floor with the lights dimmed even lower, it was all too easy to believe that centuries of stories and history could lend themselves to a family history of mingled joy and tragedy. Perhaps one day Alison would have time to write it, Cara thought hopefully.

The huge library was the next stop. Plenty here for Alison to write about. Meanwhile, she'd continue doing her best.

'This,' she began as authoritatively as she could, 'is the place that houses the stories of all the family ghosts in the vast array of books it shelters. As you've already heard, the ghosts are all eager to materialize and tell their own stories.'

There was an encouraging titter from her audience. 'There's quite a few of them in addition to the ones you've already heard about,' she continued. 'There are the murderous ones who walk again, wanting to wreak their vengeance on other more fortunate people, ghosts who merely lament their fate and keep on reliving it all again, and other more kindly ones who want to help others avoid the same pitfalls.'

She paused to see whether she still had her audience with her, and sensed she did. She pressed on. 'Their lives on earth were all in the past, many of them from an age that precede the building of the Towers. Even so, you can see that all these high shelves have an enormous number of books, so goodness knows how many ghastly secrets are looking over our heads here.'

Was she still on the right track? she wondered, mentally crossing her fingers. Or were some of them sounding too fanciful? She had embroidered them a little. 'We're in the twenty-first century now and have the ability,' she continued, 'to disentangle folklore from the supernatural. Tanton Towers is planted in the past but flowers today. Your society contributes to that because it deals with the supernatural as it examines the evidence for the stories of the past.'

Where did that come from? she wondered. Whether it was nonsense or had some truth to it, it seemed to have worked, as the murmurs didn't seem to be hostile. Only one room now remained before the butler's pantry would end the tour and her personal part in the tour itself would be over. Her only task would be the superintending of the champagne in the Happy Huffkin after the tour ended. It couldn't come soon enough.

Unfortunately the billiard room seemed uncharacteristically unwelcoming today. Cara realized she was shivering although, despite the sun having gone down by now, it wasn't a cold evening. She must be reacting to all these tragic tales from the past. She related the story of the ghost of the billiard room with as much gusto as she could garner. The story of the two gentlemen who vowed that whoever won at billiards that evening could have the hand of the eldest daughter of the house went down exceptionally well with the group. According to a snippet she had unearthed in the archives, the unlucky loser shot himself and his ghost reappeared every so often to replay the game.

The group left the room seemingly satisfied, although Cara had no doubt that the stories she had related would be dissected and probably dismissed by ghost hunters far more knowledgeable than she was. She looked round her flock. Rachel seemed relaxed enough, even chatting happily (it seemed) to Charlotte; Pete was talking to Luke who was clutching the spirit box he'd insisted on bringing with him; Harry had his arm round Emily, and Jamie was holding her hand on the other side; Len and Josie were behind them; and Virginia was scurrying back from the library, which boasted a special section of antique cookery books that Cara knew well, as they had inspired her own love for them. To her surprise, Sammy had turned up too, and was bringing up the rear.

'To the butler's pantry!' Lady Izzy shouted happily. 'And afterwards we can return to the Happy Huffkin for champagne.'

The end was truly in sight. Cara placed herself at the back of the group with Sammy, now that her task – thankfully – was over. She was beginning to relax. Lady Izzy had positioned herself on a dais at the corner of the row of huge cupboards that lined one wall of the pantry and the curtained windows on her other side. Behind her was a small table. Journals, writing equipment, table and chairs made a business-like array. The butler's pantry was usually more comfortable than it appeared now, she thought, obviously cleared for tonight's onslaught. Alison had told her that Lady Izzy had been fussing over this climax for a week or more, and visited the room practically every day. Now she had positioned herself at the far end of the dark curtains with the screen on her left.

'And I'd like to end this tour,' Lady Izzy almost cooed at her audience, clearly aware that her moment had come, 'with a little talk about my darling late nephew, Thomas Chalcott. Let me introduce you to him as some of you never knew him.'

Not quite what Cara had expected of Lady Izzy's speech, but reasonable enough so far, she thought cautiously.

'I didn't see much of Thomas as he was growing up because I lived abroad,' Lady Izzy continued conversationally, 'but in these last few weeks he's been very close to me. Some of you here knew him. Hands up those who did.'

No one moved at first, then Cara saw one tentative hand rising up, followed by others.

'Excellent,' her ladyship said approvingly, 'because we're all going to meet him again *now*!'

Now!

What was happening? Cara fought panic as the lights went out, plunging everybody into darkness. Something frightening was going to take place, but what? Tension shot through her – and in everybody around her, judging by the noise, the fear and panic that was spreading.

And then it happened. Thomas Chalcott was standing in front of them against a pale background, as though about to step forward. Cara recognized him immediately from the photo she'd seen. Glasses, slim, short dark hair. A grey suit. Neat. Smart. Serious. *A ghost.* It had to be.

Cara could no longer see anything else in the darkness, though she could dimly make out Lady Izzy next to Thomas. As the immediate shock calmed down, she realized they must be looking at a huge life-size photograph which was gazing out at them, all the more stark because Thomas Chalcott seemed to be alive. No, this wasn't a photograph; it must be a slowly moving video, but that combined with the shouting and screaming left Cara grappling with reality. People all around her were pushing, breathing hard, panic-stricken. Only seconds could have passed before one voice rose above the noise, a voice that boomed:

'Good evening, ladies and gentlemen. I'm Thomas Chalcott.'

The noise all around her intensified, with indignation replacing the initial shock, but the mere name halted efforts to escape from the room. Cara couldn't move, hemmed in with bodies, heavy breathing and the smells of fear all round her. She felt she was choking, stifled by the noise and unable to push her way out because of the darkness. She had to listen. The noise, the voice went on and on.

'I'm here to tell you what happened on the night I died.' No emotion in it. Just a statement. This certainly couldn't be for real. But it seemed so. It can't have been Tom Chalcott himself. It had to be something to do with Lady Izzy. A relation perhaps. Somebody anyway. Cara snatched at rational thought, but it vanished again as the voice went on: 'I was murdered, though no one seemed to care. Something hit the back of my head, a darkness came, stifling and killing me.'

The uproar was growing. This was crazy. Surely something would end this pantomime. It was the darkness that was making it so terrible, with everybody struggling to get free in their effort to escape as the booming voice continued. 'I could do nothing. I was no longer alive. But I saw who did this to me.'

He'd seen? Cara couldn't think clearly. What was behind this? What had Lady Izzy planned? There had to be more to this than merely one of her jokes. Joke? This was no joke. It was a stab in the dark.

The dead silence lasted for perhaps two or three seconds more and then uproar. The whole room seemed alive with noise and movement again. Someone was yelling for lights. Whoever managed to reach the light switch was croaking out that it wasn't working; someone else that this was a cheap shoddy trick, a woman was screaming. Some people were trying to get past to the door in the darkness, others making for whatever machines were causing the video and soundtrack, others were tearing down the life-size photograph.

Cara focussed on that screaming woman. She recognized the voice. It was Rachel, shrieking time and time again:

'It was Alice! *Alice*.'

THIRTEEN

'Who on earth is Alice?'

Wearily, Cara sank into one of the comfortable chairs in Max and Alison's living room. Sammy had disappeared from the butler's room with Virginia Harding, and everyone else had softly and silently vanished away like the victims of Lewis Carroll's Boojums. No doubt the guests had slipped away to their respective homes, and all talk of their concluding the evening with a celebratory glass of champagne had been forgotten. So here she was with Alison, Max, and a complacent Lady Izzy, who seemed at first to think the evening had been a tremendous success.

It was Max who replied stiffly. 'I've no idea who Alice is or was. Was Rachel thinking of you, Alison? The names are similar.'

Alison shook her head. 'Not very likely. I didn't exchange girlish secrets in my brief talks with her.'

Cara made another effort. The atmosphere suggested that they were far from happy with Lady Izzy. 'She's probably a friend of Rachel's. If not, it must have something to do with Tom Chalcott. Do you know of any Alices in his life?' she asked Lady Izzy.

For once Lady Izzy looked beaten. Perhaps the evening's events were having their effect on her, after all, or perhaps Max's displeasure was becoming all too obvious to her. Nevertheless, she made an attempt. 'I do not. I shall investigate this matter further,' she announced regally. 'It seems that my humble attempt at forcing the truth about dear Tom's death might have failed. That was the reason for my recent absence from your hospitality, Max. I needed assistance from one of Tom's cousins, who was only too willing to oblige.'

Max and Alison were clearly struggling to look grateful that she would still be blessing them with her presence, and Cara followed suit. The chances of Lady Izzy's gimmick being successful seemed remote. What could she have been hoping for? That everyone would quietly watch, go home, and write a letter of confession to the police? Or stand up and say, 'Yes, I remember that evening. It was old so-and-so who frightened him to death.'

She was longing to get home, where no mysteries and nothing supernatural would be facing her, and politely made her excuses to leave. Never had home seemed more welcoming. Lights could be switched on without having mysterious consequences, there would be no screaming, she could blank out until tomorrow – a wonderfully comforting word that demanded nothing of her until then. Perhaps the memory of tonight's catastrophe would have vanished, a nightmare that had cast its shadow and disappeared.

No such luck awaited her. She had made the effort, paid her adieux and set off for home, with Max having insisted on accompanying her to the car park. As she pulled up at her cottage, however, she could see another car parked nearby. Nothing unusual normally. But this one she recognized. As she slammed her car door shut, Andrew got out of his car. Before she could speak, he did.

'I'm not taking any chances. You need police protection,' he informed her. He seemed to loom over her, although she could see he was keeping his distance. 'At least during the nights,' he continued. 'I'll be watching the situation.'

She was too tired to protest but had to try. 'But Lady Izzy is the one who needs protection. She—'

He interrupted her. 'She's not alone. You are. I'll sleep on your sofa tonight.'

He didn't even ask whether she minded. Did she? No. Too worn out, too confused.

She awoke to noise – her mind was blank at first but then the whole horror of last night's performance returned, together with its ending. The noise, she realized, had been the slam of a door, so she trudged to her living room to see what was happening. At least it had been agreed that police protection should only be at nights as she'd only be alone then. Even so, she was taken aback to find that Andrew had departed. Without a word, without signs of breakfast in the kitchen, save for a mug, fallen not smashed. It was that mug that galvanized her into action. Lying there on the kitchen table, it seemed to be telling her there was no time to waste.

Andrew was no ghost, but she could certainly feel his presence. It brought her fully awake. 'Who's Alice?' was her first thought, followed by, 'What am I going to do about Andrew?' She had no answers for the latter, but that would have to wait. The question of Alice had to come first. Was she someone in Rachel's life or was she something to do with Tom Chalcott? In which case, how was Rachel involved?

Whatever might face her, last night's events meant she had to spring into action on Lady Izzy's behalf, regardless of the calamitous end to last night's proceedings. No ducking under the blankets again for her. A quick breakfast – toast and marmalade helped along by two mugfuls of tea – and she was off to work, although what kind of work would be needed today brought a big question mark. At least one thing was certain, she thought gratefully. Sammy would be waiting at the Happy Huffkin. Sundays were busy days for the Towers.

Sammy was not the only person waiting for her when she reached the folly. Lady Izzy, clad in bright blue and lime green today, was sitting inside clutching a cappuccino. This lady was indefatigable, Cara decided, forcing herself to look cheerful. It was good to see her, if only because it meant that hopefully nothing even more disastrous had happened since yesterday's drama.

'Morning, Cara! Who's Alice, you still wonder?' Lady Izzy greeted her cheerily, thus rubbing salt into the wound. 'A rhetorical question,' she added. 'I have at last recalled an Alice, although she has no connection with Rachel, or with Tom, merely an Irish friend of his parents.'

Any straw to clutch would be good at the moment. 'Is she still alive?' Cara asked hopefully.

'His parents are no longer with us, and alas that must be the case with Alice. She was older than them, I recall. The generations don't tally with Rachel's Alice. She must be in Rachel's own circle of friends or family, although I grant you it was an odd time to faint if it wasn't through shock.' She chuckled. 'I'll leave you to solve the mystery, Mrs Sherlock.'

With that, Lady Izzy rose to her feet, waved her stick in the air to signal farewell.

'Thank you,' Cara muttered to herself.

Rachel, to Cara's surprise, seemed only too willing to talk later that day. True, it was a Sunday and therefore busy – to say the least – at the Happy Huffkin, but the sooner she could speak to Rachel the better – even if Andrew had the same idea. The fresher Rachel's memory of what had happened yesterday, the more valuable it might be. Even though she had warned her that she couldn't tell her much, her idea of 'not much' could be gold dust to Cara. First, she had to get Sammy's blessing for abandoning him at such a busy time. That should be easy enough as Virginia was present together with Lucy, but she had to go through the ritual apology.

Ellum Place looked even more imposing and less welcoming than it had done on her earlier visit. What lay behind those uniform rows of windows and that forbidding dark red front door today? It was almost declaring that what went on behind it was its own affair, Cara thought. She had marched – or rather scuttled – along the long drive with that same sense that behind her those trees were awaiting their opportunity to strike her down. Nonsense, Cara told herself, but all the same she was glad to reach the front door, despite the fact that the real ordeal would lie within.

Perhaps her diagnosis was wrong, however, because when Rachel opened the door, she seemed her usual composed self. Far from being upset by last night's drama, she appeared unperturbed as she led Cara into a large drawing room, impressive but soulless, elegant but dull. She ushered her to a large Chesterfield sofa, but there was no offer of coffee. Indeed, there was an open iPad on a table by the window, together with a chair that had obviously been pushed aside when Cara rang the doorbell. This declared that business matters were the order of the day, Sunday or not.

'I'm having to take on extra work having lost Berowne; he was good at his job,' Rachel remarked dispassionately.

Rachel, Cara decided, was an odd mixture. There was the self that she presented to the outside world, and a totally different version when the barriers were down, which had been displayed with a vengeance last night. Today, her barriers were definitely back up. Not perhaps a good omen, however.

'Unfortunately, there's nothing I can tell you,' Rachel continued almost regretfully almost as soon as Cara had settled herself on the sofa, 'as to why I made that scene last night. It just happened. I'm told I cried out for somebody called Alice. I have no idea why I did so. Who is she?'

'That's the puzzle. Have you friends or family past or present of that name, or did the name crop up in any discussions you had with anyone about Thomas Chalcott?'

'I think I had a great-aunt called Alice, but goodness knows why I should have called out for her,' she replied. 'I'd love to be able to help you, but I can't. If I do think of anything else, I'll let you know.'

To Cara's astonishment, that had a brisk air of finality about it, and after a short amount of polite chit-chat it was clear she was expected to rise from the sofa and depart, even though there was surely more to be learned here. Was this dismissal her own fault? No, she decided. She wasn't going to get the full story from Rachel, only the one she had prepared in advance. It had been like chipping ice off a frozen pond without knowing whether any water suitable for ducks lay beneath. Cara didn't quite see herself as a duck, but the thought pleased her as she took her leave. She would waddle back to the Happy Huffkin to see if any breadcrumbs might have emerged there.

Sometimes ducks are rewarded. When she arrived, Oliver Bright was sitting at one of the tables – already glaring at her. 'Wondered how long you'd be,' he growled. 'I want to talk to you.'

Sentiment not reciprocated, but Cara pulled herself together. She was here, safely at the Happy Huffkin with the gloom and imaginary threat of Ellum Place behind her. No evil spirits had been tracking her on the way back. That was another illusion brought on by Andrew's harping on the need for safety. Now she was here, Oliver might have some insight into what had happened last night. It might have some simple explanation. The more talking she did with the society members, the more everything might begin to make sense. She would treat him like the meek little woman she wasn't.

'Fine show you gave us last night,' Oliver barked. 'What was all that about?'

'Is anyone called Alice known to the society?' she asked, placing a slice of walnut cake on the table to tempt him. 'Or to you?'

''Course not. That's a load of old rubbish anyway. What was going on?'

'No one yet knows, including Rachel.'

A grunt. 'She didn't know Tom Chalcott. I did. Told me she'd only met him the one day when he called at their house. There was no need for that pantomime. Was it you pretending to be a ghost?'

Cara blinked. 'No.'

He ignored this. 'Fine way to carry on. I'll have you know, we're serious about our ghost hunts in the society, and there you are using gimmicks. That's what I told Tom Chalcott too. All that machinery he used. Ghosts are ghosts I told him, and phantoms are phantoms. They don't take no notice of electromagnetic field meters nor those voice recorders. We don't need that sort of thing. The society's for those who understand presence, have a feeling for atmosphere. We don't frighten them away with electrics. If I was chairman again, we'd do things proper, like I told Mr Chalcott. Then that Berowne fellow comes along and says he's the new leader. Now look what we've got. That crazy aunt of Mr Chalcott's says she's stepping in – only for a while, she says, but I've met her sort before.'

'Difficult for you,' Cara replied, the moment she could get a word in edgewise. The power games for the leadership of the society seemed to her to be more important than the hunts, but perhaps that was unfair. But could they have been a factor in two deaths?

'I'll make her ladyship see sense. If not, we'll vote her out,' Oliver said grimly. Another glare at her. 'Well, what have you got to say for yourself?'

'About what?' Cara was genuinely puzzled. 'If you're still talking about last night, it was a straightforward event put on by Lady Lendale in the hope of finding out more about Tom Chalcott's last hours on earth. It somehow went wrong.'

A snort from Oliver. 'No one murdered Mr Chalcott. Poor chap died, that's all. Well, young lady, you'd best get going, and if you want something to do you can find out who killed Berowne.

And why. Maybe this Alice had a go at both of them. Or did she only have her sights on poor Mr Chalcott? Maybe you think I did him in?' Oliver was getting into his stride. 'Or maybe you've got me down for doing in Berowne, eh?' he shouted. 'Them police have got their eyes on Pete Brandon, but maybe I'm next. Maybe it was me who had a go at both of them? All rubbish. How did I do it then? Hid in the bushes until Mr Chalcott came by on his way home, then sprang out saying "Boo!" which scared him to death?'

Shaken by his vehemence, she expected one of his gusty laughs to follow this challenge, but none came. His challenge might be pure rant, but that didn't rule out the fact that it could have happened that way. If Tom Chalcott had indeed been murdered, it would have been by a very different method to the one that killed Berowne.

This gave her pause for thought. She'd been working on the link theory that if Tom had been murdered, the same person had killed both victims. Suppose she was wrong and there were two different murderers? There was no evidence of that, and the introduction of the name Alice raised a whole range of question marks. Tom Chalcott's death, it now seemed to suggest, led to two different paths – and they might have diverged with the sudden appearance of Alice. Alice could well be a red herring – but until that morsel had been tasted, no decent cook would put it on the table. Andrew might still believe that her safety was at risk, but the addition of Alice to the scene would do away with that fear since this Alice could have had nothing to do with Berowne's death. It would also, she realised, rule out her theory that there was a link between his death and Tom's. Instead there would be two unrelated deaths to consider. She would fire a parting shot at Oliver. Gently does it, she warned herself.

'Are you worried because the police might suspect you or any of the society members of being connected with Berowne's death? Have you been able to help them?'

'Slept like a log that night.' He folded his arms and sat back, as if challenging her to go further.

He wouldn't succeed. 'Are you absolutely sure that the name Alice doesn't ring any bells with you?' she asked in a last attempt, seeing that he was preparing to depart. 'The only Alice that Lady

Lendale has heard of was a remote one, an Irish friend of Tom Chalcott's parents.'

'I don't know any Alices. And if you're thinking there was one in my family, my late missus was Eileen, not Alice, see?' he replied promptly.

So that was that, Cara thought. No further on. Where next?

Cara was still pondering this the next day. With the groundwork of the society members' recollections of Tom Chalcott done, all she could concentrate on was the mysterious Alice. It was a weak line, but it had to be followed to its end – wherever that might be. The name Alice might have lain in Rachel's subconscious mind as having to do with Tom, even though she had not been present at the hunt after which Tom had died, nor could she have known him well. That made it hard to see it leading anywhere.

Be positive, she ordered herself. What motivations were there that suggested Tom's death was murder? Leadership of the society would be a feeble reason for the loss of a human life, although there seemed to be a continual battle for the honour. Anything else? Not yet.

She was still musing on this when she arrived at the Happy Huffkin. At least it had taken her mind off stupid ideas that she was being followed by vengeful spirits – or murderers. Now she could stop musing – there couldn't be any while Lady Izzy was around, and there she was striding towards the folly.

'About the society's leadership,' her ladyship said briskly, once she had settled herself down inside, stroked the cat that had accompanied her from the Towers' family wing, ordered a huffkin with cherries from Cara and looked as though she was declaring herself monarch of all she could survey. Fortunately, that wasn't a great deal at present, as the Towers was closed to the public on Mondays. Then Sammy emerged from the kitchen to inform her that she would have to wait an hour or two for the huffkins as the dough wasn't even in the oven yet. One good thing about Lady Izzy, Cara thought, was that she always knew when she had met her match. She had met it in Sammy. It turned out that a cinnamon biscuit would do just as well.

Nevertheless, Cara geared herself up for trouble. Lady Izzy had that look about her.

'You're not to worry about the society leadership,' Lady Izzy continued comfortingly. 'I've fixed it. They didn't want me around,' she explained in glee. 'Nevertheless, I told them I was going to shake them up a bit, and I will. When I'm ready, the society can take over and run itself, but until then I'm in charge. It can't do without my patronage – for that, read money – so I'll get my way. Don't fuss, I'll see we get young Jamie aboard at the next proper meeting. We want some youth around.'

Jamie? Cara was stunned. This was coming out of the blue. Was it a joke? Surely the appointment of a young man in his twenties would result in the dissolution of the society? Instinct told her not to express her views on this. '*Proper* meeting?' she queried instead.

'Oliver has called one without informing me and is all set to persuade everyone he's in charge. I'll be there together with a couple of lawyers to frighten him. He's set it up in the village hall, the daft old man.'

Cara agreed. It was quite something for a small village to have a village hall at all, but the current one was uninspiring, in her opinion. It was chilly, maintained only by stoical volunteers, and refreshments were usually unavailable. Nevertheless, she supposed it looked businesslike.

'I'm not having that old man in charge. I'll be chairing the meeting, not him,' Lady Izzy continued happily. 'Forget the village hall venue. It's going to be held here in the Happy Huffkin.' She must have seen Cara's shocked reaction. 'Don't worry. I'll be there, if only to see if I'm forgiven for my irreverence towards the paranormal.'

Cara grappled with this fait accompli. *Try* to be present? And being held here? A nightmare flew through her mind. If she wasn't careful, she might find herself elected chair. She rapidly dismissed this horror. 'I'll put you all on the upper floor so that you'll be able to battle it out without being disturbed,' she said firmly. 'And positively no dramas like Saturday's please.'

'Dramas? My dear Cara, of course not,' Lady Izzy said meekly, 'even though Detective Chief Inspector Mitchem was most grateful to me for my little show.'

Why? Another surprise to grapple with, Cara thought grimly. That man was getting everywhere – including perilously close to her bed. Perilously? All right, she silently told her conscience, I withdraw the perilously. It was more as she'd felt as a child while waiting for the annual travelling fair to arrive, excitement mixed with tension for the unknown glories that might lie ahead. She could do with them. Once again, she'd thought there was something evil lurking in the bushes on her way here.

'Before that,' Lady Izzy continued, 'I wanted to give you advance notice of probable visitors.'

Caution definitely needed here. 'To what? To the Towers and Happy Huffkin?'

'Probably. You wouldn't want them calling at your home, would you?'

'No. But who?' she asked even more cautiously.

'The ghost hunters,' Lady Izzy said blithely. 'They see you as the fount of all knowledge – not only about Saturday's little drama, but about the police investigation and of course your own on my behalf. I fear I might have given them the impression that my little show helped you enormously in working out what happened to my poor nephew.'

'But it hasn't.' Cara stared at her, aghast. 'I'm not any further forward on finding out how he died and, even if we discover who Alice is, she is only one piece of the jigsaw.'

'I'm aware of that – and of the danger to you, even though you are not investigating poor Berowne's murder. Fortunately, Detective Chief Inspector Mitchem – what a nice man he is – has told me that he has taken care of the safety issue. But, my dear, please do nothing rash.'

Rash? All Cara was capable of doing at the moment was sneaking off home. If only she could but although this wasn't an open day for the Towers, running the Happy Huffkin still involved hard work with preparations for the rest of the week plus supplying the Towers' staff with sustenance. This evening she'd cook a nice supper *for herself* and fall into bed, she vowed. *Alone* – for the time being. But for the moment she had the Happy Huffkin to run.

She had one more shock to cope with. As she parked her car after driving home later that afternoon, a stout, rather jolly-looking lady, some years older than herself, detached herself from the car against which she had been leaning.

Cara was instantly on guard. Who was this?

'Cara Shelley?' she asked cheerily. 'Police Constable Jackie Smart – and don't ask me if I am. I know I am.'

Cara's momentary fright vanished. So Andrew had been serious. He'd meant it and here it was in person. Her guardian angel. Making bad jokes. She couldn't cope with this, even if it was supposed to be for her own safety.

'Are you with me all evening?' she asked her new companion wearily.

'And night. Shall we get going?'

Cara opened up the Happy Huffkin on Wednesday morning with renewed energy. PC Jackie Smart wasn't as bad as she had feared. After two nights there, and now that she was over the shock, Cara rather welcomed having a companion. Once again she pushed away ideas of that companion being Andrew – yet! She and Jackie had made up the bed in what was usually her daughter Kate's bedroom, occupied all too rarely now. Jackie Smart had disappeared on both days with a cheery word after breakfast, to which she had so far contributed a melon, six eggs and fruit juice and cooked a delicious omelette. Cara had set off to work with no grudge at all against Andrew.

Now it remained to be seen whether the usual day's events at the café – as Wednesday was the first open day of the week – would be enlivened by visits from the ghost society. The now familiar hitch cropped up. Combining her duties at the Happy Huffkin with her role as Lady Izzy's agent meant that she couldn't always follow her own routine. Such as now, in the midst of serving coffee and chatting to a couple from the Czech Republic, she saw Charlotte sitting at a table on the lawn. That was unusual – she normally tried to escape notice. Had the police called Pete in again? It was clear she was here on a mission. She didn't seem to be interested in the menu but politely ordered tea. She looked ill at ease as Cara hurried to serve her.

'It's about Tom Chalcott,' Charlotte blurted out, just as Cara was about to tactfully bring up the subject of Pete. 'I thought I should talk to you about that awful show Lady Lendale put on. And Rachel screaming out.'

'Alice?' Cara suggested helpfully as Charlotte came to a halt.

'No. It's more about Rachel herself.' A pause, then she burst out, 'She's been spreading lies about me and Berowne. People are looking at me oddly, but it isn't true. I don't want the police to think that Berowne and I were an item, especially as they keep questioning Pete about Berowne's awful death. I'd never have an affair with anyone, and certainly not with him. So why is she telling all these lies?'

'Have you talked to her about it?'

'I daren't. We owed money to Berowne – Pete got into debt – and now we have to pay it to Rachel so I can't plead with her. Pete believes everything she says.'

'You might find her accommodating over the money,' Cara said sympathetically. 'But why does she think you had an affair with him if you didn't?'

'Because Berowne could have lied about it. If he was having an affair, it wasn't with me.'

Cara's ears pricked up. Who then? The mysterious Alice or Josie or even Emily? she wondered. 'Have you told the police about this?'

'I think Rachel did, because they asked me about it. I didn't tell Pete, because he might not have believed me. And now this awful thing about Tom Chalcott has cropped up. Do you know who this Alice is?'

'Not yet,' Cara said. 'Have you any ideas? Do you remember Tom talking about an Alice?'

'No, but I liked Tom. Pete didn't like me being friendly with him, though, and this awful Alice thing has stirred it all up again.'

When Charlotte departed after some counselling on Cara's part, she looked slightly happier. Would she be capable of murder? Cara wondered. If passions were raised, perhaps. Given the way in which Berowne had died, perhaps those passions had been raised despite her denials.

Still no further on the Alice question, though. It was possible, Cara decided, that there was more to the Tom Chalcott story than she knew, and probably more than Lady Izzy knew either. He wasn't married but he did have girlfriends, so is that where Alice came in? Here we go again, she thought. Don't let your theories get too far ahead of the facts. Get on with serving that couple on the table over there.

Charlotte was no sooner out of sight than her husband strolled into the Happy Huffkin. Great. This was not how Cara had planned her day, and Pete had a determined look on his face. She was a sitting duck here, and she didn't want to get drawn into talk about his being taken in for questioning. Surely he wasn't going to blame her for the interest in him that the police seemed to be taking. Furthermore, Sammy was not going to be pleased if yet again she left him to prepare for the afternoon rush. At the moment, though, she had no choice but to talk to him.

'You've just missed Charlotte,' she sang out to Pete as she went over to the table at which he'd sat down. His folded arms indicated he was not here on a pleasure visit.

'What did she want?' he hurled at her. 'Still carrying on about Saturday's festivities, was she?'

'We were all somewhat shaken,' Cara said hastily. 'I imagine you were friendly with Tom Chalcott.'

'Friendly? Publicans don't get chummy with the upper classes. We doff our hats.' He seemed quite serious. 'Anyway, this is nothing to do with Chalcott. It's about that Berowne. It's a plot to get me hauled into the police station again. Blaming me. It was your chum that policeman who set me up. A plot,' he repeated savagely, 'and you're in it.'

'What on earth are you talking about?' she asked indignantly. 'I've nothing to do with your being questioned. What plot?'

He ignored this. 'She didn't care two hoots about Chalcott. It's Berowne, isn't it?'

'Who is *she*?' Cara demanded. 'Lady Lendale?'

'Maybe,' he said darkly. 'Maybe not.'

Cara took this nasty bull by the horns. 'If by any chance you're referring to Berowne's private life: firstly, it's none of my business; secondly, in my opinion he didn't have his sights set on anyone in the Tanton Ghost and Phantom Society, including,' she added bravely, 'your wife.'

That shook him. 'Rot. He was after her all the time,' he threw at her. A silence and then: 'But if you think I did him in, you're wrong.'

Keep the subject firmly on Tom Chalcott, Cara thought. 'Is there anything more that you can tell me about that last hunt with Tom in the grotto?'

Pete hesitated. 'Maybe a bit. Didn't tell you before, but I reckon it's all in the past now, so no harm's done if I tell you. Berowne was on the make as the new chair that night – but not with my Charlotte. I made sure of that, in case he made a pass at her. I knew his type, even then. I kept close to her when we all left to go back to the car park – everyone except Chalcott, of course. He would have come up on his own once he'd collected all the records and stuff. I lost sight of Charlotte on the way back – she was talking to Oliver or someone maybe. But when I looked around, I couldn't see Berowne either. Then I saw her with Oliver, so Berowne must have gone for a pee.'

Berowne wasn't with the group? Cara held her breath. At last, some new information. 'Did Berowne come back to join you?' She waited on tenterhooks for his reply.

'Didn't see him after that. He bled me dry, that swine. Good riddance, say I. Reckon he lined his own pockets with the money he got from me.'

At last. Cara could hardly believe it. A positive step. It could probably never be proven now, but if Tom Chalcott had been murdered, it had to have been someone present at that last meeting. They had all left together, save for Tom himself, who was delayed. He was found near the car park, so he couldn't have been attacked while he was still in the grotto. It would have been a long way to drag him. Berowne was the only one in a position to have killed him, probably by asphyxia. That cushion could have been deliberately put there beforehand. There was plenty of evidence that everyone save Tom had left the grotto together, but no evidence that they all reached the car park together.

No, she reasoned, Tom would have fought back, shouted, yelled. Someone would have heard. Unless, he had been silenced by that stone. Muffled. No. Hit from behind – yes. That was possible. A stone from behind to stun him. Blood? If there was any, it would be from the stone, but it could, she supposed, be put down to his tumbling to the ground after a heart attack. He might have been stunned with it, then asphyxiated, probably with the help of the cushion, which must have got left behind by mistake or more likely tossed away.

There could be no proof now. Worse, Cara thought, there seemed no motive. But if Lady Izzy was right and Tom had been murdered, then either some stranger from the village had been lying in wait to kill Tom or it was someone on the ghost hunt. Someone who wasn't with the group returning to the car park. So Tom's killer was obvious.

It could only have been Berowne Dyer.

FOURTEEN

'It's a viable theory,' Andrew finally agreed.

Was that all he could say? Cara was taken aback. No, there was more, it seemed.

'So, if Berowne Dyer killed Tom, who killed Berowne – and why?' he continued.

She was floored. Intent on Tom Chalcott, she hadn't yet thought this through. She had asked for an appointment and had been allotted one straightaway. She had been so sure of her ground, but now his simple question threw her. It had been so obvious to her that if Tom had been murdered, his killer must have been Berowne. True, perhaps, but now she had to speedily consider his story as part of a wider picture. What had she expected? A pat on the back from Andrew? Admittedly there were snags in her theory. There had been no overt hostility between Tom and Berowne, so far as she'd discovered, and the hiccup in her story was that she could see no motive for Berowne to be driven to murder Tom or for Berowne to be killed ten years later. In other words, there was no link between the two deaths.

'I don't know,' she was forced to confess, not something that would help her case, especially with Andrew sitting opposite her with gimlet eyes. Steady the Buffs, she thought – her grandfather's way of progressing an argument. 'Nor do I know why Berowne should have wanted to murder Tom. He'd already taken over the leadership, so there must have been some other reason for their falling out.'

'Evidence?'

'None, m'lud,' Cara admitted ruefully, aware that he was letting her off the hook. She had rushed here too quickly. She hadn't yet dismissed the Alice line, remote though its relevance was. She should have waited to follow it as far as she could.

A slightly raised eyebrow emphasized that she was in official territory, which didn't encourage wild accusations. Anyway, her role was over as far as the police were concerned, although she could continue looking for any back-up to her theory. She would have to report to Lady Izzy that her job seemed done, however. Why did she feel so reluctant to do that, she wondered. Was she *still* thinking there was a link between the two deaths? Without an answer to the vital question of why Berowne and Tom might have been at odds with one another, she could see no way forward – yet. The truth about it lay buried ten years ago, but it surely affected the other issue she had to raise with Andrew.

'There's no real need for PC Smart to guard me any longer,' she said awkwardly, as she prepared to leave. 'Everyone knows I was only following up the Tom Chalcott death, and if Berowne was responsible—'

'She will remain on duty,' Andrew interrupted.

Of course she would. Cara had a sneaking sense of relief. Jackie was a comforting presence in a way. She had to admit that she never liked walking home alone in the dark – or at any time recently, come to that. She was always imagining people hiding in the bushes about to leap out at her. Stupid. She'd get over it once the shock of the ghost tour had subsided. Even though she could get no further over Tom Chalcott's death, she still had all the background knowledge that she'd picked up from society members, which she was aware could have relevance for Berowne's murder. Whether she liked it or not, she was in the thick of the uncertainty and shadows that were affecting Tanton Towers, and so she owed it to Max and Alison to carry on. This reassured her that she was on the right path – until she remembered the caveat. She had been sensing this imaginary threat for good reason. Out there somewhere was a murderer.

As usual, her best-laid plans could go adrift. As soon she reached the Happy Huffkin, it was clear that Virginia had been summoned. Lucy too, thankfully, as the tables were nearly all full. Worse, Sammy was waiting for her at the main door. 'What's wrong?' she asked, alarmed. Fire? Flood? Run out of teabags?

'Luke.' Sammy was looking so grave that her alarm grew.

'What's happened to him?'

'Wants to talk. Waiting upstairs.'

Terror promptly subsided, even though she hadn't bargained on this. Would this visit be about Tom or Berowne? If it was about Tom, it might be useful now that she had a theory to prove. If it wasn't and he was merely here to criticize everybody else, it would probably be the opposite.

She repented of such negative thoughts as she rushed up the stairs. She found Luke huddled by the windows, staring out at visitors to the Towers peacefully having their coffee on the lawn. He did not look happy.

'Hallo, Luke,' she greeted him warily, sliding into the seat opposite him.

He was staring at her as though she was about to perform a citizen's arrest. 'That show of yours,' he said abruptly. 'What was all that about Alice?'

This sounded hopeful. 'Do you know who she is?' she asked eagerly.

''Course I do. My wife as was. Walked out on me fifteen years back.'

Not so hopeful. 'Did Rachel know her?' Cara asked. 'I don't think she was living in Tanton then, so it can't have been the same Alice.'

'Died five years back in Australia, did my ex-wife. I reckon Rachel's one of them clairvoyants. There she was yelling for my Alice, you see. Well, she can yell all she likes, but you can tell her she won't get no reply.'

One thing was certain, Cara thought. She was going to get no help from Luke. Anyway, whoever Alice was, the odds against her being involved in Tom's death were minimal. When the rush at the café was over, she'd have another go at finding out more about the night that Tom died. Berowne, Luke, Oliver, Pete and Charlotte were the society members there, and any of them could have caused his death. But who? There must have been staff members around too. Len was one, and she hadn't talked to him about it. Yet. She'd try right now.

She was in luck. Len was just unlocking the door to his shed as she hurried along the path round the Towers. 'I'm still trying to help Lady Izzy find out more about her nephew's death,' she said hopefully. 'I know it's a long time ago, but if you were working here then, were you by any chance on duty that night?'

He nodded. 'Under-gardener I was. Made sure of that. There were some good classics in that car park. Don't remember much about that Chalcott chap, but I saw his car there. Alfa Romeo it was. One of the early Jags there, too, and Mr Berowne had his Porsche. Last to leave that was – except for the Alfa Romeo.'

Evidence! She had some proof at last. Berowne's car had not left with the others. Even if Andrew didn't think it strong enough, Lady Izzy would fasten on to it.

'Are you sure you didn't see Tom Chalcott that night?' she asked eagerly.

'You're doing this detective stuff for the old lady, aren't you?' Len asked crossly. 'Well, can't tell you much more because I never saw him that night. Died on the way to the car park, they said. Old Oliver found him. Bit of a shock for him. And me. I was only a young 'un. Shame it wasn't that Berowne.'

He was looking gratified at this chance to speak his mind. He was welcome to it. She now had her evidence safely in the bag. All she needed was a motive.

Of course there was also still the puzzle of Alice to follow up, and indeed a puzzle it was. It still might have nothing to do with Tom Chalcott. If by chance it did, then the case she had put together was surely connected. How though?

At least she felt she had now made a giant leap, if not for mankind on the moon then at least for Lady Izzy.

Now to switch back into work mode. She could see Jamie sitting peaceably with Emily at the only occupied table on the grass outside the café. The first afternoon tour round the Towers would only just have begun, judging by her watch, so it was surprising to see them there.

Mistake. Cara realized as she approached that it wasn't Emily with Jamie. It was Lucy, Virginia's niece. So her first thought that there had been a reconciliation between Jamie and Emily was a mistake. The long blonde locks common to both girls had misled her at first sight.

Highly amused, Cara could see that she and Jamie were clasping hands across the table. None of her business, though. Lucy looked so happy that for a moment Cara wondered if she was missing something in her own life. She'd managed perfectly well without a man permanently present, but occasionally of late she had found herself wondering how that might work. Purely objectively of course, but she admitted it was happening more frequently now. Business first, however.

'I reckon we're like a scene from *Midsomer Murders.* My gran watches that,' Jamie said cheerfully, when she went over to greet them. This was a change in outlook. Emily must clearly now be firmly in the past. 'We're here having a nice cup of tea, and you turn up to accuse one of us of murdering Berowne.'

'Not me,' Cara replied. 'I'm only on the Tom Chalcott trail.'

'My aunt says you think their deaths are linked,' Lucy piped up.

Virginia had clearly been called in too often not to be genned up on why Cara had been missing from her post rather a lot recently.

'I went home after we cleared up from the party that night,' Lucy said virtuously. 'So I've no idea what Jamie got up to in the grotto,' she added innocently.

'None of your business,' he replied amicably, kissing her hand. There must have been a serious reconciliation between them, Cara thought almost tenderly. Jamie looked genuinely smitten with his former love. 'My Miss Happy Huffkin here reckons I was bedding everyone in town, but hand on heart I slept alone,' he said virtuously.

'You didn't sleep much though,' Lucy retorted. 'That's what you told me next day.'

'For love of you, sweetheart.'

'I bet.'

So did Cara. In his position, he might well have been patrolling the grotto in the hope of reclaiming Emily from Harry's bed. Harry had been the lucky recipient of Emily's charms that night.

Harry, who had been first to find Berowne the next morning.

The kitchen, Cara told herself. This afternoon had to be dedicated to the Happy Huffkin, and when she left the lovers' idyll, she went in to report to Sammy. He was looking distinctly bothered about something.

A jerk of his head. 'Phone. That was Mrs Redman. Wants you to go right over there. Now. Private, she said.'

'But—'

'We can manage. Virginia's on her way.'

What was this about? This sounded like a crisis. Cara was puzzled as she hurried towards Josie and Len's cottage. Every jigsaw has a final piece to fit in, but this one was an evasive one. She couldn't see what it could be. Private? That sounded worrying.

Life was a snakes and ladders board, but she had hoped that if she, Cara, found the right ladder, someone might be at the top to pull her up. Was this summons going to help?

She remembered her first visit to Josie and Len's home when the ghost celebration and hunt were merely events of the future, exciting experiments for the Happy Huffkin in evening catering. Today it was a far different matter, although it was hard even to think of that when there was clearly a crisis of some sort. Especially on a day like this, with the summer smells in the air, which lulled one into the comfortable feeling that no killer was going to leap out of the bushes she was hurrying past.

Josie was waiting for her anxiously at the door and led her into their living room without any ado or explanation.

'Are you OK?' Cara asked.

Josie paused, then said awkwardly, 'I must tell you the whole story, because with all these awful things happening here, I'm working on the principle of a secret shared is a life spared.' Another pause, then it came out in a rush: 'Rachel isn't the easiest of people to get on with, and this is only between you and me. It all starts off with her. I've only just remembered someone called Alice.'

Cara's hopes shot up, although Josie really was in a state, she realized. She was definitely nervous about something, almost scared. She had already left her job at Ellum Place, so what was still an issue?

'With Rachel involved?' she asked. 'Even though she shouted the name out that night, Rachel says she can't recall any Alices in her life, except a great-aunt, let alone any that might have had a connection with Tom. All Lady Lendale remembers is an Irish Alice who was friendly with Tom's parents, so I'm not getting very far . . .'

Cara stopped, aware that she must have said something significant.

'Tom's parents,' Josie half whispered. She looked alarmed, almost terrified. 'So it is that Alice. I've heard of her.'

Cara held her breath. Could this be a breakthrough? Unlikely, but perhaps pigs might fly if this was her lucky day.

'I was a chum of Tom's,' Josie blurted out. 'Lady Lendale may not know that. He and I were at university together. We weren't close, but we met again here. I was knocked for six at that show of Lady Lendale's, but when that stupid woman Rachel started yelling Alice, it never occurred to me that it could have anything to do with Tom's parents. Why should it?'

A bull's eye. And Cara hadn't even been hoping for one. This was progress, she rejoiced, hardly daring to believe her luck. At least the trail was still open.

'Tom had once told me an Alice Seton who lived in southern Ireland was a friend of his parents,' Josie continued.

'Not of his? Not a girlfriend?'

Josie managed a grin. 'No way. Alice would have been about sixty years old when he told me all this.'

Cara's faint hope dwindled. 'So Rachel's Alice is unlikely to have been the one Tom was telling you about?'

She could see Josie deliberating. For a moment Cara thought she'd say no more, but she sent up a blessing to the stars when Josie picked up the story again.

'It was. It might not have been Alice herself that's the focus of the story. Tom relayed it to me about it two or three years before he died, when Berowne and Rachel first came to the village. Alice Seton had told them she had a friend in Ireland whose daughter had married someone called Berowne. He had deserted her after a year of marriage, and she had not heard from him since. Alice remembered the story because Berowne is an uncommon name – and she had been told his parents were travelling actors and had drawn the name from Shakespeare's *Love's Labour's Lost.*'

Cara's hopes shot up but then collapsed. 'That can't be *our* Berowne,' she said uneasily, remembering his story of how he had acquired his name, 'because if it were, he would have had to divorce the girl in order to marry Rachel.'

'There was no divorce,' Josie said bleakly. 'She was a farmer's daughter, a devout Catholic, and not in a position to chase after him when he vanished. She wouldn't have divorced him anyway because of her religion. That was the story. As to whether it was "our Berowne", as you put it, I'd assumed that if it was the same man, Rachel and he weren't married legally. Bigamy is of course a crime both here and in southern Ireland – I checked and there were over twenty convictions there last year but, even if she wanted to pursue it, I doubt whether it would have led anywhere in this case. Anyway, I work freelance, I have other customers, and it was none of my business whether they were married or not,' she said defiantly.

She paused, then said awkwardly, 'What I didn't know was the name of Alice Seton's friend, but I had no reason to probe further when it didn't seem relevant to Tom's story.'

It was obvious what was coming. 'And you think this was Rachel's Alice?'

'Yes.'

Cara was appalled at the thought of where this was leading. 'Why—' she began.

'Why do I think it could be the Alice that Rachel was screeching about? It was Rachel herself who by accident set all this off? Easy,' Josie said evenly. 'You know that I stopped working at Ellum Place two or three weeks ago. Jealous spouses lose all sense of proportion, and Rachel and I were never on chummy terms. She went berserk. She had this crazy idea that I was having an affair with Berowne. No way. I wouldn't dare to do that with her beady eye on me. First it was Charlotte she accused, then me. So, yes, I lost my cool and told her that if she thought she was married to Berowne, she was wife number two. She was not amused.'

This was even worse. 'Not easy breaking that to her,' was the best Cara could manage to say.

Josie seized on this. 'You're right. And where Rachel's concerned, you're *very* right. So I realize that you'll have to tell the police this story, but don't bring me into it.'

FIFTEEN

This bombshell left Cara reeling. She'd been wound up like a corkscrew not knowing what this investigation would now reveal. She struggled with it as she left the cottage because it raised questions galore. It might have nothing to do with either Tom or Berowne's death, but on the other hand it could be the key to one or both.

It was normally a pleasant walk back to the Happy Huffkin but not today. Too much to think about. Was it true for a start? The story could have been embroidered over the years. Perhaps there had never been a marriage service with this girl? Perhaps over the years she had acquired a divorce somehow, with or without Berowne's knowledge. Perhaps the marriage hadn't been legal in the first place. Maybe the girl had refused to divorce him and Rachel knew all about it. The Republic of Ireland had a different jurisdiction from the UK.

Think, Cara, think, she told herself. You can't just stroll back into the Happy Huffkin and ignore it for a while, so she took the longer path round the front of the Towers. The downside was that the path brought her closer once more to the grotto, and she would again be reliving that awful moment of her first sight of Berowne's body. Nevertheless, visitors would have left by now, and perhaps seeing the grotto again might help rather than hinder. It might produce some kind of solution, and that she sorely needed.

Not such a good idea. The minute she stepped inside the grotto, she felt on alien territory. Still, she was here now, and she'd brave it. What struck her first was how cold the stone was. It wasn't only cold to the touch, it *looked* cold, as though the Olympian gods were accusing her of trespassing on their preserve. Apollo was staring angrily down at her and Aphrodite was smirking at her discomfiture. Even Hades looked as though he had a few plans for her. At least there was no sign of any police presence here now, nor any trace of the ghost hunters who had stayed here on that fatal night.

Rachel's room was only a short walk from where Berowne had died. Don't jump to any conclusions, Cara warned herself. She now knew that Rachel might have a motive for his murder, and she had known that in time to plan ahead. Perhaps she had ensured that her quarters would be on this convenient corner, perhaps to prevent anyone else creeping along to share Berowne's bed that night – or perhaps because she intended murder.

Cara peered up the passageway to the room where Berowne had died. Perhaps the ghost of the Laughing Lady might reappear and give her a clue about what happened here on her patch. No laughter now though. Just silence. There was no sign of ghosts now, or even of a ghostly atmosphere. It just felt empty and cold.

This was no time to ask herself whether her questioning was clashing with Andrew's case. This would be a major turning point if it was as new to him as it was to her. They would both have to deal with it.

When Cara arrived at the Happy Huffkin on Thursday morning, she found Rachel herself waiting inside, courtesy of Sammy who had arrived early. Quite how she had managed to get past the gatehouse wasn't clear but, knowing Rachel, she could easily have climbed over the gate if she was set on entering. Now what? How much to say, how far to dig? Cara thought, as she hung up her anorak and went over to join her.

'I had a call from dear Josie,' Rachel began coolly. 'It seems she has told you her fairy story about Berowne and myself. She really didn't like my sacking her, did she? Her tale came as quite a surprise. My lawyers are looking into it now, so I do advise you not to join the Josie slander club.'

Grasp this one by the horns, Cara decided. 'Whatever the situation, the shock must have been dreadful for you on top of everything else.'

'It was. But I do suggest, Cara, that we both leave this matter for my lawyers and the police. Do you agree?'

'I do,' Cara said courteously. 'I shall tell Lady Lendale, however, as it does affect her. There is the wild possibility that if the Alice you recalled so vividly at the ghost-tour evening was indeed the same Alice known to Tom Chalcott's parents, it could affect his death.'

A step too far, because Rachel retorted immediately, 'I hate to contribute to the fairy story, but if you recall I was not with the society that evening.'

But she was very much present at Berowne's death, Cara thought, as Rachel swept up her jacket, politely presenting a ten-pound note for her coffee. She could have heard about Alice well before Berowne's murder, which meant that she would be on the suspects list. So what should be her own next step? Step slowly, she told herself. Think about it. By the time Cara had returned with the change, Rachel had gone.

Where now? She had no choice, Cara knew. She had to face it, she decided. She had to talk to Andrew again. Surely now the two cases must collide.

'Come now please,' he replied as soon as she was put through to him.

From the detached tone of his voice, it sounded as if this was going to be tough going, and she was glad that at least talking to him in his office would be neutral territory. As her information affected his case more than Tom Chalcott's, this was just as well if the Rachel story was going to be news to him.

Sitting behind the desk, looking at her stony-faced, it was clear he wasn't going to help her through this. Which card should she play first? The evidence against Berowne on the night Tom died? Or the bombshell of his bigamous marriage?

He spoke first. 'I need to talk to you primarily about Thomas Chalcott's death, Cara, not about Lady Lendale's evening performance. We can come to that afterwards.'

So, she need not have stepped so gingerly onto the thorny ground of the Berowne case. 'Very well. That's in my remit,' she pointed out, nettled at his taking charge of the conversation so early. Then she pulled herself together. Don't be ridiculous, she thought, marshalling herself to deal with this.

'Just to make it clear, however,' he added. 'There is still no evidence that Tom Chalcott's death was murder.'

Relief. She was on safe ground here. 'But there is evidence,' she replied, noting that he had used the word 'murder'. That meant he was at least considering it, which was a step in the right direction. Now to make her case. Deep breath. 'We assumed at first that the group all went back to the car park together except for Tom who stayed behind. The evidence is that although all the members of the group left the grotto together, they didn't all arrive at the car park together.' Thankfully, she could see that he was listening attentively. 'Berowne disappeared from the group at one point, whether to pee or otherwise, and he didn't rejoin it.'

Andrew replied immediately. 'Is the implication that he murdered Tom Chalcott when he walked by a little later? That's a big leap, Cara, given that there's still no proof that he didn't die a natural death. Naming Berowne is an even bigger leap.'

A pause, and she tensed up. 'This isn't an official case for me, Cara,' he continued, 'but it's looking as if the situation is changing. I'll talk to Lady Lendale. I need to see her anyway, but whether the Alice story affects the Chalcott death or not remains to be seen. Either way, I agree a different light has now been thrown on at least one of the two deaths. What still concerns me is the danger both for you and others.'

Cara failed to see why this should be so, since it must be common knowledge that she was sharing any information she had with the police. She was going to push ahead anyway. The poker face that Andrew donned when discussing police business had vanished, she noted with pleasure – tinged with a tiny bit of apprehension. Could he be right about the danger involved? Forge ahead, she ordered herself. No point giving up now. Anyway, she'd agreed to PC Jackie Smart still coming to the cottage at night and had to admit she was glad of it.

'Alice,' she began firmly. 'She is very definitely in both your remit and mine. I've discovered that Berowne was already married when he married Rachel ten years ago.'

She waited for his reaction. Would it be 'Well done, Cara,' or would the axe fall on her neck?

It didn't fall. Instead: 'Yes,' he said quietly. 'We already know.'

A damp squib to end all damp squibs. What a let-down. 'You didn't tell me.' The words were out of her mouth before she could stop them and, instead of the brave collaborator, she sounded like a petulant child.

He let her off lightly. 'Have you talked to Rachel Dyer about this?'

'Yes, but it was she who came to talk to me,' Cara replied.

'Not to discuss it, only to say it was in the hands of her lawyers. Josie Redman told me the story. She'd known for some time, but I gather Rachel only found out recently. It makes a difference.' That was putting it mildly.

His face was a mask. 'We make background checks on victims, including births, marriages and death certificates. I agree it's a serious factor in this case. Just as we check not only on the suspects but also those around them.'

'There's a lot of ambition and jealousy in both cases,' Cara said forthrightly, 'both Tom's and Berowne's. There were the battles over leadership of the society, there were the emotional doubts, false assumptions and betrayals – and there was Berowne, the figurehead in the middle.'

Andrew looked almost human as he said, 'Yes, I agree, but there's more to be uncovered.'

He might be indicating that she could make a move forward. She'd risk it: 'I'll ask you two questions then,' she began. 'What was the weapon used to kill Berowne?' She tried to ignore the ghastly image that that summoned up.

A slight hesitation on his part. Then: 'An ordinary kitchen knife. Not found.'

'And could a woman have inflicted those wounds?'

'I can't say whether or not it applies to this case, but generally, yes.' A pause. 'I'm set on bringing this case to an end quickly, Cara. I want that.'

She steadied herself. 'So do I.'

'Let's meet this evening. Just us and the English countryside. Nothing heavy duty.'

The Farran Arms was a good choice, Cara thought. Well, it had been, sitting in this pub garden by the stream and peacefully awaiting his lordship's arrival. Now the sound of dissenting voices spoilt that. There were no obvious contenders for the source – until she saw the two men some way away in the wooded area further along by the stream. There was something familiar – oh no! One of them was Jamie, now rushing towards her – no, she realized, not towards her, but to Emily, who had just appeared round the side of the pub. Emily again? Weird. What had happened to Lucy? Warning signs began to flash up in Cara's mind.

Everything seemed to happen in seconds then, amid a lot of yelling both masculine and feminine. Harry had appeared and was in hot pursuit of Jamie – no, he was after Emily too. A leap from behind by Harry sent both the young men into a sprawling heap on the ground, with Emily hopping up and down squealing.

Cara went into action. She'd dealt with a similar situation at least once at the Happy Huffkin. Nothing like cold water to dampen the pugilists' ardour. She snatched the jug of water on her table, rushed over, pushed Emily out of the way, chose her moment and emptied the whole jug over them, making sure their faces caught a good whack of it.

'Get up!' Cara ordered them. 'And one of you look after Emily.'

By the time the two men had clambered to their feet, though, Emily seemed to have disappeared. The whole pub had emptied to enjoy the battle, and now the two men took flight too – probably into the toilets to dry off. Then Emily reappeared from wherever she'd been hiding and began to giggle.

'They did look ridiculous,' she observed.

'Men often do,' Cara said cheerfully.

'Thank you.' A familiar masculine voice behind them made Cara jump. Andrew had arrived for their date. 'Dare I enquire what's going on?' he asked.

Emily eyed him doubtfully. 'You're that policeman. They didn't mean any harm,' she pleaded. 'Don't take them away.'

Cara laughed. Clearly Emily thought Andrew had arrived to arrest them.

'I'll give them another chance,' Andrew said grandly. People were drifting back inside now that the fun appeared to be over. 'Do you mind telling me what's going on, Cara? And why you're clutching an empty water jug to your bosom?'

'Somehow,' she explained, belatedly aware of what she was doing and hastily put the jug down, 'it got emptied over two gentlemen.'

'Did they deserve it?' he enquired.

'Yes.'

'Do you make a habit of pouring cold water over gentlemen?'

'Only on Thursday evenings,' she assured him.

'Emily,' he turned to the young woman, who was still looking wary, 'kindly explain what has taken place this evening.'

'I was going with Harry to get a Chinese,' she muttered. 'Then Jamie saw us and started shouting at us and we ended up in the wood over there. He said he'd dump Lucy if I'd come back to him.'

'Then I suggest you use your feminine charms to convince them both of their great value to society and the need to avoid fisticuffs. Then quietly pop off home alone,' Andrew said.

Emily looked at him doubtfully. 'I don't think I'd know how to do that – apart from the going home bit.'

'Off you go then, Emily!' he commanded.

She didn't need to be told. At that moment Cara saw Harry and Jamie emerging back into the garden, apparently now the best of friends. She decided the sooner she was out of this the better, or Virginia would think she had something to do with this change of heart on Jamie's part.

'Leave it to them to sort out,' Andrew told her as Cara began to stroll towards the two ex-fighters. 'Jealousy is straightforward. You either put up with it and let it smoulder or you take action as they've done, rather pleasantly in their case. Take Pete, though – he's in there merrily chatting up all the ladies while Charlotte's left behind the bar, doing her best to get on well with the customers.'

Charlotte. Cara stopped in her tracks. That reminded her of Rachel, who seemed so fixated on Charlotte having had an affair with Berowne. Cara doubted that. It was merely the green-eyed monster on Rachel's part, linked with possessiveness. 'Rachel knows about Berowne's earlier marriage,' she told Andrew. 'She is also convinced that he had affairs with Charlotte and Josie Redman. I don't believe Rachel. Neither of them is the type.'

'Is there a type?' he enquired politely.

Cara laughed. 'I suppose not.'

'Jealousy isn't based on fact anyway. Insecurity perhaps. Possessiveness? It sits there, lurking, ready to pounce.'

'That's very profound.'

'Then I'll be even more profound. When it's let loose it can hit out at random. Take care, Cara. Take a great deal of care.'

SIXTEEN

The world looked a whole lot brighter the next day. Cara felt that some obstacle had been clambered over successfully in her relationship with Andrew. That, however, had to be put to one side. There was too much to do for the day ahead to ponder on that, and the problem centred on Rachel – and Alice.

Rachel was a cool woman. She had to be on the suspects list for Berowne's murder and could have easily insisted on having the room nearest to him in the grotto. The perfect position for revenge for his affairs – if they existed – and for his bigamy. Nevertheless, to cast her as a murderer was a big step, just as it was for all the society members. Still, if Sherlock Holmes could do that, so too could Cara Shelley. She would turn herself into a modern Sherlock once more. How about the dog that didn't bark in the night? If Rachel had interrupted Berowne's sleep, he'd have been annoyed but he wouldn't have screamed. That was food for thought.

Another consultation with Lady Izzy was next on her 'to do' list. The family wing seemed quiet as Cara rang the bell. There was no reply from Max and Alison's bell, so she tried the guest suite. No answer, but the family wing door was slightly ajar and she could hear voices from above. Raised voices.

Very raised voices. Lady Izzy must be up there but who was with her? It sounded sufficiently like Rachel to make Cara push her way inside. The screeching seemed to be more or less continuous, and alarmed she rushed up the stairs. The noise was indeed coming from the guest suite and Cara hurled herself inside. What was going on? To her horror, Rachel, back to the door, seemed to be looming over Lady Izzy, who was unable to escape from her chair. One hand was gripping Lady Izzy's shoulder, clearly painfully.

'Leave her alone!' Cara shouted.

Surprised by the unexpected, Rachel did so. 'What do *you* want?' she yelled at Cara in fury.

'To see Lady Izzy.' Cara monitored her voice down. This was the woman whom she had dismissed as calm, yet here she was about to stifle someone. 'Just what are you here for?' She injected quiet menace into her voice in the hope it might have some effect.

It did. Rachel calmed down and she collapsed into the chair. 'Sorry. It's getting too much for me. All this and Berowne's death.'

She had a point, Cara acknowledged. Whether Rachel was a victim or not, it was only a short time since his death, and she could hardly be expected to be 'normal', especially when she'd only recently been told she was not legally married to Berowne. Nevertheless, attacks such as the one Cara had just witnessed were over the top.

Lady Izzy was regaining her composure and Rachel sat upright again.

'You knew all the time, didn't you?' Rachel said accusingly to Lady Izzy's obvious puzzlement.

Cara turned to her. 'Rachel discovered only recently that at the time she married Berowne, he was already married.'

Lady Izzy's eyebrows shot up. 'My dear,' she said gently to Rachel. 'A frightful shock on top of all this horror.' Her eyes travelled questioningly to Cara, who nodded slightly. Lady Izzy was obviously wondering whether that was before Berowne died.

'Thank you,' Rachel said bitterly. She was clearly gathering strength, for another outburst followed: 'And did you realize, Lady Lendale, that your dear Berowne had not one but two whores, mistresses, affairs – whatever you like to call them?'

'I do now,' Lady Izzy murmured.

Rachel was in her stride again now. 'There's Mrs Prim and Proper Charlotte. Her grovelling husband probably chucked her in as part of the rent he owed my company, for which Berowne nominally worked. I certainly never saw much of the cash. He was too busy spending it on dear Charlotte.'

Cara fought to restrain herself from commenting on this, but Lady Izzy was looking mildly interested.

'And,' Rachel added with venom in her voice, 'there's darling Josie too. I informed her two or three weeks ago that Berowne's breast and other regions were no longer available to her. A very cunning lady, that. She's older than me too but – for Berowne – age didn't matter.

'She actually had the cheek,' Rachel swept on, 'to tell me she'd found out about this stupid marriage. She was smirking with pleasure at telling me. She had some cock-and-bull story about being at school with Tom Chalcott.'

'University actually,' Lady Izzy said gently.

Rachel looked at her rather shamefacedly. 'Well, anyway, I *had* heard of an Alice. Your nephew called at our home a day or two after he'd handed over the chairmanship of the society to Berowne and I remember him saying something like "Alice is never wrong" at the door as he left. I had no idea then what they were talking about. Poor Josie though,' she added sarcastically. 'She did so worship Berowne.'

'Well, my dear, how much of that do you believe?' Lady Izzy asked, when Rachel had left – the session had ended in a pool of tears.

'Carefully selected?' Cara said. 'Carefully edited?' The one thing of which she was sure was that there was a lot of unfinished business here.

'Much of it,' Lady Izzy agreed. 'It has, however, made my mind up. We are now sure that my dear Tom died at the hands of Berowne. The case will never come to court, but that's not important. Tom must have been threatening to reveal his nasty little secret. My part in this ugly story is finished, as that's what brought me here. I shall oversee the election of a new chair for the society and then depart. I have imposed myself on Max and Alison too long. But before that . . .' She paused.

'Yes?' Cara asked warily.

'Let's have one other gaudy night.'

'*What?*' Once again Cara reeled with shock. This sounded ominous to say the least. Not again, not again.

'Shakespeare always had such a clever way of putting things,' Lady Izzy murmured. 'And of course there's the splendid Dorothy Sayers crime novel of that name. She too understood life so well.'

Cara swallowed. 'You want another celebration?' she managed to ask. Surely not, not after the disaster of the last one.

'Such a marvellous way of my handing over the baton of responsibility. First voting Jamie in as the new chair – after I have arranged that,' she added blithely. 'Then the champagne. No doubt a donation from me will smooth his passage into the role of chair.'

The Tanton Ghost and Phantom Society was in for a shock, Cara thought. She'd assumed that this particular brilliant (or otherwise) idea of Lady Izzy's had quietly disappeared. It clearly hadn't – and, she reflected, perhaps it wasn't so crazy after all. If Jamie's leadership attracted a young generation of ghost hunters, it could be a big plus.

'And where—?' Cara began to ask. There was no need though. It was all too clear.

'The Happy Huffkin.'

Cara walked back across the lawns to the folly, still getting to grips with the idea of another celebration. Inviting the society members to a party seemed innocuous on the face of it. What had happened last time could not be repeated. And yet she had this foreboding. Trouble, here we come again.

What was Lady Izzy's aim now? Her last great idea had ended in a shambles, so what had she in mind? Whatever it was, there would surely be a big question mark over it. Rational thinking told Cara nothing would happen, apart from a nice farewell drink or two. Experience had told her differently. Instinct told her the same but even more strongly.

Here she was sitting in the cool of the day still trying to figure this out. Sammy had already left, and she was getting nowhere. Back at home, PC Jackie Smart would be waiting for her. Cara got on with her well; they would begin chatting and there would no more time for mulling things over. On the other hand, she wasn't achieving very much anyway.

She made a determined effort. She'd begin with Berowne's murder. Rachel must surely now be a prime suspect, but Oliver, Pete, Charlotte, Harry, Luke, Jamie, perhaps even Emily had to be considered as well. One of these eight people had blood on their hands. Which one of them was it? Where motive was concerned, the answer seemed to her fairly obvious but it needed checking. Too late she reminded herself that this was Andrew's job to solve and not hers. So what? He had listened to her earlier on the subject.

Take Oliver, she reasoned. He was bent on getting somewhere in life as old age crept on. His driving force seemed to be power.

Was that motive enough for murder? Did he feel neglected, his talent wasted, the end of his life approaching and nothing to show for it? Is that what was rushing through his head? Envy of his fellow members?

Then there was Pete. Now there was a motive. Jealousy. He was not only in debt to Berowne – or rather Rachel's firm – but in his view Berowne was his wife's lover. As for Charlotte herself – if the story was true – then Berowne had dropped her in favour of another. That would have given her motive, revenge, and it would get Pete out of financial trouble as he'd been dealing with Berowne. Luke was another person eaten up with envy – full of bitterness at seeing Berowne in the position he thought he should occupy, not only recently but also ten years earlier. Harry was a puzzle, Cara thought, now seeming a different person than when she had seen him on that fatal day. Why was that? Obviously, it was probably shock at finding Berowne's body, but theoretically it could have been because he'd just committed murder. Emily – surely no murderer but possibly the inspiration for murder, if Berowne's amorous intentions had fallen on her. And Jamie – whom Lady Izzy was now planning to push into the Tanton Ghost and Phantom Society chair. Had he too seen his future as its chair? Unlikely, but if he mistakenly thought Berowne was making a play for Emily, that could have wound him up. Nothing on that front so far, but it was something to follow up perhaps. And lastly, and by far the most likely, there was Rachel, who had so recently discovered that her husband was a bigamist.

Strong or weak, these could all have been motives for Berowne's murder, a ferocious murder committed with passion, Cara reflected. A passion that must surely pinpoint Rachel. The band was playing the right tunes, but the facts surrounding the murder weren't quite dancing in step. She had thought she knew the score, and Andrew was no doubt marching along with it, but could it be that they were dancing to the wrong music? Passion had its own tunes.

'A feast, a thank you. A farewell,' Lady Izzy crowed, as she flourished a glass of champagne at the society members assembled on the Happy Huffkin's upper floor a week later. Clad in a turquoise tunic over turquoise trousers, with a purple blouse peeping out, she was her usual striking figure.

'I've been at a few ghost hunts in the time I've been an honorary president,' she continued, 'and after that do in the butler's pantry went wrong, Tom must be waiting in the wings to pop down again. And I've been told there's a list of sightings around these parts just waiting to be followed up. Exciting stuff. Too exciting for an old lady like me, who'll soon be a ghost herself and popping down with him to keep an eye on you. I'm going back to being a silent honorary president now. You need a youngster to lead you. And young Jamie here will make a fine leader. I shall put my money where my mouth is, and my mouth is with Jamie here and no one else.'

A few moments of appalled silence followed, and then the fireworks began. Should she linger here while the din of dissent roared on, Cara wondered, or retreat downstairs? She was surplus to requirements, as Len and Sammy had set up the table and chairs here while Virginia had taken care of the food and drink, together with Lucy who had apparently insisted on taking the place of Josie. Josie had claimed she wasn't well, but Cara had suspected that she was nervous of facing Rachel. There was a glint in Lucy's eye that had suggested trouble as she served Jamie, but nothing had happened. Max and Alison were tucked away at a small table as onlookers, although Cara wasn't sure of the wisdom of this. It could be merely a tedious meeting or all hell could break loose. And amongst this group, so intent on the society's future, there was a murderer.

Lady Izzy had just blithely informed guests that this was a farewell to her active participation in the society's activities, but was that really going to be the case? Cara looked round at the assembly, all now shouting at each other and at Lady Izzy. Oliver was sitting like the patriarch he considered himself to be, but his red puffy cheeks told a different story. Harry was next to him, looking uncharacteristically subdued, perhaps because Lucy wasn't here and Emily was being protected by Jamie's arm firmly round her. Harry did then join in the shouting, perhaps aware that Oliver's eye was upon him. Pete was watching Rachel, perhaps to see how she was taking it – which was not well. She and Charlotte seemed to be acting together in contributing one side of the argument, but which it was, Cara couldn't tell in the general hubbub. Luke seemed to be leading the protest.

Lady Izzy had sat down and was listening to the ongoing racket with apparent interest. In the first lull, she rose to her feet again. 'So, I gather it's agreed. Jamie is your new chair and I shall be delighted to support the society if so.' A pause. 'But not otherwise. What do you think, Jamie? Is that acceptable to you?'

All eyes were on Jamie, including her own. Cara held her breath. Jamie had said and done nothing, except withdraw his arm from around Emily. As a sullen silence reigned, he rose to his feet and shrugged.

'OK,' he said. 'I'll do it.' Then he sat down again.

Cara watched as the champagne flowed and Virginia's best party fare was enjoyed. And yet she knew differing emotions must be at work. Just below the surface of this gathering simmered jealousy and envy. They were all marching onwards, but to where, Cara wondered. To another murder? The more she thought about it, the more certain she had become that she had been following the wrong music. It was time to rethink.

There was nothing, but nothing, to compare with the early morning sun at the Happy Huffkin, Cara mused. She had arrived at eight thirty, earlier than Sammy for once, but on a day like this it was sheer pleasure to be here, especially with so much on her mind. She could take this time to think everything through in peace and quiet until Sammy arrived. Virginia wouldn't be bringing her supplies up from the village for several hours, and there was little to do here as yet. Sammy would be cross that she had beaten him to it, as he would interpret it as a slur on himself.

Cara put her boxes of biscuits out for the day, and strolled through the café to the rear doorway and the mock temple balcony that overlooked the village. Below her the hillside sloped downwards and she could see the roofs of the houses bordering what had once been a river and was now a mere imitation. Where to go from here? If she'd been dancing to the wrong tune, what was the right one? She suddenly felt uneasy. Pull yourself together, Cara, she told herself sternly. The sun was shining, she reasoned, and she should be facing the day and its challenges with determination, but here she was missing the beat. Where was the elusive right tune?

What was the matter with her? Had one of the ghosts lost his way and got stuck in the Happy Huffkin by mistake? What nonsense. It was true there was still a murderer in their midst as Andrew had made no arrests yet. That would surely happen soon. She was fairly sure that his team had been unobtrusively present at last night's celebration, if it could be called that – very probably to keep an eye on Rachel. In any case she wouldn't have been in Rachel's or anyone else's firing line, as it was the police who were handling Berowne's murder and not Cara Shelley.

Now that they were drawing closer to an arrest, there was surely no need for PC Jackie Smart's watchful eye on her any longer. Andrew must be wrong about her being in danger, Cara thought, whether she had been dancing to the wrong tune or not. Why the delay to an arrest though? Andrew had had all those people in his sights last night, the people who had gathered in the Italian garden on that fateful evening. Only one of the nine was bent on murder. No, not nine of course, she remembered. There were others there, such as Josie and Virginia.

Cara stopped short. Josie Redman and Virginia. *That was the right tune.* People who were at the grotto but not sleeping there. That included Josie, who hadn't been present last night, she had assumed because Josie had feared Rachel would be there, full of fury. Josie, who had been so upset at what she'd discovered about Berowne, perhaps because she was indeed having an affair with him, had been in the background of this murder case all the time.

There was something else, though, and it was *here. Now.* A presence of someone being around, nearby. A ghostly presence? No, stupid of her. Mountains out of molehills. Of course. She was safely in the Happy Huffkin. It must be Sammy moving around inside.

But it wasn't Sammy. It wasn't Rachel either. Cara whisked around to find Len Redman standing behind her. What could he want? She relaxed. Probably something to do with the opening of the grotto. Then it registered. This wasn't the usual Len, the placid, helpful Len. He was furious about something, his face contorted with rage. What . . .?

'You couldn't keep your mouth shut, could you?' he hissed at her. 'Telling my Josie her husband did a murder.'

What did he mean? She hadn't done anything like that. Fear gripped her. Murder? Him? *Len?* 'I didn't—'

'You won't be telling no one else,' he snarled, grabbing her close to him.

The smell, that breath, stifling her. 'Josie—' she tried to say.

It was too late. He was clutching her, hands round her throat, choking her, pulling her off balance. She was choking, choking . . .

She heard a snarl, there was noise in her ears. She couldn't move, she couldn't speak, she couldn't see; it was pain, pain, pain becoming ever stronger. He was breathing, gasping, into her face. Then she was aware of something flying through the air – something, someone, and a noise, a clang of some kind; then nothing more.

She managed to open her eyes. Had time passed? There were people. There was some kind of cushion under her head. Sammy was standing there with a relieved smile and his heavy frying pan clasped in his hand. And surely that was Andrew rushing towards her, face white as icing sugar. That comparison pleased her. She stopped thinking and let things flow through her mind. This had happened to her once before, a long time ago . . . She'd survived, hadn't she? And now she was going to survive again. Hers not to reason why, but at least she was alive, and already beginning to recall what had happened. That faint flickering of doubt over Rachel's guilt had been justified. She'd been attacked by someone – yes, she remembered now, it was Len Redman. *Len?* Why? She struggled to think about that and at last she realized the answer. It had to be because it was he who had murdered Berowne Dyer – even though she couldn't work out why. Or could she? She grappled with this in vain until she felt herself drifting off . . .

The word jealousy was swirling round in her mind in the hospital, although she was confused. She wasn't sure what jealousy was or why she was thinking about it. She'd been aware of a man sitting by her side. Was it Andrew or was it Detective Chief Inspector Mitchem? Did it matter? Not really. She loved both of them. With this comforting thought she dozed off, but when she next opened her eyes, he was there again. This time she managed a grin. She knew who he was. She didn't know why she was here and why she felt so strange, but Andrew was looking happy enough.

'Tomorrow,' he said. 'I'm taking you home tomorrow.'

Now that was an interesting statement. Home. Her home? His home? Tanton Towers?

He answered it himself. 'To the Towers. Max and Alison refused to let me take you to anyone else. Too afraid I'd make another bad job of it, as I did this time.'

That clinched it. Of course. It all came flooding back to her. She was alive and well and in her right mind – she hoped. Just as well, because Lady Izzy was approaching her bedside and she needed to brace herself for what would undoubtedly be an energy-sapping visit. Even the mere sight of the scarlet trousers and bright blue jacket made Cara feel exhausted. But she made a huge effort and allowed herself to be kissed.

'Ah,' Lady Izzy announced. 'I'm glad you're here, Inspector. I wanted a word with you.'

'Business or private?' he asked guardedly, pulling up a chair for her.

'Neither. This is nothing to do with the case, but it's not private. My goodness no. It's already shouting at me from the rooftops.'

Cara shrank under the coverlet. This introduction did not bode well, so let them get on with it, she thought.

'Detective Chief Inspector Mitchem,' Lady Izzy began firmly. 'It's high time you married Cara. She needs a keeper.'

What? Cara struggled upright at this insult. Andrew might be laughing, but she wasn't going to be joining him. 'I don't, I don't,' she managed to gasp. What was this daft idea all about?

'I agree,' Andrew said peaceably. 'But it won't be me.'

He *agreed.* What the blazes was this? Her stomach seemed to be turning over. Was this the man she thought she knew? Why wouldn't it be him? Was he going away again?

'Having a keeper,' Andrew continued peaceably, 'isn't a role that I feel Cara would welcome.'

This sounded a whole lot better. Cara listened carefully. It was interesting having her life being arranged on her behalf. That's if this *was* her. Perhaps it was someone else called Cara. She felt herself drifting off again . . . and she still didn't understand what had happened to her.

The Towers. That's where she was. Safe and sound in an armchair with Andrew at her side. She had still been groggy when Andrew had brought her back here, but once back in the familiar family wing of the Towers, she felt at home. Max and Alison had tactfully departed, as had Lady Izzy thankfully. And thankfully she was now thinking clearly. Remembering all those times she had felt under threat, as though the trees and bushes were closing in on her, with malicious intent. Could that have been Len, awaiting his moment to strike and finally succeeding? But he hadn't succeeded, and here she was – granted she wasn't feeling at her best, to say the least.

'I'm better now,' she announced brightly. 'So, let's get it over with, Andrew. What happened? Why did Len Redman pounce on me? All I was doing was investigating whether Tom Chalcott was murdered and I think Berowne killed him. Is that right?'

'Yes, so we now believe. No proof and there never will be. Off the record, his motive was that Chalcott was going to tell the world that he was a bigamist, starting off by telling Rachel.'

So, she thought triumphantly, there was a kind of link between the two cases, even if it wasn't the one she had expected. Berowne himself was the link. Even so, the big puzzle still remained. 'I understand that,' she said, 'but why did Len kill Berowne?'

'Jealousy.'

Of course. That was the word that had been drifting through her mind in hospital. 'Of whom? Not of me,' she said doubtfully, aware that perhaps her brain was still not functioning at its best.

He laughed. 'No. You can rule yourself out on that one. It was his wife, Josie. As far as we can make out, he thought—'

It was beginning to come back to her now. 'Did he think Josie was having an affair with Berowne?' she interrupted eagerly. 'Rachel told me about that but I still can't believe it, especially as she said that Charlotte was also on his list. Len must have got the wrong end of the stick and killed him on the spur of the moment.'

'Hardly spur of the moment,' Andrew replied. 'It was well planned. Len Redman was admirably placed to creep into the grotto at the far end, sufficiently far from any equipment picking up signals – and even if it had, he could easily have had some genuine excuse for entering during the night as he was in charge of overseeing the grotto's safety during the night. Redman had armed himself with a sharp kitchen knife, carefully purchased ten days earlier from a London store,' he continued, 'and marched into Berowne's quarters, killed him, and then muffled and smashed the equipment, including cameras. We think from the post mortem that Berowne woke up, but he wouldn't have been overly startled to see Redman, only concerned that something was wrong.'

Cara struggled to take this in. 'Blood. There'd be blood everywhere.'

'All planned. Redman had his hut and even more importantly he had the garden incinerators and compost heaps all at hand. He quite proudly told us about those. Disposal of the knife was also simply planned. Buried in the woods, to be thrown into the sea once we'd finished our initial investigations. That was the plan. Unfortunately for him we found it first.'

She was still struggling. 'But why attack me?'

Was he at the root of her constant uneasy feeling that she was being stalked? If so, how fortunate she was to have had Jackie Smart guarding her, Cara thought. And how fortunate that Andrew had insisted on arranging that. But she still couldn't see why Len had stalked and attacked her.

'Simple,' Andrew replied gravely. 'He thought you'd worked out that he murdered Berowne and that you had told his wife.'

That took her aback. 'Had I?' Surely her memory wasn't still that bad.

'If you had, I didn't hear about it. I wasn't present at the ghost tour of the Towers, but he's been burbling on not only to us but to all and sundry that on that tour you suggested men who'd slaughtered their wives' lovers should inform their spouses about their actions. In addition, I gather that when he was absent one day, you seized the opportunity of visiting Josie in order to inform her that it was he who had murdered Berowne. It wasn't only you who suffered from Redman's revenge on these mistaken interpretations. I'm afraid he beat Josie up.'

Cara could scarcely take this in. 'That's all nonsense. It was Josie who rang me, and I went over to see her about Alice, not about him. That's crazy. *He's* crazy.' Now she remembered that Josie hadn't been at that final party at the Happy Huffkin. He'd attacked her and the signs of it would have been obvious.

'Maybe he is crazy, but I doubt if he is so clinically. We have DNA evidence linking him to Berowne's murder, and now there are the attacks on you and Josie to clinch it. He announced that he'd been tracking you, waiting for a good opportunity.'

So her sixth sense had been right. It wasn't evil spirits stalking her, it was Len Redman. 'Josie must be devastated,' Cara said. 'Was she badly hurt when he beat her up?'

'She's recovering. Anyway, she blames herself both for that and for the attack on you, because she was the woman having an affair with Berowne, rather than Charlotte – and as Charlotte denies it too, that's probably the case.'

'Pete's her keeper,' Cara said wryly. 'Another jealous controller.'

'You're safe with me in that respect.' A pause. 'By the way, Jackie Smart's been stood down. The case is over. I thought I might take her place when you move back to your cottage. Unless of course you prefer to try mine.'

Cara gazed at him suspiciously. Maybe her head was still swimming. Maybe he was still talking about the case in some way. Surely he wasn't seriously talking about the future? This was just an add-on from the case. Better be sure though.

'You'll be protecting me?' she asked cautiously.

'Definitely not. You may recall that the rabbits are due to prance.'

No add-on. No doubts now. She looked at him straight-faced. 'And you won't cage them up? You won't be their keeper?'

'Only a lover.'